They
Had Never
KNOWN

J. S. Helms

Gods
They
Had Never
Known

ISBN-13: 978-1724966216
ISBN-10: 1724966219

Cover design and original serpent illustrations artwork created by Mary C. Findley • https://elkjerkyforthesoul.com/image-displays/

Map by Oscar Paludi "Exoniensis"

Book production by David Bergsland • http://bergsland.org

Selections were adapted and modified from 1 Enoch: Book of the Watchers. This is free from copyright and in the public domain available at http://book-ofenoch.com/

Visit the author's website at www.godstheyhadneverknown.com

VALLEY OF
SHALLIYT

They sacrificed to demons that were no gods,
to gods they had never known,
to new gods that had come recently,
whom your fathers had never dreaded.

—(Deuteronomy 32:17,
English Standard Version)

PROLOGUE

(About Ten Years Ago).

"Brethren!" Aarkaos stood above the assembly on a rocky ledge, his voice booming through the clear night air. He strutted back and forth, jeweled skin flashing in the light of the torches blazing in the darkness. Complete silence settled on the expectant crowd. His hooded gaze swept across the thousands craning their necks to look up to him from the plateau below.

"Who among you have noticed the women of the valley?" A sly smile spread his lips and a forked tongue flicked out briefly tasting the excitement in the breeze.

A murmur rippled through the Guardians, building layer upon layer to a muffled roar, their curiosity palpable.

Aarkaos raised his hand to quiet them. "And who desires to live among these women?" His voice lowered here, but as one, the throng leaned forward, enthralled, to catch his words. He smoothed his hands down over the gold and onyx, sapphire and emerald that encrusted his body like scales. "To live amongst them, and…" he quirked a brow, "to take them as your own?" This was a dangerous game he played, Aarkaos knew. But greater than his physical brilliance, his unrivaled wisdom garnered admiration, loyalty, and, at times, blind trust.

A stunned silence followed the final echo of the question, then whispers swelled in the shadows as the Guardians turned and spoke to one another.

Someone shouted, "What about the laws of Shalliyt? Are we not forbidden?"

Ah, Aarkaos thought, the laws. The laws of Shalliyt versus the unfulfilled passions of the Guardians. That was his game. His gamble.

The crowd settled once again to hear their leader's answer to this. But instead of responding immediately, in an unprecedented action, he turned and climbed the final few steps from his perch to the highest peak in their mountain realm…the venerated, yet seemingly abandoned, seat of Shalliyt. The stones of the mountain here glowed and throbbed with molten intensity.

He spun around, exultant in the shocked looks now directed toward him. He employed his final, arguably his greatest, strength: reasoning. "Shalliyt? When last did we hear from Shalliyt?"

Guardians had been created to watch over men. But in the present age, they were relegated to primarily observing from a distance. Shalliyt seldom summoned them to intervene in the affairs of men anymore.

Over time, some of them had begun to indulge in fantasies of being with the women of the valley. There were no women of their race. An immortal breed, these sons of Shalliyt, procreation was not ordained for them. But the daughters of men seemed soft and alluring, with eyes that sparkled, cheeks that glowed rosy with their blushes, and wet lips that enticed. Their silky hair flowed thick and long over soft skin, and their full hips swung from side to side.

These particular Guardians, being in every way superior to men, yet compelled to serve them, began to wonder why they had been denied the pleasure of women. But this was the first time the desire had been spoken aloud publicly, boldly.

Aarkaos allowed a look of anger to flash across his face. "How many generations of men have come and gone, and we have no word from Shalliyt?" His voice echoed with authority and conviction across the mountains' peaks.

After a long pause, as if theatrically waiting for a response, Aarkaos answered it himself in a quieter, sibilant voice. "Shalliyt has deserted his senseless human sons." He chuckled. "He has left *us* to rule over them for eternity. We are their gods now."

The length of his back flexed in anticipation of the illicit pleasure he had planned. Then with a frenzied bellow, he stretched his fists high to the glittering stars overhead. "We can do that which is right in our own eyes. The women are ours for the taking!"

Many Guardians cheered at this pronouncement. Many more did not. Aarkaos gathered to himself those loyal to his cause, those burning with the same fiery lust pulsing through their bodies. He made them swear an oath to carry through to fulfillment the plan to invade the valley and take for themselves the daughters of men.

PART ONE

1

Haven gazed up the cliff face, his eyes sweeping from side to side, searching for any sign of danger descending from within the dense mist. A slight breeze blew cool and damp on his cheeks, ruffling the hair at his temples. He paused to stare through the dimming light at each shadow, confirming nothing lurked within, then continued his scan. The mist curled in tendrils that clung to the mountains, obscuring soaring peaks; it was utterly impenetrable.

The mountains stood in a rough circle many dozens of miles around, forming a sheltered, verdant valley at their feet. Passes wended between occasional breaks in the mountains, connecting the valley— known as the Valley of Shalliyt—to the outlying wilderness. Few saw reason to venture out to that sun-burnt desolation, the haunt of the jackal and vulture alone.

Haven tapped his fingers against his thigh, aiding his concentration while he searched. He finally gave a nod, having yet again spotted nothing, and tore his gaze away from the misty borders above him.

The Guardians preferred to descend in the evening, so he had heard, their forms uncannily slipping down the rock sides, when lengthening shadows obscured their incursion into the valley below. No man could scale the surface of the mountains, either up or down, but the Guardians were not quite men.

He massaged his neck where a twinge had formed from staring upward too long. He rolled his broad shoulders to loosen them up. The fabric of his shirt scratched his skin as it slid over his back. It was time to get going. The Telling of Shalliyt would begin soon, and Haven did not want to be late.

He sprinted along a path that wound its way along the base of the cliff. The smell of wood smoke hung in the air, reminding him that he had missed dinner in his vigilance for the Guardians. It would have to wait. He had anticipated the Telling all week long. It often gave him peace of mind during this time of apparent madness filling the valley, a touchstone of truth and reality.

His rock-toughened bare feet leapt over and dodged boulder edges with familiarity as he skirted the mountain's edge.

He arrived at the cave, where a narrow doorway led into the base of the mountain itself. Haven bent his head forward to duck under the low-slung rock of the lintel and stepped into the ancient gathering room. The scents of mildew, candle wax, and warm bodies enveloped him. He paused to let the familiarity of it wash over him as his pounding heart and breathing began to slow. He tap tapped on his thigh again as he looked around the room.

The space spread out before him with row upon row of wooden benches leading up to a platform at the front of the room. At either end of each row stood a waist-high stone pillar topped with a fat, white candle flickering in the dimness. Waxy blobs dripped down their sides, mounding up at the base. A luminescent moss covered the cave walls so they glowed a faint green. The glow ascended as far up as could be perceived, hinting at an impossibly high ceiling to the cave. Moisture trickled down, watering the moss and forming damp spots at the edges of the room.

Haven slumped onto a bench at the back near the doorway where he had entered, running a hand through his hair, causing the chestnut curls to spring askew. Everyone's backs were to him so his slightly late arrival went unnoticed…almost.

Up front on the platform, flanked by a pair of pillars and candles, sat the ancient Teller, cross-legged. His milky-blue blind eyes were turned toward Haven as if they clearly saw him. Haven knew the elder missed nothing, his inner sight more than compensating for his lack of physical vision.

The Teller's gnarled fingers stroked a snowy beard that cascaded downward over his woolen robe. His powerful voice filled the cavernous space: "…It was then that the Guardians chose to turn against their creator Shalliyt. Lust filled their hearts and their minds, clouding their thinking, perverting their reasoning. That for which they were created to guard, they now conspired to exploit. It was no whim; this was carefully orchestrated, shrewdly premeditated. The consequences of their actions would be dire, eternal, and yet they forged onward with their plan."

The aged one paused, licking cracked lips. Heavy creases bracketed his mouth and eyes. A prominent brow ridge framed the top of his face, sporting tufts of white eyebrows; a long, narrow nose dominated his countenance. No one knew exactly how many summers the Teller had seen. Children whispered that he came from the beginning of the valley, maybe eternally formed like the Guardians.

Haven glanced around the room. Attendance had dwindled in recent months—many seats on the benches remained empty. Fewer than twenty people came tonight. Years ago he could remember the cave packed with several hundred—benches and aisles filled to capacity, heads craning through the door from outside. His father would perch Haven on his shoulders and stand in the back. Haven could see over everyone from that height, his fingers clamped into his father's hair, thick and shaggy like his own.

His young eyes always stared in rapt fascination at the blind man up front, who spoke of strange things, and who always seemed to look straight at Haven at some point during the Telling. The ancient's sight pierced even into his soul—young Haven would quiver at the connection he felt to the Teller.

"You listen to him, Haven. Always. He is a teller of truth and life," his father once told him. He missed his father, terribly at times.

In the sparsely occupied cave, Haven scanned for one person in particular: a young woman with a head of black curls that tumbled down her back. He frowned. Rachel had promised him she'd be here. Maybe she hadn't promised, but she said she would try. He thought she would come.

His attention shifted back to the Teller.

"The rebellious leader of the Guardians compelled his horde to take an oath—that they would not change their minds, thus leaving him alone to face the unquenchable fire of judgment. Two hundred agreed, sealing their fates. Their wild eyes now turned down toward the valley, toward the beautiful women for whom they lusted."

The skin on Haven's arm prickled. He could not fathom how such perfect creatures could so casually throw off their immortality for the greed of their unsanctioned desires. The women of the valley were in great danger. Nay, the whole of the valley would languish, maybe perish, if this invasion were permitted to continue.

His thoughts turned once again to Rachel. The lust of the mutinous Guardians must never approach her hearth. Whether or not he could ever have her, he would protect her from this evil.

The Teller continued, "They plotted and schemed to determine the best way to unfurl their wicked plan. Straightforward ravishment was considered a viable possibility. But would it not be more cunning to find a way for the women to accept them willingly, or even seek them out? Or better yet, to have the women's fathers heartily agree to hand over their daughters? How clever to incite the passion of the women and the greed of their fathers to accomplish their purposes!

"First they had to choose an enticement, but this was easy. Not only are they guardians of man, but they are guardians of the wisdoms of the mountains, ancient knowledge that is forbidden to man. This is knowledge that mankind, in its depravity, craves. Shalliyt had withheld these wisdoms from the valley of men, not as a punishment as some suppose, but as a protection. The Guardians would exploit this weakness in man, offering their illicit knowledge in exchange for the women..."

At the end of the Telling, Haven trudged down the path toward his home on the outskirts of the village. The occasional candle-lit cottage window glowed lighting his way, but great black gaps stretched between the warmer pools of light. Discouragement dogged his heels, and fear shadowed close behind.

As he walked, Haven thought about the Guardians and his changing world. He didn't want it to change. Even though he couldn't see much in the dark, he knew his path wound between everything familiar: fields and vineyards that yielded their bounty year round; sheep, goats, and cattle which fattened easily on pastures watered by the dew that settled after sunset and the streams meandering across the landscape; days that dawned sunny and mild without fail; and people who tended toward a good nature, working in harmony with one another, though this beneficence was less steadfast than the weather or crops.

But things were changing now, and this settled in his belly like a weight. He had never actually seen a Guardian, but he never doubted the words of the Teller.

Haven could see his thatched-roof cottage aglow with candlelight in a grouping with several others a short distance ahead. Most of the homes in the valley outside of the village were arranged this way: a cluster of four or five cottages surrounded by pasture and fields held in common that stretched outward, finally abutting a neighboring cluster of cottages' fields.

Instead of heading directly to his home, he veered off the path, hopped a stone wall with one arm, and jogged the short distance to another cottage through a pasture drenched with dew. Sheep and goats glared at him with their reflective eyes, mouths halted in mid-chew, hunks of grass dangling from their lips. Then as if a single organism, the herd began to bleat and scattered into the night. He had to check on Rachel; he needed to know she was all right.

Standing before the door of her home, Haven paused, a little breathless. He could hear the muffled voices of men talking within; their tone was amicable, though he could not distinguish any words. Curling the knuckles of his right hand into a fist, he rapped on the heavy wood. The voices silenced and footsteps padded toward the door. He tapped his fingers on his thighs as he waited.

The door creaked open just enough for Rachel to put her head out. Her expression brightened when she saw Haven. She squeezed her body out through the narrow opening in the door, shutting it firmly behind her. Haven arched an eyebrow at her odd maneuver.

She wore a gauzy full-length skirt, bare toes peeping out underneath. Her shirt was the same fabric but tightly wrapped around her torso above the flare of her hips, outlining and lifting small breasts that swelled slightly above the material. She looked dressed for something special.

"Haven, it's good to see you!" Rachel reached up and laid her hand on his chest. The warmth from her hand seeped through the fabric of his shirt, heat flushing his face and longing curling his toes. The top of her head came only up to his chin, but tonight she seemed taller with her curls piled up and artfully held in place with a length of cord.

"Are you going to invite me inside, little one?" Haven glanced toward the door, then back at Rachel.

"Not tonight. Father has an important meeting and cannot be disturbed." Her smile faltered a bit as her eyes flicked over to the cottage.

He wondered what kind of meeting a carpenter could possibly have, but he was distracted when Rachel raised her hand from his chest and softly laid it against his jaw, now stubbled with a day's beard growth. Her thumb stroked back and forth across his cheek. His eyelashes fluttered closed.

He dragged his eyes back open, gently gripped her hand and removed it from his face, holding it loosely in his own larger hand. He looked directly into her pale green eyes. "You weren't at the Telling tonight."

Breaking away from the intensity of his stare, Rachel looked somewhere over his shoulder instead and said, "Something came up. It's of no great concern." She twisted a finger from her free hand through a lock of hair that bobbed by her ear.

"It *is* of great concern. Danger has breached our valley, and we must be prepared. The times are perilous and the days are evil."

"Oh Haven, you are always so serious. How can the ramblings of an old man get you this overwrought?"

Haven's mouth dropped open in disbelief. "Ramblings of an old man?"

"You are just barely three and twenty, but you carry the weight of the world on your shoulders." She finished this with a light laugh.

"He is a prophet to our people, Rachel. The mouth of Shalliyt. He speaks only of truth."

"Well, if Shalliyt wishes me to hear something, he can come right here and say it. But we both know that is not likely to happen."

The blush on Haven's cheeks intensified with the beginnings of anger. "Rachel, that is heresy. Who's been filling your mind with these ideas?" He squeezed her hand in emphasis.

Rachel yanked back her hand and put both hands on her hips defiantly. "Father agrees with you that the valley is changing; though he says it is not for evil but for…enlightenment, for advancement. New things are being discovered, our lives are improved.

"Father is excited about new metals he can use alongside his carpentry. Old Naomi told us of new tonics that help her lambs grow faster and stronger, and increase the egg production of her chickens." She paused to suck in a breath. She leaned forward, tapping Haven on the chest with her finger and lowered her voice. "Those who do not embrace the change will be left behind in the old ways. Is that what you want, Haven? To be left behind…left out of the excitement to come?"

Haven was silent, perplexed. Rachel shifted under his gaze, wrapping both of her arms around her waist.

Haven reached for her. "Rachel…"

But his thought was interrupted when the door of the cottage swung open. His attention turned toward the door; Rachel looked down at the ground.

Two men stepped out onto the stone stoop next to them. Rachel's father, Jared, was bearded and portly with the same pale green eyes as Rachel. His hair a shimmering black shot through with silver and cropped short.

The other man stood tall, nearly a head higher than both Rachel's father and Haven. He wore a finer cut of clothes and was clean shaven. His shoulder-length hair was pulled back neatly at his nape and tied with a leather thong. The man smiled as he shook hands with Rachel's father. As they concluded their farewell and turned toward the younger pair, Haven could see the taller man's smile did not reach his eyes.

Those eyes…

The pupils were flat and inky black. They did not shine or reflect at all, but sucked the candlelight spilling through the door into their depths.

Haven shuddered as he realized he was staring into the beautiful, ageless face of a Guardian.

2

The next day, another brilliant and sunny day in the valley, Haven walked into the village to speak with Rachel's father, Jared, alone. The night before he had left abruptly after seeing Rachel's guest. It occurred to him later, the man was the reason she hadn't come to the Telling. He had done nothing untoward, but Haven's scalp prickled fiercely as he had walked away from them.

He followed along the winding packed-dirt streets; homes and shops hunched together on either side. Most of the buildings were two stories tall, with the upper story protruding out, creating a shaded walkway underneath and providing a place to get out of the way of horse and donkey riders and herds of sheep as they were driven along to the market.

All night and during the walk into town, Haven had thought of his father. Seeing the Guardian had brought to the forefront all his father's warnings. Haven missed him so much that a heavy ache settled into his chest. He rubbed at it to try and ease it.

"Haven, boy, you must be strong." Baruch had coughed into the rag he clutched in his fist, then wiped away the blood that stained his lips. "You will need to care for your mother—"

"Father, you will get better." Haven scrubbed his hand through the unruly curls on his head. His heart beat erratically as he looked down at the wasted body of his father. All the strength had fled Baruch's bones and muscles so quickly, and now Haven could see the color seeping from his face. It was a shock of white against his dark hair that lay sweaty and matted along his scalp. The smell of decay filled the room.

"You have fifteen summers, Haven, old enough to be a man." Baruch shifted a bit in the cot as if he were trying to get more comfortable. "You know how to run this farm and you will provide for your mother." He coughed again, then motioned for Haven to lean closer. "But more importantly, you must stay faithful to Shalliyt."

Haven nodded. He bit into his bottom lip to keep it from trembling.

"You were born with a strong faith, but never turn your back on him. Do not rebel as many your age do. He is faithful and just. Follow him always." Baruch broke into wracking coughs, the sound of wetness in his lungs undeniable.

Haven helped him sit up, then held his father's bony back as he handed him a cup of water from the bedside. Haven wiped up the splatters of blood the best he could, then laid his father back down on his pillow.

Baruch closed his eyes for a moment. He opened them again and pinned his gaze to Haven's. "Mind what the Teller has spoken to us about the Guardians. They will be coming and they will be the destruction of the valley. They may already be here—there is talk…"

Haven nodded.

"Many will disregard the Teller's warnings. But you must never do that. First and foremost in your life, love Shalliyt and hear his words through the Teller's mouth. Fight for righteousness. Protect and warn those you love…"

Haven nodded again with absolutely no idea how to do what his father just said. Tears ran down his face as he had watched Baruch slip back into that deep sleep where he spent so much time now.

That had been eight summers ago. He had never doubted his father or the Teller, and the time had finally come that he had seen a Guardian. And it was with Rachel. Bile rose in his throat.

And his brave response at seeing the two of them? He had essentially run. He had made his excuses and left, neither warning nor protecting anyone, completely overwhelmed. His face grew hot with shame now. It was good his father wasn't around to witness his cowardice.

Haven came to Jared's wood shop. The door stood open, propped there with a chunk of wood to allow the afternoon breeze in. The shop was roughly divided into two areas: one for finished goods for sale—chairs, cabinets, a table and bench, along with smaller wooden objects mostly for kitchen use. The other half housed the workshop area, and this is where Haven saw Jared.

In contrast to the fine clothes he had been wearing the night before with his meeting with the Guardian, today he wore

14

rough-spun trousers, belted with a thick piece of twine, and a loose long-sleeved woolen tunic.

"Good day, Haven! I suspected I might be getting a visit from you," Jared said as he straightened up from a small table that he had been sanding.

"Good morning, sir."

"You seemed troubled last night, and Rachel said you had some...concerns." The tang of fresh-cut wood and piney tar saturated the air. Dust motes twirled in the stripes of light coming through the open windows and door.

"Yes, I—"

Jared motioned him over to another table. "Let me show you something." The older man swept aside some rags and chunks of wood. Out of the debris he pushed two objects toward Haven. One was a fist-sized mottled green rock. The other snagged Haven's attention: a shiny, brownish-gold lump like an egg.

Haven reached his hand out toward the lustrous chunk. It was cool and smooth under his fingertips. "That is the oddest-looking nugget of gold. The color...and the size!"

"Ahh, my boy. It is not gold. It's copper. Before," he pointed to the rough greenish rock, "and after processing." He lifted the polished piece, Haven still petting it.

"Incredible..."

"This is much harder than gold, and therefore more useful. It is also a good deal less expensive, again, more useful. I'll be working with a blacksmith to fashion pieces to improve certain wooden implements. Can you imagine the share of a plough formed of metal instead of wood?" Jared beamed with pride.

"What is this process that changes it from rock to shiny metal?" Haven pulled his hand back and fisted it at his side. He wondered if this was some of the improper knowledge spoken of by the Teller.

"Trade secret, and Aaron isn't talking. But he will sell me however much I need." Jared set the copper back down. "Now then, come have a seat over here, son, and you can tell me what occupies your mind."

He brushed wood shavings off a bench and indicated that Haven should sit there. Walking over to the back of the workshop, Jared pulled back a curtain revealing a small closet.

A crock covered with a cloth sat on a sideboard. Jared removed the cloth, took a dipper and ladled some water from it into two ceramic cups. He walked back to Haven, handed him a cup, and sat on the bench next to him.

Haven gratefully took a swig from the cup. The water wasn't cold but it was wet, soothing his throat from the dusty walk through the village. It also gave him a moment to collect his thoughts. Jared waited patiently.

Haven took a deep breath. "Sir, I was concerned to see a Guardian at your house last night and with Rachel right there." He slowly rotated the cup around in his hands, his eyes seemingly transfixed to its gritty bottom.

Jared just stared at Haven for a moment then laughed, though not unkindly, and laid his hand on Haven's back. "A Guardian? Wherever did you get an idea like that?"

"…and you're doing business with him—"

"Sure, he's not from the valley, but he wasn't exactly hiding his wings under his coat now, was he?" Another good belly laugh shook Jared.

Haven's eyes widened. "He's no *man*, sir! You saw how tall he is. And where does he come from if not the valley… there is no place outside the valley. Refined men do not live in the desert."

Jared set down his cup and pursed his lips. "That's enough, Haven."

"And his eyes…you saw his eyes! He is a danger to you, to Rachel…" Haven realized his words were just tumbling out.

"Yes, he's tall and, according to Rachel, exceedingly handsome. I hardly think that qualifies any man to be one of the ancient sons of Shalliyt. He is from the mountains, and I believe he might be quite wealthy." Jared paused here and began stroking his chin lost in thought. "We did speak of business. He has some interesting ideas, and if I could interest him in investing some capital into my business, this…," he swept his hand over the raw and polished copper chunks, "I could make a real go of this."

Haven was stunned. How could Jared not be aware of the nature of his visitor? "Sir, did you see his eyes? He is *no* man!"

"His eyes? Why on earth would I be interested in looking at his eyes? This is ridiculous, Haven. I know why you're here, and it has nothing to do with Guardians and eyes." Jared sighed heavily, shaking his head. Haven saw him take several deep breaths. He was usually a patient man and had always treated Haven kindly.

"You and Rachel practically grew up together. I know you are fond of her and she of you. Maybe you have hopes of a more permanent alliance with her. But I also know you would only want what is best for her. Am I correct?"

Haven thought *fond* was not the word he would use for how he felt about Rachel. He was no fool. He knew Rachel didn't return the kind of love he felt for her, not yet. Often Rachel treated him like a brother. She saw him at times as a nuisance, but more so lately as a confidant. Sometimes she was affectionate with him in a way that gave him hope and made his heart pound. His mind flashed to an image of her face, her wide laughing smile and her slanted green eyes fringed by smoky lashes. He had loved her for a long time. He sighed. Maybe he was a fool. Jared was right about one thing: Rachel was *fond* of him.

Haven realized that Jared was looking at him, waiting for an answer. "I would give my life for Rachel. Of course I only want what is best for her."

Jared nodded and seemed to choose his words carefully. "Even if what is best for Rachel isn't you?"

His words stung.

Haven mumbled a thanks to Jared for his time and the cup of water, and he left the shop.

On the walk back to his cottage, Haven desperately tried to sort through his feelings. No, he did not want Rachel to marry another man, but this wasn't about some petty jealousy. If she were truly better off with another man as husband, so be it. But that wasn't what was going on here. The Teller had been issuing clear warnings of the emergence of the Guardians for a few years now. How is it that Haven could look at one and clearly identify him as a Guardian, but Jared could not? Maybe Haven was mistaken, and the visitor was just a man. A wealthy, attractive, older man that Rachel would be foolish not to pursue. But Haven felt it to his marrow that he was right—this man was a threat.

Haven felt overwhelmed by panic. If he couldn't make Jared see the truth how could he protect Rachel from what he knew deep in his heart was a huge mistake?

3

Haven sat among the flickering shadows in the cave waiting for the Teller to emerge from his chamber and begin the Telling. His best friend, Jonathan, sat next to him, looking distinctly uncomfortable with his knee bouncing up and down. Having arrived a bit early, they had taken a bench near the front of the room by the platform.

Men and women huddled in groups, murmuring in low tones. Something about the cave inspired reverence, and it would feel inappropriate to speak too loudly. The acoustics were such that even a normally pitched voice carried, winding around the rock walls so that those on the opposite end of the room could hear as clearly as if they stood next to the speaker.

"It feels strange in here, Haven," Jon whispered and ran a hand through his black, wiry hair. The dark skin of his face beaded with nervous perspiration.

Haven nodded. Getting Jon to come today had been a real chore. Haven had left home early to stop in at Jon's cottage before the meeting.

"Come on, Jon," Haven had urged. "This IS important." He had wanted to smack his hand on his thigh where he sat on a hay bale, to make sure Jon knew he was serious. But he kept his hand still.

Jon turned his back to Haven to scoop up the soiled hay with his pitchfork. "I know..." He walked out the door of the small shed that housed his few head of cattle, balancing the soggy load out in front of him, and tossed it in a large mound. Coming back in, he jabbed the fork into the dirt floor and leaned against it. "I know I should go, but there are chores and dinner and—"

"You used to make time for the Tellings." Haven grabbed a chunk of the hay to keep his hands occupied. "What changed?"

"Nothing. Just busy, I guess."

Haven raised an eyebrow at him.

Jon fidgeted, scratching the back of his head, his arm. He huffed. "I think the old man is strange, okay?" He grabbed the pitchfork with two hands and jerked it out of the packed dirt and rammed it back in again. "He makes me uncomfortable, you know?"

Haven stood and walked toward Jon. He pulled away the pitchfork that Jon tightly gripped and leaned it against the wall. "Yes, but that's why it's more important now to come and hear what he has to say. It's supposed to make us uncomfortable."

Jon clearly didn't know what to do with his hands. They waved around a bit, till he folded them across his chest. "Maybe he's crazy or wrong. Honestly, Guardians walking around the valley like men? It sounds like a story my grandmother would tell me to make me mind her....when I was *much* younger!"

What was it with both Rachel and Jon reacting to the Teller this way? "You're my best friend, Jon. Will you come along tonight for me? It's important to me..."

Jon sighed dramatically. "Fine!" He stomped over to where Haven had put the pitchfork and grabbed it. "But I'm finishing this stall first."

Haven had sat back down on the bale, content to wait a bit.

The satisfaction of convincing Jon was short-lived as other issues began pushing back into Haven's mind as they sat on the wooden bench, waiting. He was still troubled from the brief encounter he'd had with the Guardian at Rachel's the week before, followed by the unsettling meeting with Jared. He slept poorly all week. Haven clasped his hands together to stop them from trembling. He hadn't shared any of this with Jon. It was still too raw, and Jon wouldn't have believed him, anyway.

Haven had come up with an idea. He would try to speak directly to the Teller. The Teller didn't generally mingle with the people of the valley, but he wasn't completely inaccessible. Besides, he had always felt some connection to the Teller, though it had never been spoken about. Haven could only try. The stakes were too high not to.

The small wooden door to the left of the platform opened and the Teller bent his large frame to fit through, then unerringly made his way to his usual seat without assistance except for his tall, knobby staff. He folded his legs under him, settling

20

onto the platform between the flickering candles. Once again Haven had the sensation that the Teller was completely aware of his surroundings: who was present, perhaps who was not, even without his sight.

He began the Telling reciting much of what Haven had heard before. But tonight the Teller had new prophecies concerning the offspring of the Guardians:

"…each Guardian chose a daughter of man, and went to her and married her, defiling himself with the mortal flesh. They shared the eternal wisdom of the mountains with the women and their families, teaching them charms, metal working…"

Haven's heart pounded.

"… the power of roots and plants, the reading of the stars and clouds, and the methods of beautifying their faces for seduction.

"And the women became heavy with child and gave birth to monsters. The offspring were beautiful with the height of giants but with vacant souls. They grew quickly and consumed all the food of the valley, all the grain and all the meat. Man could not keep pace, could not supply them with enough to satisfy their voracious appetites. And when the food ran out, the offspring turned on the men and consumed them, too…"

Haven noticed the Teller had moved into future prophecies, even though he spoke it as if it had already passed. Before this, his tellings were explaining what had happened in the past and was happening now, but from a point of view the people couldn't see themselves. This new future revelation was even more disturbing—birthing monsters, starvation, and cannibalism—how could that even be possible?

At the end of the oration, the Teller stood and walked back to his chamber, the door thunking closed behind him.

Soft weeping swelled in the cave. The air tonight was oppressive, nearly suffocating. Haven remained seated as the rest of the assembly shuffled out. Everyone headed into the night, subdued as they returned to their homes and farms. Jon stood up.

"Are you leaving?" Haven asked. "I thought you might come with me to speak to him." He nodded his head toward the Teller's door.

"Uh, no. I need to leave. I did what you wanted…" Jon had his hand combing through his hair again. "I came and listened, you know. I'm no good with…" then he glanced toward the still-closed door and started backing away.

Haven gave him a weak smile. "It's fine, Jon. I'll see you later."

The room was quiet now, heavy. Small rivulets of water snaked down the walls. Haven twisted his hands together; he had not anticipated being this uneasy approaching the Teller. He took several deep breaths and dragged his hands through his hair. Just as he prepared to stand and knock on the Teller's door, it opened.

"Haven, please come in. Bring a candle with you."

How does he do that? Haven leapt to his feet. "Yes, sir." He took hold of a nearby fat candle, using his other hand to shield the flame from drafts as he walked, and ducked through the chamber door. The room had stone walls like the rest of the cave and contained a narrow bed covered with a cowhide blanket and a stool in front of a table piled with animal-skin scrolls. Another blanket hung from the frame of a doorway on the opposite wall, the access to what must be the rest of the Teller's chamber.

There was no light in the room except for the candle Haven held. It cast shadows that jumped along the wall as the Teller walked over to the bed, turned, and sat on the edge. He pointed to the stool. "Sit, Haven."

Haven looked for a place to set the candle since it shook in his hand. It didn't look safe to place it on the table by the scrolls so he just held it on his knee after he sat. Utter stillness settled around them.

The Teller broke the silence. "You are troubled by the proximity of the Guardians." It wasn't a question.

Haven stared into the flame of the candle and took a deep breath. "Yes, I am. You have warned us about them for years. Their purpose here is an abomination, yet many people tolerate and even encourage them. What clearly should be a thing from which to flee, a thing to rebuke, is instead embraced." The words spilled from Haven's mouth. He needed to rein himself in. He finally looked directly into the Teller's eyes and spoke more slowly. "And something of which I have just become aware… not all men seem capable of identifying them. How can that be?"

"When a man's mind is filled with the distractions of this world, he will easily miss the truth that stands before him." He paused. "Tell me, Haven, what specifically is bothering you."

Haven felt the Teller already knew, but it was likely for his own benefit that the Teller wanted him to actually speak it. "It's my friend Rachel, Jared's daughter. I fear that Jared will promise her to a certain man, um, Guardian, I believe, who has begun to visit their home. Rachel and Jared seem…enamored of him. They are impressed by his appearance, his confidence, his knowledge…" Haven looked away from the clouded eyes that pierced deep into his being. Hopelessness began to close in around him, the candle shadows dancing on the walls seemed a living, malignant thing taunting him.

"And what concern is this of yours?" The Teller spoke softly. Normally he boldly pronounced his prophecies, his voice unaffected by any hint of emotion or self-awareness.

Haven felt a burning behind his eyes. "Sir, I care for her."

The Teller stroked his snowy beard for several long minutes. "Haven, Shalliyt has seen you. You are pure in heart, only wishing to please him."

Haven tried to swallow past the tightness in his throat.

The Teller continued, "You need to stay the course you are on. Maintain your vigilance and discernment, and you will always remain under his protection." He let go of his beard and folded his gnarled hands on his lap. "As for Rachel, if she is destined to be yours, Shalliyt will open her eyes to the truth, at some point. Do not give up hope with her."

Haven would never give up on her. He just needed to be more forceful, more persuasive. He'd find a way, any way, to convince her. He would come up with a plan of action and formulate an argument she couldn't refute. He would make her see the truth of the situation, show her how much he loved her, and then she could love him in return.

"Haven, are you listening to me?" The Teller tilted his head a bit. "*Shalliyt* will open her eyes. You are to simply remain faithful to him."

Oh. But what if Shalliyt didn't understand how important she was to him? What if he chose not to open her eyes to the monster she was inviting into her life…?

"Haven!"

Haven was jarred out of his depressing train of thought. "Yes, sir."

The Teller paused and closed his eyes. After a few moments, he spoke again. "Shalliyt wants to show you and

Rachel something two days hence. Take her for a half day's ride, following the foot of the mountains to the east, southward. Stay on the path and do not go into the South Village. There is much turmoil there, even now as we speak. At midday, you will meet a man whose face is marked. You will know him immediately. Speak with him and see what Shalliyt must show you." The Teller stopped speaking.

The silence pressed in hard on Haven as he thought through what he had just been told.

"That is all. You may go."

Haven stood, gripping the candle. "Thank you, sir," he whispered and turned toward the door.

"Oh, and Haven?"

Haven turned back toward his elder, now sitting deeply in shadow.

"As I said, remain vigilant." He paused, stroking his beard. "But stop watching the mountain tops. The Guardians' descent cannot be seen by man. There is enough for you to attend to down here."

"Yes, sir." Haven, thankful for the dim room to cover his blush, opened the wooden door. Taking one last look over his shoulder at the Teller still sitting quietly at the edge of his bed, Haven ducked out through the doorway closing the door behind him, leaving the prophet in blackness.

4

Kharshea inhaled deeply, smelling the earthy mix of odors around him: fragrant herbs and flowers, roasting meats, and fresh animal dung. Being in the valley limited him in many ways, but the variety of stimulation in the sights, sounds, and smells enveloping him invigorated his senses.

He strode forward into the outdoor market from the South Village. The market sat centrally within the valley and at the juncture of the four regions of the village.

Flocks of aproned women toting baskets tucked under their arms filled the narrow avenues that formed the grid of the market. Vendors' booths stood hip to hip along the way, offering a cornucopia of fruits, vegetables, meats, cheeses, herbs, small livestock, and an abundance of wine.

The sound of the vendors hawking their wares rose and fell as Kharshea weaved his way around the shoppers, the merchants, and the occasional rope-led livestock.

He drew a good deal of attention to himself. At nearly seven feet tall, he towered over the throng. He carefully kept a kind and gentle smile upon his face, with eyes crinkled at the corners, so that women, eyes wide with fear as they dragged their gazes up the alarming height of his frame, would be eased at once by his friendly expression. Then they would scurry away.

Though Kharshea may have appeared to be meandering through the market, his path was intentional: he had a destination in mind. Months ago, he had selected Hadassah to become his. Her blonde hair waved past her face and down over her shoulders. It swished back and forth along her back as she walked, like a ripened field of wheat tossed by the wind. She was beautiful in form and lighthearted in temperament. Her cheeks were round and pink, and her eyes sparkled when she spoke. Gazing at her incited a hunger that coursed through his body.

25

Kharshea knew the family, had watched them for generations in his diligence as a Guardian. The women tended to be beautiful and passionate. Hadassah was young yet, maybe 15 or 16 summers at most. He could see she was beautiful, and he would train her passion as it blossomed. He had descended for her, and now the time had come to claim her. He headed toward her booth now.

He spotted her but stayed back a bit to watch. Hadassah stood among herbs, dried and tied in bunches with bits of twine, hanging along the top and side of the booth. Cut flowers and bouquets in pottery lined the ground around her feet. Next to her, Seth, her father, haggled with an elderly woman over the price of his potatoes which overflowed bins and bowls, some set on a table, some on the ground. The woman's gnarled hands were waving about in the air, apparently emphasizing her argument. Kharshea waited for the gesticulating woman to make her purchase and leave.

He approached the booth, and Hadassah and her father noticed him immediately. "Good morning!" Kharshea greeted them, smile firmly in place.

Seth frowned but then recovered quickly. "Good morning, sir. How can we be of assistance to you?" A compact, wiry man, Seth had skin darkened from the sun and forearms corded from years farming the land.

"I could not help but notice your beautiful selection of blooming flowers." Kharshea directed his comment directly to Hadassah. "Did you grow these yourself?""

She blushed and craned her neck up toward him. "Yes, sir. I have a yard where most grow happily enough and a small greenhouse for the more delicate blooms."

"They are as vibrant and beautiful as their gardener. What is your name?" He was leaned in closer to her, one arm braced against the side of the booth.

Hadassah's teeth sank into her bottom lip as the blush spread down across her chest at this stranger's bold question and manner. She stepped back slightly, glancing toward her father.

"I am Seth, and this is my daughter Hadassah. Dassah, gather a few fine stems to show…," he paused.

"Kharshea," he said, offering his hand to Seth.

Seth shook the larger man's hand. Tilting his head to the side a bit, he said, "You're not from around here."

"I have just recently come from the mountains."

Like most of the villagers, Seth had undoubtedly heard rumors of these men from the mountains. Some feared their sudden presence in the valley, others embraced the wealth of knowledge they brought with them. Since most people at this point had yet to meet one, they tended to believe the rumors of their unusual height had surely been exaggerated or even that the whole story was fabricated. Whatever Seth thought, Kharshea could see him struggling to absorb the undeniable fact of his encounter with one of the rumored tall men. Before Seth could further question him, Kharshea spoke again, his attention focused solely on Dassah.

Kharshea's hand stroked over a twined bundle with silvery-green leaves and small purple flowers pinned to the wall. "Do you know that we use many of these same herbs you have here back home. And also the roots. They make fine tonics for keeping health, curing illness…and other uses. If you were to make some of these tonics, people would flock to your booth. Only you would know how to brew them!"

"Curing illnesses?" Seth crossed his arms over his chest.

"Absolutely." Kharshea shifted his gaze towards Seth. "And people would pay good money for their illnesses to be cured, would they not?"

Dassah passed a small bouquet to Kharshea. He accepted it in his large hand, surreptitiously stroking a finger along the back of her hand as he did. She looked up at him through lowered lashes and smiled.

"Beautiful," he murmured.

Seth missed the exchange between the stranger and his daughter as he gazed off, distracted. Kharshea could practically see Seth counting coins in his head as he visualized the impact a new miracle cure could have on his money pouch.

Seth turned back toward Kharshea. "And you are offering to share these recipes with us?"

"I am."

"Why? What do you want?"

Kharshea made a show of sighing and allowing dismay to dampen his smile. "Why? Because I am alarmed at how the people of this valley struggle along without the life-giving knowledge to better themselves and their circumstances. My heart goes out to them."

"And the cost to me?"

"No cost. I came by it freely and will share it freely with you." Kharshea shoved down the urge to laugh since he knew Seth would take these 'miracle cures' and charge others plenty for them. Actually, he was counting on Seth doing that. "Though perhaps I would appreciate the chance at a friendship, an alliance of sorts, with your family? I am new here and don't know many people."

Kharshea was invited back to Seth and Dassah's cottage and garden over the next few weeks to share his familial knowledge of plants and roots, knowledge that was unknown in the valley. They naturally shared meals together and this soon led to a courtship and marriage between Kharshea and Dassah.

Dassah's mother, Hannah, was never in agreement with Seth about including this outsider in their life, giving their daughter to him. But by this point, as Kharshea had calculated, Seth probably felt tremendously indebted to Kharshea. His daughter *was* making the tonics and they *were* selling well and with high praise. Besides, Kharshea was a strong, healthy man and appeared to be wealthy. In fact, Seth would have reasoned, as a father he could not have done better for his daughter!

5

Kharshea leaned back in the chair with his legs stretched out in front of him, tapping the rim of his drinking glass absently with a long forefinger. The amber liquid within rippled from the vibration of the tapping. Behind him, a four-paned window set high in the wall of the sitting room showed only the profound blackness of late night. Two squat candles sat on the sill, their flames reflected back into the room. Several more candles were on the fireplace mantel. The fireplace itself contained only soft piles of gray ash. The silence was broken by muffled screams coming from the bedroom with some regularity now.

Kharshea glanced over at Seth, his wife Dassah's father, sitting across the room. He usually exuded an air of capable strength and a bit of arrogance, but at the moment the man appeared to be wilting into the horsehair bench he occupied. Seth's booted feet were planted on the wide wooden planks of the floor, his elbows set on his knees and his head sagged forward into his hands.

"Are you all right, Seth?"

Seth startled at Kharshea's question. He looked up at the huge man that filled the space in his sitting room and rubbed a calloused hand against the back of his neck. "No, I'm not all right." His adam's apple bobbed as he swallowed. "Can't you hear my daughter's distress?"

"Seth, she's a strong one. You give up too early." Kharshea sipped at his drink.

Seth sank back into his torpid state, appearing to completely shut down, no longer reacting to the nearly incessant screaming.

Kharshea shook his head, disgusted at how this man could behave as if he were so helpless, impotent.

The bedroom door flew open and Hannah bustled out with her arms wrapped around a large wooden bowl laden with a heap of bloody toweling. She passed by the men without looking at them, her expression like stone and mouth pressed into a grim line. Kharshea watched as she went into the kitchen and dumped the towels into a short barrel where they landed with a squelching thump. She set the bowl down and arched her back a bit to stretch out the knots and heaviness settling into her tired muscles. She tucked some hair escaped from the bun at the base of her neck back behind her ears and picked up the bowl again. Returning to the bedroom with fresh towels, she glared at the men as she strode by.

Kharshea's mind burst with pride and excitement. His child would be the first of its kind to grow up in the valley, the first ever Guardian offspring since time immemorial! This pending achievement helped to offset the bitter pill the Guardians had been forced to swallow. None of it seemed fair.

His race had been created to watch over the valley of men, but not interact with them except by command of Shalliyt. At least that was so since the day the impenetrable mist cloaked the mountains generations earlier. Before that, humans and Guardians had mingled to some degree, the way up and down the mountains open to men, and Shalliyt lived among them in the valley.

But since the mountain path closed to men, when their fickle human hearts turned them from the face of Shalliyt, Guardians watched from a distance and were rarely summoned to intervene. Some of the Guardians, these sons of Shalliyt, had desires prone to wander. They began to lust for the women of the valley, and prodded to action by their leader, Aarkaos, they acted on these desires.

Shalliyt made known his wrath to his sons for their disobedience through a message delivered by the prophet of the valley. The Guardians who swore the oath to Aarkaos were damned, if the Teller were to be believed, and would one day stand in the council of Shalliyt himself, face to face—for the last time—and be condemned to die like men.

This proclamation made the accursed Guardians more desperate for their plan. Now they had to achieve immortality in the way of man—through the begetting of offspring: a feat unknown to the Guardians to that point.

And this child, here in Seth and Hannah's small home, would be the genesis of the Guardian offspring and Kharshea's

30

path back to his forfeited immortality. Oh, technically he knew the child would not be the first born; that honor went to his brother Rhyima.

Kharshea sipped his drink and laid his head back against the chair, closing his eyes, remembering the disaster that was the birth of Rhyima's son.

Rhyima had married a delicate flower of a girl shortly before Kharshea descended through the mist. He had bullied his way into the family, not being particularly interested in courtly ways. But given the proper inducements, the parents gave over their young daughter easily enough. His harsh and dictatorial control over her paid off when she quickly became pregnant. Her belly swelled alongside the constant bruises that bloomed on her face and arms.

When the time came for Rhyima's child to be born, it had clawed its way out of its mother's womb, ripping her apart. The girl's father had come into the room and seen the child wheezing in a pool of blood between its dead mother's thighs. It was pink and wrinkly in the normal way of babies, a thatch of dark hair covered its head.

But then it opened its black eyes, and the father looked into their soulless, prescient depths. The truth of what he had allowed, what he had done to his daughter, slammed through him.

As soon as the midwife cut the cord, the father grabbed the now-howling baby by its heels with one hand and ran out the door, the child flopping against the back of his thigh. In front of the cottage, he swung his arm in an arc, smashing the child's head against a large rock half sunk in the grass. He brought his arm down over and over, blood splattering in every direction, till there was nothing left of the babe but a pulpy lump. Rhyima only got to him then, crushing the father's throat in his fist, a frothy substance squeezing out between the dying man's lips.

Soon after, Rhyima had taken his dead wife's younger sister as replacement. Fury constantly radiated from him and no one had dared to contradict his choice of recompense. She was only thirteen and lived in terror of her new, savage husband. As of yet, their union had proved unfruitful.

Kharshea took a lesson from Rhyima's experience. He would carefully watch Dassah's father around his newborn baby. Glancing over at Seth, he felt assured that this man was too broken at the moment to even lift himself from his bench. He was no threat.

Through the window, the first hint of dawn seeped over the mountains. The tiresome screeching had long since faded to a whimper, then winked out altogether like the spent candles on the windowsill. Heavy silence fell for several moments, and then a woman's weeping filled the cottage. The door to the bedroom opened and the midwife, Maddie, stocky and efficient with a blood-stained apron wrapped around her, stepped into the room with the men.

With hands clasped in front, Maddie fixed her eyes on Kharshea. "Sir, you have a son." She paused and breathed in deeply. "But your wife is dead."

Seth began to sob as his haggard body collapsed further into the bench.

Kharshea looked down at the drink in his hand. It bothered him that Dassah had died. She was pleasant to spend time with and beautiful to behold. She had soothed the ache that ran through his veins. But there were many more women available. He lifted the glass to his mouth and tossed back the contents. He stood, his frame filling the room, a smile slowly spreading across his face.

"Bring me my son!"

6

(Two Years Ago)

Hannah stood at the counter in her small kitchen, bundling different branches of herbs to hang above the windowsill to dry. She glanced over her shoulder at the child who played in the background just outside the kitchen door.

Briysh, her grandson, climbed trees and whooped it up like any normal boy. Hannah trembled. But he was anything but normal. At two summers old now, he was taller than the neighbor's child of eight. Much stronger, too. That neighbor's child had been forbidden by his father from ever coming over again to play after Briysh's cruelty to him.

When he thought no one was looking, Briysh had taken the older boy and shoved his head under the water of the rain barrel. Thankfully, Seth had rounded the corner of the cottage just then and rescued him. After Seth assured that the boy was okay and sent him home, he turned toward Briysh.

"What do you think you were doing?" Seth demanded.

Briysh shrugged and made some comment about wanting to see how the boy's legs would thrash up and down when he couldn't breathe.

Later, when Kharshea returned home, for the huge man continued to live with them after Dassah's death, Seth had told him of Briysh's disturbing behavior.

An expression flitted across Kharshea's face. It almost looked like...pride? "Well," he boomed out, slapping Seth on the back, "I bet that neighbor boy will be more careful next time!"

Word had spread, and none of Seth and Hannah's friends visited the cottage any more. Hannah couldn't blame them and was relieved they would continue to stop by the booth on market day to visit. Kharshea always took Briysh on market day. She had no idea where they went, but it was a huge relief having a day off from watching the boy.

At first Hannah felt guilty for feeling this way about Dassah's baby. But that soon passed as she disconnected in her mind her beautiful, laughing daughter from the offspring that could only be thought of as evil. Maybe evil was too strong of a word. But he was clearly without conscience or empathy. Because his father indulged him completely and ignored his poor behavior, there was no control on the boy at all.

Hannah realized she had gotten lost in her thoughts again and spun around to check on Briysh in the backyard. She could see the top of his black hair where he sat in the tall grass out a bit. What was he doing? Briysh never sat still unless he was plotting his next evil move. "Stop it, Hannah," she whispered to herself. "He's just a little boy."

She wiped her hands on her apron and headed outside to see what he was doing. As she crossed the back lawn, whisper-quiet, she saw him cock his head. Among his other abnormal features of height and strength and early speech, he had wolf-like hearing. He quickly shoved something under his leg.

"What do you have there, Briysh?"

"Nothing."

"It's something. Let me see it." Hannah extended her hand.

"I said it's nothing," the child snarled.

"Show it to me now."

At that, Hannah's little grandson smiled the most feral smile. Hannah wanted to jerk her hand back.

Briysh reached under his thigh, pulled out something, and flung it at Hannah.

She leaned over to pick it up where it landed at her feet. She ran her thumb over the braids of leather that formed a circle. Some fabric was woven in among the braid. Crusts of blood caked the leather in parts. Only one of these existed in the world and Dassah had made it.

"Briysh, where is the dog? This is his collar."

Briysh laughed and jumped up on his still slightly chubby legs and ran off to the nearest tree. He scaled it, still laughing, till he was hidden in the leafy branches.

Hannah closed her eyes while she gripped the collar. The dog had disappeared last week. Seth and Hannah figured Briysh had something to do with it, but they hoped he had run the dog off. The blood on the collar indicated otherwise.

34

Hannah vomited into the tall grass, wiped her face and her eyes with the apron, and headed back into the cottage still clutching the braided collar.

7

(Present Day)

Haven lay awake staring at the ceiling in the early hours of predawn. A mockingbird outside his bedroom window had begun running through its cache of stolen birdsongs and ambient noises—a repertoire that would only repeat itself with appalling merriment for the next few hours.

He sighed and got up off his pallet knowing that sleep would not return to him again this morning. He crossed over to a small table that held a pitcher of water and a bowl. He bathed himself by the silver wash of moonlight slanting through the window, though he could have done it in the dark just as well. He toweled himself off and quickly dressed. With silent footsteps he moved through his cottage, not wanting to disturb his sleeping mother, and stepped out into the brisk air of the early morning.

Stars still dotted the night sky, but Haven could see a faint pink limning the edge of the mountains to the east as he headed toward the small stable behind the cottage that sheltered their two draft horses. He eased open the oaken stable door. The horses sensed his presence immediately and began to shuffle around in their stalls.

"Easy, girls. Good morning to you." Haven spoke softly, reaching out to run his hands down their broad, velvet noses. Sheba and Shiloh occupied adjacent stalls. They would put their heads over the half doors of the stall to touch each other, tossing their heads and flipping their manes around. But now, they nuzzled into Haven's hands, their lips twisting to suck at the flesh of his forearm. They were seeking treats more than affection. Haven gave them their breakfast of hay and oats, then sat back on a bale of hay to wait till they finished.

He thought back over the day before. Convincing Jared to let Rachel come with him on a ride and picnic for the day had been surprisingly easy.

"Sure, sure, Haven, that sounds like a fine idea." Jared had waved him off distractedly as he continued rummaging through a drawer searching for something.

Rachel had beamed at the idea, which relieved Haven a great deal since he wasn't sure where he stood with her at this point.

Haven had turned to Rachel and said, "Wonderful. Then I will see you first thing tomorrow morning."

Rachel said nothing, but nodded and smiled, bouncing on her toes. Haven hadn't been completely forthcoming about the purpose of the journey as the Teller had relayed to him, but they would indeed be going for a ride and having a picnic.

The horses were done eating and began to get restless.

"Sheba, we are going on an adventure today." Haven opened the mare's stall door and reached up to slip a rope halter over her nose and behind her ears. Then he stepped back and led her out, her heavy hooves clopping along. Shiloh nickered in protest at being left behind. These mares did most things together, so Sheba's absence would be felt. Sheba snorted in the cool air outside and stomped her foot, ready for her adventure. Both mares were heavily muscled, their coats gray with flecks of black all over and tails and manes of white. The tails were kept braided and folded under, so as not to get caught in the plowing equipment.

Haven tied Sheba to the fence and began to rub her down. She leaned into him with the pleasure of it. When he was done currying her, he went back into the cottage and grabbed the cloth bag that held their picnic meal of crusty bread, cheese, and fruit. He slung the strap of the bag over his shoulder and headed back to the waiting horse. The sky was pinkening quickly and birds all around noisily greeted the new day.

Haven untied Sheba and walked her over to a stone wall. At nearly five and half feet tall at the withers, she was too tall to mount without a step up. He climbed up onto the wall, grabbed a fistful of her mane, and heaved himself up, throwing a leg over her broad back. He picked up the rope to her halter and turned her toward the path, plodding off toward Rachel's cottage.

When he arrived, the edge of the sun had just peeked over the rim of the misted mountains, throwing long shadows. Rachel was already outside waiting for him. She clambered onto a large rock and Haven pulled the horse alongside. He was glad to see she was sensibly wearing a pair of loose-fitting woolen pants conducive to sitting astride a horse. Her curls were pulled back into a ponytail. Her nose and cheeks bloomed a rosy pink.

"Good morning, Rachel."

She returned his greeting with a shy smile. "Morning."

Haven reached down to grab her arm and hoisted her up behind him on the mare's back. She clasped her arms around his chest, and they headed off.

"Has your father left for his shop already?" Haven spoke over his shoulder.

Her reply gusted against his ear. "Yes. He left just before you arrived." She paused, "Where are we going on this grand adventure of ours?""

"It's a surprise," he chuckled, giving away nothing.

The morning was beautiful, and he had his heart's desire nestled warmly against his back. For the first time in days, Haven felt at peace. But he had a feeling his surprise was not going to be a good one, though he had no idea what the Teller foresaw for them.

Rachel prattled on at length, but then fell silent and rested her head against Haven's back. Haven noted that she didn't mention the visitor from the previous week. They both enjoyed the warming of the morning and the comforting scenery of livestock grazing in pastures as they passed by on the rhythmic cadence of the horse's gait. Haven veered toward the path that followed along the foot of the mountains, as the Teller had directed, though it wasn't the most direct route to the south.

Several hours passed and the two were now in an unfamiliar area of the valley. They hadn't seen another cottage for some time. The path led them through meadows and copses; chattering squirrels leapt between branches overhead and snuffling badgers dug in leaf litter under the trees. In the distance they saw a hamlet of sorts.

Haven's back stiffened as they got closer. He kept his eyes focused on the settlement, trying to make sense of what he saw.

Sheba plodded in measured pace, a stacked stone wall along one side of the path and a brook burbling on the other side.

"Rachel, look at that." Haven pointed beyond the stone wall. A field stretched out before them. Instead of being green and leafy with crops or grass, it was blackened and barren.

Rachel had been drowsing but sat up straight. She shaded her eyes with one hand, still clutching Haven's chest with the other, and looked where he indicated. "The field looks burned. Why would someone burn their crops?"

"I don't know, but it looks to continue on through a number of fields."

They fell silent again as Sheba plodded onward. Haven noticed she was shying away a bit from the side of the path with the stone wall as it ran alongside the acres of scorched field. Haven spoke softly to Sheba to settle her. She responded to his tone and relaxed slightly, though her ears were at full-alert, pivoting forward.

"Haven, what is that black pile over there?" Rachel leaned to the side trying to get a better view. Haven set his hand on her thigh, urging her back. He knew Sheba would pick up on the shifting around and get nervous again.

Haven steered Sheba up to the wall and halted her. He handed the rope to Rachel and slid off Sheba's back. "Wait here. I want to check it out."

He hopped down from the wall onto the blackened dirt and trotted over to the pile Rachel had indicated. As he approached, a stench filled his nostrils. Haven had seen dead animals before, but this sight roiled his stomach. Up close, he could see a pile heaped up of a dozen partially burned sheep or goats—it was impossible to tell which. The hair or wool had all been singed off leaving behind a blackened film on the hides, which were brittle and curling off the bones. Their flesh was charred but not completely burned away, accounting for the putrid smell that hovered in the air here. The horns and hoofs remained fairly intact. Large black flies droned in a cloud around the pile, startling upward when Haven approached. He could see maggots as they writhed in the unburned flesh. He was thankful for his empty stomach as he felt it heave involuntarily at the smell and sight.

Haven spun around and headed back to Sheba and Rachel. He could see Rachel was struggling to keep the mare still. He didn't doubt Sheba could smell the rotting flesh. She tossed her head up and down, snorted, and pawed the ground.

Haven reached them, took the rope from Rachel, and got Sheba against the wall. He mounted her and adjusted Rachel back into place properly behind him. "We need to move on."

Sheba eagerly surged forward. Haven let her trot for a ways to get her past the foul pile in the field. He didn't explain what he saw to Rachel, though he knew she was probably curious, but she didn't ask as they bumped along the path.

As they came to the end of the last field, Haven pulled Sheba to a complete stop. They were at the edge of a grouping of four cottages—or what remained of them. They had all burned. Some heavy timbers and fireplace chimneys stood skeletal in the yard. The roofs and walls were gone.

"What do you want?" A gruff voice barked out from behind, startling Haven and Rachel.

Haven spun Sheba around. A middle-aged man stood in the middle of the path. He wore rough clothes and battered leather sandals. He leaned on a gnarled walking stick. One half of the man's face seemed to be badly damaged. Red welts and white lumps contorted his cheek down to his chin. His lip hung loose on that side. An empty eye socket gaped above the ruined flesh. A sheen of fluid oozed from the wound.

Haven swallowed and focused on the man's remaining eye. "Sir, we have ridden for a distance and would like to dismount and water the horse." He looked beyond the man and saw a small wooden shack that had been hastily cobbled together. They had walked right by it because their eyes were focused on the wrecked cottages.

"Fine," the man grunted.

Haven swung his leg around the front of him and leapt off Sheba. He turned and reached up to help Rachel down. Her eyes were wide.

She whispered to him, "Are you sure about this?"

"Yes, I need to find out what happened here," he said under his breath. Haven gripped her waist and pulled her off, setting her gently on her feet.

The man grumbled and motioned for them to follow him. Haven held Sheba's rope and trailed the man, with Rachel close behind. He led them to the center of the grouping of cottages, a squared-off area like a courtyard, to a wooden hand pump. A

41

rectangular trough sat underneath the spout. Haven tied Sheba's rope to a ring on the shaft of the pump and began to crank the handle up and down. Water splashed into the trough.

The man appeared with several cups in his hand. He dipped them into the spray as the trough filled. He took the filled cups and headed to the stone wall. He mumbled something that may have been "follow me." Haven stopped pumping and Sheba leaned down and began to suck in the cold water.

Haven reached out for Rachel's hand as they headed over toward where the man sat. He swung the cloth bag off his shoulder and began to open it. "We would like to share our meal with you."

"Thank you." The man barely spoke above a whisper. His good eye looked glassy with moisture. He passed them each a cup.

Haven sat on one side of the man and Rachel on the other. Haven passed out the bread and cheese. "I'm Haven, and this is Rachel. We live several hours north of here."

The man reached for the food, and Haven saw his hands were scarred, though not as badly as his face. "Eli."

Haven nodded. "Eli, will you tell us what happened here?" Haven swept his hand toward the fields and burnt-out cottages.

Eli tore off a chunk of bread and chewed thoughtfully. He swallowed and took a deep breath. "Ruffians brought this destruction to us."

"Ruffians?"

"Guardian spawn," Eli spat.

"Guardian spawn?" Haven could hear his heartbeat pounding in his ears.

"Yes. Those men from the mountains have begun breeding with our women. They birth monsters." His solitary eye blinked rapidly.

Haven heard Rachel suck in her breath.

Eli continued. "They grow quickly. Individually they are ill mannered. In a pack, they are savage." His nostrils flared. "Several weeks ago, four of them came here and demanded food. Jonas, my good friend and neighbor, fed them. But it was not enough. They burned our homes with a torch—"

Haven cut in. "Could you and your neighbors not stop *four boys*?"

Eli slammed his scarred fist onto his thigh. "You understand *nothing*!"

Rachel laid her hand on Eli's bulging fist. "Tell us, Eli," she spoke softly. Haven had never seen her so serious.

Eli looked off into the distance, going deep inside his mind, remembering that horrible day. The four boys had come into the courtyard that connected their cottages. Briysh, son of Kharshea, had stood in the middle of the group of boys, clearly the leader of the gang.

"Jonas!" Briysh bellowed, his legs spread and hands on hips. "Feed us. We hunger!" All the boys laughed. Briysh had thick black hair that swung free to his shoulders. His facial features were attractive but boyish and rounded.

Jonas's wife scurried out of her cottage carrying a platter with a lamb leg roast and potatoes. It was the dinner she had prepared for her family. She stood in front of the boys, looking directly into Briysh's eyes—he was the same height as she—and bent over to lay the platter on the ground before him. Another boy—Eli didn't know his name but noted that he had six fingers on each hand—lifted his booted foot and kicked Jonas's wife in the back end. She stumbled but recovered and turned directly back to her cottage.

No one else ventured out while the boys ate. They quickly finished the meal. "More, Jonas. We need more!"

Eli emerged from his cottage, going nose to nose with Briysh. "Go home, you brat. We've shown you generosity and hospitality, and you have returned hostility. Leave us."

Briysh leapt onto Eli—moving faster than seemed possible—and smashed him to the ground. He held Eli on his back, pinned by the neck. "Watch your mouth, old man." Eli saw hatred blazing in the boy's eyes. "Araza, bring me that torch," Briysh said.

Eli began to struggle fiercely, clawing at the hand around his throat.

Briysh laughed, his dark eyes dancing. "You are such a fool, Eli."

Araza grabbed the torch from in front of Jonas's cottage. It was perpetually kept lit to start the hearth fires in the evening. As Araza sauntered toward Briysh, he reached up and dragged the torch along the edge of the thatch roof of first Jonas's, then Eli's cottage. The dried grasses blazed in a whooshing vortex, sparks shooting skyward. Eli tried to scream to alert his wife to get out of the cottage. But Briysh held his throat tightly, and no noise escaped. Araza tossed the torch to Briysh, who deftly caught it with his free hand.

A red-haired boy, the fourth member of the gang, grabbed handfuls of burning thatch and tossed them onto the other two cottage roofs. Eli saw Araza and the six-fingered boy rounding up his wife and neighbors, herding them into a circle to watch helplessly as their homes burned.

Then Briysh laughed, spittle landing on Eli's face, and brought the torch down against his cheek. Searing pain bolted through Eli as flames licked up the side of his face, his beard instantly scorching. Eli screamed. Blessedly, he had passed out quickly.

◦❯❮◆❯❮◦

Rachel held both of Eli's hands in her own, tears tracking down her face. "Your family? The other cottagers? What happened to them?"

"They were not harmed. They went to find shelter in the village. My wife stayed with me for a time and nursed my wounds. But I sent her to the safety of her mother and father's house. I wished to remain here. This is my home, my land!"

"What about the livestock and fields?" Haven's voice came out in a croak.

"They burned the fields and pastures while I was senseless. I suspect they stole some of the animals, but they killed many, too. Everything…is gone."

The three sat without speaking for a few minutes, Eli dejected and Haven and Rachel stunned. The sun was high; billowy clouds drifted overhead in the azure sky, oblivious to the deadened, charred earth unfurled beneath them.

Haven rubbed his chin. "Eli, there is one thing I don't understand."

Eli swiveled his good eye toward Haven and waited.

"The Guardians only arrived a few summers ago, maybe ten at most. How old could their sons possibly be?"

Eli nodded and fixed his gaze off into the distance again. "Briysh is the oldest. He was born four summers ago."

44

Haven and Rachel headed back toward home. For a distance they rode without speaking. Sheba's steps were faster, as if she felt anxious to return to Shiloh. Rachel shivered against Haven's back even in the heat of the afternoon, and Haven clasped her hand in his, threading his fingers between hers.

The path turned closer to the mountains putting them in shade. Out of the glare of the sun, Rachel broke the silence, her chin resting on his shoulder. "Haven, you knew we were going to meet that man. How?"

"The Teller sent us there, Rachel. It was Shalliyt's will that we learn from him."

Rachel remained silent.

Haven decided it was time to press her on this issue. "Do you understand what we were to learn from this?"

"That it is important for me to go to the Tellings, because the Teller does speak truth?"

Haven wondered if it was really possible she did not see it. "And?"

"And what? Just say whatever it is you need to say, Haven," she huffed.

Haven slowly shook his head. "It's a warning to you, and your father, about your Guardian visitor."

"My Guardian…" her voice trailed off. "What are you talking about?" Her posture stiffened.

Haven pushed his hand through his hair. "The man, at your house last week. Exceedingly tall, black eyes, meeting with your father?"

Rachel barked out a most unladylike laugh. "You think he is a Guardian? Haven, that's ridiculous!"

Haven's heart sank. She couldn't see it either, just like her father.

She continued on. "He's just a man. Well, not *just* a man, he's quite a good man and a handsome one, too. He's intelligent and witty and…Haven, are you *jealous*?"

"No, I'm not jealous." He rubbed the heel of his palm against his chest. The pain from this conversation was almost physical. "I'm terrified," he said softly.

Rachel fell silent. The horse plodded on, her head nodding in rhythm with her step. Haven could feel Rachel shifting a bit behind him on the horse.

At length, she spoke again. "Haven, listen to me. That man is a good man. Even if he is a Guardian—and I don't see how that's possible—he is not evil. Not like these boys Eli spoke of, not like the Teller warns of. He is a gentleman."

"You barely know him," Haven ground out between clenched teeth.

"My father knows him better than I. His character seems without defect, and he has no feral children terrorizing the countryside!"

Not yet. He wants to breed those children with you. But Haven kept his thoughts to himself. They rode the rest of the way home in silence.

8

Rachel sat on her chair with a large wool-swathed distaff clenched between her knees and a spindle held out to one side, twirling. She pulled some wool from the distaff into a thin, even strand before wrapping it around the spindle in a consistent thickness.

She had been spinning since her mother taught her as a child. It came second nature to her now, and she used the time to think. She was making the thread that she would later weave into a blanket for Haven's mother with the lovely multishaded natural wool she had gotten from her favorite sheep. It had strands of silver and tan mixed in with the midnight blackness of the bulk of it. Haven's mother seemed to be always cold now, so Rachel thought the extra blanket would do her some good.

Her mind whirred in time with the twisting spindle, her thoughts tumbling and repeating. Her recent trip with Haven and meeting up with Eli-of-the-ruined-face had thrown her into a state of confusion. She understood that Haven was trying to warn her, and Eli's tale confirmed Haven's fears. But she saw no connection between that and the handsome man who filled her imagination now. Ashteala was his name: exotic, beautiful, and so capable.

As Rachel had grown, she assumed she would one day marry Haven. He was a good man, known for his integrity, and handsome in a boyish way. He cared for her deeply, she knew. And she cared for him too, always would. But maybe her feelings were more that of a sister toward her brother. She just couldn't be sure. Haven tended to be overly serious, often seeming to disapprove of Rachel's carefree manner.

Ashteala, though, was a thoroughly different type of man. So far he had only visited their home to see her father as they discussed some sort of business ideas, mostly involving the new metals. But he had taken time to speak with her, too. He laughed with her, seeming to enjoy her buoyant view of the world.

Just the week previous, Rachel had sat on this same chair, her distaff bundled with white wool that day, when Ashteala had startled her as she was deep in her thoughts.

"Oh!" Rachel had jumped when a large hand gently rested on her shoulder.

"Forgive me, Rachel." Ashteala smiled down at her with affection. He crossed the short distance of the room and grabbed a plain wooden chair that he then set near her.

He wore a fine linen shirt of bright white with a gold thread patterned in a crisscross at the seams. Rachel would love to know who did the needlework. The garment must be quite costly. It covered his massive chest, then tapered down to a narrow waist where the shirt was cinched in with a heavy leather belt. Full-length leather leggings were form-fitting on his muscular thighs and calves.

Rachel found herself staring at him as he folded his impossibly large frame on to the too small chair. She realized her mouth gaped in a ridiculous fashion at both his overwhelming masculinity and his attention toward her, so she schooled her features into a more well-bred expression. "Are you finished speaking with Father?"

This man that had gazed into Rachel's eyes was so charming, so beautiful. Haven completely misunderstood this fine gentleman. After all, Haven had only ever seen him for a few minutes before so rudely bolting away. Rachel had never known Haven to be particularly judgmental, but he was being so this time, and he was wrong!

"Not quite. A neighbor required his assistance. Something about a sheep and some brambles?" Ashteala lifted an eyebrow.

"Oh, yes. That would be Old Abe and his brier patch. His sheep are forever snagging their wool on those thorns. One would think he would have cut that nasty growth back by now. It really damages the wool and lowers the price he can fetch for it…" *Stop rambling, Rachel. You are going to bore this beautiful man to death.*

"It seems you have a real talent working with wool." He reached out and ran a finger down the ribbon that looped around holding the raw wool to the distaff. He continued downward following the ribbon to the bow where it was tied off just above her knee.

Rachel stared at the slow progress of that finger, mesmerized. Then it came to rest on her knee. It gently moved in a circle. Rachel snapped out of her trance and jerked her knee away. "Sir." She meant to say it sternly, but instead it ghosted out of her mouth more like a sigh.

Ashteala withdrew his finger and folded his hands together on his lap.

Rachel felt heat on her cheeks and knew she was blushing. She dragged her gaze up to his face. She was startled to see a different expression on his face. It was almost...predatory. It reminded her of her father when he chose a lamb for slaughter for a special occasion. As he looked at the choices, he would single one out, then clap his hands and smack his lips like he could already taste it. "That's the one, Rachel. He'll make a fine meal for us!" Her father's almost child-like enthusiasm would always make her laugh. It didn't feel as comfortable having that hungry expression directed toward her now.

"Rachel, beloved. I can see you are thinking too hard." A broad grin spread across Ashteala's face. He reached over and took her hand in his. Its smallness felt lost in his massive grip.

Rachel eased immediately and promptly forgot her temporary misgivings. His smile radiated warmth and security.

Just then the front door had opened and shut, and she heard her father's footsteps in the kitchen as he muttered to himself.

Ashteala stood. "I must go." He turned her hand palm up and bent over to press his lips to her there. Rachel thought she felt his tongue flick out against her salty, sweaty skin, but the moment passed quickly. He had winked then and walked away toward the kitchen and Jared.

Today, Rachel felt the heat crawl up the back of her neck again at the memory of that tiny flicker of his tongue against her palm. It sent tingles up her arm. She shook her head to clear it and set down her spindle. She needed to rub her palms together to get rid of a phantom itch there. Her hands slid smoothly back and forth in the slightly greasy lanolin that coated them from handling the fresh wool. She began rubbing up her forearms a little ways till her hands were clean.

"Rachel, have you seen my pipe?" Her father strode into the room.

"Yes, Father. It is sitting over there on the table."

She carefully laid the distaff on the floor next to the spindle, sat up, and laid her hands on her knees. Rachel had shared with her father briefly what had happened with Haven and the trip south. Jared had simply dismissed it with a wave and mumbled something about young people these days. She wasn't sure if he was referring to her and Haven or the destructive offspring Eli spoke of.

"Father, what do you think of Haven's concern about these supposed Guardians?" Warm afternoon light spilled through the window forming stripes along the polished wood floor.

Jared rummaged through items piled haphazardly on the table. "I think it's preposterous. And he thinks Ashteala is one of them. Did you see Ashteala levitate and fly away from here as he left? Ridiculous."

He finally looked at Rachel directly. "Look, I think Haven is a good man and he has certainly been a good friend to this family. I'm not sure why he has gone to the extreme on this. He just parrots back what he has been hearing from the Teller, who I think is too old now to be competent in his mission. The old man deserves a rest! …and we deserve a rest from him and his ideas."

"I agree that Ashteala is nothing but a good man." *Though maybe a bit lusty*, but she didn't voice that. "But could it be possible that Guardians have arrived on the other side of the valley and are causing problems? Maybe there is some truth to the Teller's prophecy and Haven's fear. "

Jared walked over to Rachel and put out his hands to her. She laid her hands in his, and he gently pulled her to standing. "My silly dove. It is all nothing. The Teller is old with a clouded mind filled with moving shadows, and Haven does not like the idea of another man possibly looking your way.

"But Father, I saw burned fields, and that poor man's story…"

"Can you not think of a natural reason that a field would burn? And you said the man was wounded in the head—was he thinking clearly? Enough of this Rachel!" Jared leaned over and kissed his daughter on the cheek. "None of this should concern you."

Rachel wasn't so sure.

9

Dinah spun in a circle, letting the gossamer material she held against her body flutter out around her. The dress was a stunning shade of scarlet, utterly different from the usual browns and tans worn by the village women. The color reminded her of the brilliance of a ruby. It was an opulent dress, costing her father a small fortune. But it would make her even more beautiful, and that was all that mattered.

Dinah commissioned the making of the dress from her dearest friend, Rebekah. Rebekah had recently married one of the mountain dwellers during the first influx. He had taught her the skill of dyeing fabric with unique blends of ingredients. The colors were beyond imagination: blues in shades of water and sky, yellows and oranges like the flowers of the meadows, reds of precious gems, and magnificent hues of violet and purple of dusk and dawn.

Rebekah was already a skilled seamstress, so the addition of the transcendent colors to her fabrics afforded her instant acclaim among the village's wealthier women. And it was not just wealthy women, though a good deal of money was required to purchase one, but also women with a tendency toward narcissism and vanity, as the dresses tended to accentuate, and reveal to some degree, the women's feminine assets.

Dinah's handmaid, Judith, came into the room. "May I help you dress, Miss Dinah?"

Dinah had just finished bathing and wore only her thin shift. "Yes, but be careful with the material. It is delicate and expensive." She held out her arms for Judith to slip the dress over her.

The dress had a form-fitting bodice that closed up the back with an intricate criss-crossing of satin straps. Judith carefully weaved the straps back and forth the way she had been shown, starting at the neckline and working down. At the bottom, she finished with an extravagant bow. The front of the bodice plunged in a deep arc revealing a good deal of Dinah's bronzed skin. Or it would have revealed it if the shift didn't ride so high.

"This will not do," Dinah huffed, as she shoved at the offensive material that covered her modestly.

"Wait, Miss. Please let me help you." Judith smoothed out the rucked up material and began to carefully unbutton the tiny buttons on the front of the shift. As she went, she tucked under the spare material till she was down to the underside of Dinah's breasts. Then she straightened out the neckline of the scarlet dress, smoothing it as she went. "Is this how you wish it to look, Miss?" Judith's forehead wrinkled at what the dress revealed.

Dinah took a deep breath, looking down at the rise and fall of her cleavage, and smiled. "Perfect."

The skirt of the dress hugged her trim stomach, then fell straight to the floor from there. "Get my slippers."

Judith scurried to the wardrobe and removed a pair of tan leather-soled slippers. She got on her knees to slip them on Dinah's feet. Dinah had always been proud of these well-crafted slippers, but now, somehow, they seemed drab compared to the dress. She wondered if Rebekah could apply her dye-craft to shoes. She would have to mention it to her.

Dinah sat in a chair, and Judith began to style her hair. She piled Dinah's white-blonde hair atop her head in swirls, with a few pieces hanging down along her cheeks. Judith walked over to the window where a glass vase sitting on a small table held a clutch of meadow flowers. Selecting a few, she returned to Dinah and skillfully weaved the flowers into her hair.

"Let me see, Miss."

Dinah turned her head and looked up at Judith. Dinah's pale hair contrasted beautifully to her sun-bronzed skin. A long slim nose bisected large eyes that shone a deep golden brown. Pale lashes, nearly as blonde as her hair, fringed her eyes. Her lips were prettily shaped but a bit thin.

"Miss, you are beautiful!"

Dinah dismissed Judith with a wave of her hand as she stood. Judith nodded and walked out. Dinah absently tugged on one of her artfully hung tendrils as she gazed out the window, unfocused. She smoothed her hands up and down the sides of her dress.

She looked forward to tonight intensely. Marahka had been courting her and they would soon be wed. He stood tall and elegant. Dinah thought he looked regal in bearing. He had shiny black hair, deep, brooding eyes, and a trim beard and mustache.

Dinah loved his hands; they were exquisite, large, with long fingers. When he set his hand against the small of her back it felt like it spanned the width of her. He dressed in finery unknown in the valley. Marahka would be picking her up and taking her to the local inn known for its sumptuous fare.

Dinah was jerked from her reverie by several loud thumps on the front door. She waited in her room till Judith had time to let Marahka into the sitting room. She checked her nails, patted her hair, and smoothed her dress for the tenth time. She looked down at her cleavage and made sure the dress sat low enough. She grabbed a white shawl, putting it around her shoulders to cover up before being seen by her father or mother.

Dinah walked out to the sitting room. Marahka was already deep in conversation with her father, their heads bowed together as they stood together in a shaft of sunlight from the side window. Her father was nodded at something the other man was saying. Dinah crossed her arms across her chest and began tapping her toe. *What could they possibly be discussing that is so important?*

Dinah cleared her throat. The men promptly turned toward her. A smile spread across Marahka's face as he pointedly looked at her from head to toe.

"Ah, there you are dear. You look lovely. Marahka and I were just discussing some business, but I shall leave you two to continue on to your dinner." Dinah's father walked toward her leaned down and kissed her cheek.

"Thank you, Papa." Dinah's fingers fidgeted with the edge of her shawl as she waited for Marahka to speak.

Her father left the room and Marahka slowly strode toward Dinah. "You are a vision, Dinah. There is no woman as beautiful as you." He reached out and ran his finger along the edge of her shawl where it crossed her chest. "Surely a shawl isn't necessary on such a warm evening?" He raised an eyebrow. His smile shifted slightly from sensual to almost feral.

Dana shivered with pleasure. "I'll just wear it till we leave the house."

Marahka offered her his arm. "Then we shall leave at once."

She put her arm through his and they stepped out onto the street. It was a quiet evening, the sun just starting to dip toward the mountain in the west. Several children were in front of the next house down, sitting in a circle, playing a game with stones.

Marahka turned toward Dinah, and with his free hand, carefully unwrapped her shawl and laid it over her arm that was entwined with his. "Much better." His gaze was boldly directed at her chest.

Dinah felt exposed. She had never revealed this much of her body in public. At first a feeling of natural modesty washed over her and she raised her arms to cover herself.

Marahka blocked her movement gently. "You are beautiful, Dinah. Let the world see that." His voice was silky.

She knew her cheeks were blushing furiously, but the feeling of shyness was replaced by a heady sense of…power. "Yes…yes, I shouldn't deprive the people of the view." She laughed, sounding more childish than she wished to.

He flashed her an indulgent smile and gestured for her to continue walking along the side of the road. "Shall we?"

They skirted the boys completely enthralled with their game. Dinah looked around and noticed with satisfaction that the few people still on the street were all looking at her. She wasn't sure if it was the brilliance of the scarlet gown, the exposure of her flesh, or the towering, magnificent man walking alongside her that attracted the most attention. She lifted her chin and stood straighter. Marahka looked down at her and chuckled.

The inn was just a short walk from Dinah's house. It was tucked in with a row of homes, only a wooden sign hung above the door to distinguish it from the rest. The rectangular sign had a burnt engraving announcing it as The Marauding Kestrel; a carved kestrel, wings spread, perched atop it. A small black eye in the bird's face peered down at those who considered entering.

Marahka held open the door and Dinah stepped into the dimly lit room. A single large area opened before them with heavily beamed low ceilings. Tables filled the room leading up to a large, blazing fireplace along the opposite wall. About half of the tables were occupied with diners, who one by one, stopped speaking and turned to stare at the couple. A steward was immediately attending to them.

"Sir, right this way. Your table awaits you," the steward said, slightly bowing. His glance flicked across Dinah's cleavage as he turned to lead them further into the room. As they wended their way around the tables, Dinah felt the stares of the men, as if they were undressing her with their eyes; the women glared.

The steward stopped and gestured at a table that Dinah noticed was right in the middle of the room. "As you requested, sir," he said and scurried off once the couple sat.

Dinah felt on display, surrounded on all sides by the mix of ogling and hostile glances. Marahka laid his large hand over hers, and gently rubbed his thumb over the back of her knuckles. She soon forgot those around them by staring into his dark eyes, thrilling her to her core.

The steward returned and poured them each a glass of red wine from a black bottle, then retreated wordlessly. Dinner was an elegant affair. They dined on roast duck and rack of lamb, warm crusty bread, and a variety of vegetables marinated in wine vinegar.

Marahka was attentive to Dinah throughout the meal, listening to her chatter about inconsequential things. He kept his eyes focused on her eyes or her mouth, and not infrequently glancing down to the swells of her breasts. When she would realize where he was looking, she involuntarily took in a deep breath, causing his lips to turn up a bit at the corners.

When the dishes had all been cleared, Marahka wiped his mouth with the linen napkin, then leaned forward to speak more intimately with her. "I would like you to come up to my room with me." He lived in quarters above the restaurant. Having only recently arrived in the valley, he did not yet have a home of his own.

Dinah laughed nervously. "Sir, I hardly think that is appropriate." There was no heat in her words as she smiled at his suggestion.

"I have a gift for you. That is all." He stroked the inside of her wrist with his finger. "I mentioned it to your father. He will not mind."

Oh. The heat that swirled through her body from his simple touch made it hard for her to think at all. She simply nodded and allowed him to gently pull her up by her hand.

They headed toward the back of the room where the fireplace was, the flames snapping and popping as they stretched up the chimney. A door stood next to the fireplace, and he opened it revealing a narrow, winding wooden staircase. He stepped aside to let her ascend first. He had to bend to pass through the doorway which was a full head shorter than he. She felt his hand come to rest on her hip, gently urging her up the dim passage. At the top of the stairs, she paused till he joined her.

A hallway led from either side of the staircase. He took her hand and led her to the first door on their right and opened it. She stepped through and immediately smelled the faint scent of Marahka in the room. It was a woodsy essence and thoroughly masculine. She took a deep breath and felt lightheaded just being this close to his personal space.

The room contained a bed, wardrobe, and writing desk and chair. Two windows framed the desk. If she was oriented properly, Dinah figured they faced out the back of the inn. But it was dark out now and impossible to tell. His possessions were few, but kept tidy. He walked over to the desk where she noticed a large wooden box occupied the center of it. He laid his hand on the box, almost reverently, then motioned to the chair. "Please, sit."

She did, her eyes riveted to the top of the box where Marahka's forefinger absently traced a design that was deeply engraved in the wood. She didn't recognize the pattern, a combination of geometric and floral motifs. In the center, three bold circles intersected one another; a flurry of leaves surrounded them in a border. His finger trailed around each of the circles in turn, over and over.

The moment stretched long, and Dinah realized he hadn't spoken. She quickly looked up at his face. Marahka gazed sightlessly off through the window, deep in thought or memory she supposed. She cleared her throat. "Is this my gift?"

"Yes!" He was suddenly back from his musings and grinned broadly. He sat on the edge of the desk and slid the box closer to her. He removed his hands and folded them in his lap. "Go ahead and open it."

She reached forward and placed one hand on each side. She nibbled on her bottom lip and she realized her heart was racing. Whatever lay in this box would be amazing or expensive. Either option was fine. She slowly lifted the beautifully engraved lid, surprised at how heavy it was. She set it aside and leaned forward, peering into the belly of the box. It contained various ceramic pots and glass vessels, containing she knew not what. Her shoulders slumped a bit. "What is all this?"

"These," Marahka said, while reaching in and extracting a pot, "are various preparations for beautifying." He looked at her expectantly.

She had no idea what he meant. Her confusion must have shown on her face.

Marahka set the pot back down and walked over to the wardrobe. He pulled out a small framed object and returned to where he sat on the desk. "This is a vanity glass." He showed her the frame that surrounded a silver-backed, hard glass surface. He slowly rotated it toward her.

She gasped when she caught her reflection for the first time. "It...it is amazing! I have seen my image in house and shop windows but it is never as clear and lifelike as this. Marahka, where did you get this?" Dinah touched her face and hair, watching her hands' movements in the mirror.

He chuckled. "That's my secret. But it will help you understand your gift." He set the mirror on the back of the desk, propping it against the wall facing Dinah. She was mesmerized by the clarity of the appearance of her own face gazing back at her.

He reached over and touched her chin with his finger, turning her away from her self-inspection to look at him. "You are already a very beautiful woman, but these preparations will enhance your appearance, highlighting the best features of your face. No woman will *ever* rival your beauty." He reached into the box and removed three different glass jars. She could see the color of the contents through the glass. They contained various shades of red.

Marahka looked from her back to the jars several times, then seemed to come to a decision. He put two of the jars back. He removed the glass stopper from the jar he still held and dipped his finger into the preparation. The small dab of red on the tip of his finger seemed to be of a creamy texture.

With his other hand, he lifted her chin more so that she looked directly at him. He slowly smoothed the red stuff on first one of her cheekbones, then the other. "This particular compound imitates the blood rushing to a woman's face when she is animated or blushing."

Dinah swung her face back to the mirror to see what he had done. He was right; it was a lovely effect. It reminded her a bit of when her friend Rebekah's cheeks chapped when a strong wind chafed them, but this was smoother…more sensuous. "That's amazing," she whispered.

"Ah, but we are not yet finished." Marahka took another dollop of the red and waited for her attention again. Dinah looked at him, broadly smiling now. "For this you need to close your lips together."

She did, and he smeared the creamy substance slowly across her lips, back and forth. His finger moving pleasurably along her lips brought back that same tight, shivering feeling in her gut that she felt earlier when he stroked her hand.

With his other hand he removed a handkerchief from his pocket and wiped his finger clean. "The lip application imitates a woman's heightened arousal as the lips fill with blood, highlighting them so that all who look at her feel her seduction." The tip of Marahka's tongue came out and quickly swiped along his own top lip. His expression became more intense as he gazed at her.

Dinah swiveled back toward the mirror. Her mouth dropped open at the change she saw in her reflection. Marahka reached over and lifted her chin, closing her mouth. "The effect is better when your mouth is not hanging open," he chuckled.

Then he continued on. "The last of your attributes we shall accent are your eyes." He replaced the red-filled glass pot and removed a ceramic one. He lifted the lid and showed her the contents. Dinah peered in and saw a solid black color. Marahka reached back into the box and extracted a small item that looked like a tightly tied bundle of grasses. Instead of using his finger, this time he dipped the bundle into the pot, blackening the tips. "I am going to draw this across your upper and lower eyelid, above and below your lashes. Keep your eyes wide open for me and try not to move."

Dinah sat frozen, terrified he might inadvertently stick her in the eye. But Marahka seemed well practiced at the application. He explained, "This will enhance your eyes, making them appear larger and more provocative."

Dinah, once again, quickly sought out the mirror. She was stunned by her new appearance, raising her hands and placing them on either side of her face. Marahka didn't give her time to gawk at her reflection any longer, as he took hold of her arms and stood her up from the chair, turning her to face him.

He stood very close to her. She had to arch her neck to look up to his face. He leaned down and whispered into her ear. "When we are married, I will teach you the art of producing these preparations. Women will flock to you so that they too can *attempt* to be as alluring and lovely as you." His breath wisped into her ear fluttering the strands of hair that fell there. "Beautiful women will never be satisfied, requiring greater beauty at any cost. Plain women will also seek improvement, older women will chase their youth. And the young will want to appear more mature. You, my dear, will be wealthy beyond your imagination. The women of the village will practically worship you." He ran his tongue along the shell of her ear and then gently sucked on her earlobe.

Dinah gasped, but was beyond speech, because of his promise of the future and because of his current seduction. She lusted for both.

Marahka pushed her slightly back then and held her at arm's length. Dinah had never seen his eyes look so black, so savage. His gaze raked down her from head to toe and back up again. She was both terrified and intensely aroused by his expression.

He began firmly moving her backwards till she felt the edge of the bed against the back of her thighs. Still gripping her arms, he leaned down and lightly kissed her. She pressed back against his mouth, wanting more contact, but he held her away from him and smiled. Dinah realized she was shaking from the intensity of this encounter.

Then suddenly Marahka released his grip on one of her arms. He reached forward to the low dipping neckline of her dress and grasped the material in his fist. Before she could react, he ripped the material straight down to the bottom, both dress and shift torn asunder. A scream began to well up from her core, more so because of the insult of the ruined dress than the assault on her modesty.

But Marahka's fingers clapped over her mouth. "Hush, my dear. I shall buy you another, and then many more." Then he shoved her backwards on the bed.

She landed flat on her back, a frigid apprehension slithering through her veins. Her mouth wordlessly opened and closed, till she finally croaked out, "We are not yet wed."

"Soon enough, my dear. Soon enough," was the last thing Marahka said, before he fell on her.

10

Haven and Rachel entered the village on a dusty road that wound in from the countryside. Flocks driven into the village market ahead of them had left evidence mounded and fly-covered along the path that required some vigilance in placing each step.

They spoke very little to each other. Rachel was distracted and remote, and she maintained a physical distance between them while they walked.

Haven was deep in his thoughts too, though the increase in people and buildings around them brought him to attention. A pair of tittering young ladies brushed by them.

Haven stopped and turned, staring at them after they passed. The ladies looked like a pair of exotic birds, with brightly colored dresses and matching, impossibly colored feathers poking up from hair swept up on to their nodding heads. Haven wasn't sure he saw correctly, and now he could only see the back of the women, but out of the corner of his eye as they passed, he thought he saw a good deal of *leg* showing.

As if one of them could hear his thoughts, his confusion, she looked over her shoulder at Haven. When she saw him staring, she spun around and stood there, one hand propped on a cocked hip. Haven's eyes dropped to see that, sure enough, her bright blue dress was pinned up high on each thigh, dipping low to her ankles between her legs. An expanse of bare flesh—thigh, knee, shin and ankle—down to a matching pair of sapphire slippers was exposed to him. His gaze flew back up to her face to see her smirking. Then she *winked*. His face flooded with heat and he spun back around, jogging to catch up with Rachel who was oblivious to the whole exchange and had wandered on. *Where was that woman's modesty?*

Now that he looked around more, he realized that a few women here and there along the road and walkways wore these highly unusual colors, ostentatious peacocks strutting amongst dull pigeons. The colors were pretty, but thoroughly inappropriate for women's clothing. The women were clearly attempting to draw attention to themselves in a brazen fashion. And the lewd cut of the dresses for the most part was outrageous. Haven glimpsed more rounded leg and breast swells in those few minutes than he had in his entire life. His face burned and he trained his gaze straight forward.

Thankfully, Jared's workshop sat near the edge of the village, so they soon arrived. The door stood propped open to catch any breezes. Haven guided Rachel in first, and followed behind her.

"Rachel, sweetheart, what a surprise!" A wide smile spread across Jared's face. Sawdust covered the front of his clothes, his sleeves rolled up. The scent of cut wood filled the air. "Haven," he said with a nod. His greeting was a little cool.

"Hello, Papa. Are we disturbing you?" Rachel's eyes flicked around the shop, her mouth set in a frown.

"Not at all!" Jared embraced her briefly. "What brings you two to town?"

Haven glanced over at Rachel. "It's a fine day for a walk," he said. "If it's all right, I'll leave you two to visit and return shortly."

"Fine, fine." Jared put his arm around Rachel's shoulders and led her to a bench in the rear of the shop. Her eyes were now fixed on the floor.

Haven sighed and left the shop. He didn't want to admit that he was a little intrigued, under the shock of it all, with what he had seen the women of the village wearing. He walked past several storefronts, glancing casually around. Across the street he saw another flash of bright. The colors stood out powerfully among the neutrals of homespun clothing. He stopped and gaped at the woman: bright yellow dress this time but with a matching scarf wrapping her hair. *Where had this trend come from?* At least this woman wasn't revealing any body parts. She walked on by, chattering with her male companion.

"Hey, handsome," a woman's voice purred into Haven's ear.

He spun around. He had stopped to gawk with his back to an alley that ran between two buildings; this woman seemed to have emerged from the alley.

"You like to look at the pretty ladies?" She smoothed her hands through her hair, long brown and hanging loosely past her shoulders.

"N-no!" Haven could not look away from her face. It was...*painted!* Her eyes were ringed in black and her cheeks reddened. She pursed her lips, juicy and red. Then her small pink tongue slowly came out and licked along her bottom lip.

"That *lady* you were admiring? You can only *look* at her. Me you can *touch.*" As she said 'touch,' her hands reached the bottom of her hair and continued on, smoothing slowly down over her breasts. "Call me Leah." She sucked on her bottom lip.

Without his permission, Haven's eyes followed Leah's hands in their descent. She too wore bright colors, though hers were filmy and transparent. His eyes dilated when he realized he could actually *see* her nipples, brown and stiff, through the gauzy material. He was slammed with a dizzying mix of revulsion and arousal simultaneously.

He took a step back at the same moment she reached for him.

She laughed. "Don't be shy, boy."

Haven's mouth opened and closed, but nothing came out. He had absolutely no idea what to say. He wanted to run. He wanted to look. He was saved from having to make a decision when someone shoved him to the side.

Leah's attention swiveled to the interloper. "Briysh. Back for...more?"

Haven noted the tone of her voice had changed. Where she had been soft and seductive with him, she now spoke more hesitantly, less temptress and more like a fearful little girl. The dark-haired young man gave her a feral grin but said nothing. Haven looked at him hard. His name sounded familiar but he didn't recognize him. *Briysh......Briysh...it's an unusual name that I should be able to place.*

Briysh, completely ignoring Haven, reached out putting his large hand around Leah's throat and thrust her against the stone wall. With his other hand, he dipped into her transparent decolletage and roughly squeezed her breast. She squeaked but did not struggle. He released her throat, now pinning her to the wall by her breast, and bent to reach up under her dress.

Haven finally shook off his shock and lunged toward the man, grabbing at his shoulder. Briysh let go of the woman's breast and backhanded Haven across the face, slamming him into the opposite wall.

Haven was stunned by the strength of the hit. He took in a deep breath, swiped at his bloodied nose, and pushed himself off the wall. Even with Leah's complete lack of modesty, Haven would not stand by and let her get mauled. Briysh turned away from Haven and crushed his mouth against the woman's.

Her eyes were open and on Haven. He locked eyes with her over the man's shoulder and headed toward them again. She broke off the kiss and gasped, "No! It's okay." She grabbed Briysh's hand and began to drag him toward a door in the wall part way down the alley. "Come, Briysh. You can have what you want." They disappeared through the doorway, the woman throwing a quick glance back to Haven, offering him a small smile. The door slammed shut.

Haven leaned back against the wall and slid his back down it, exhaling loudly, and just sat. He rested his head in one hand, elbow propped on his knee, and squeezed his nose with the other, to stem the bleeding. *What just happened?*

Suddenly Haven slammed his head back against the wall. *Briysh! Eli's story. The feral manboy, spawn of a Guardian, who'd burned Eli's face and destroyed his property.* Haven remembered asking Eli why the men with him couldn't stop four such boys from attacking them. A brittle laugh escaped Haven. The strength of just one was inhuman. They were inhuman. According to the Teller, they were *not* human.

Haven pulled himself off the ground. He worried about Leah disappearing with Briysh. He walked over to the door and tugged on it, but it was locked. He pounded on it with frustration. Realizing he could do nothing for her, he headed back to Jared's shop.

Haven used his sleeve to wipe his nose as he walked over the threshold into the shop. It had stopped bleeding and Haven hoped Rachel and Jared wouldn't notice it.

Rachel stood when Haven entered. She had a softer look about her face. She wasn't smiling but she looked more at peace. Something was bunched in her hand.

"Look what Father got for me." Rachel reached toward him and Haven saw a brilliant flutter of red unfolding from her fist. "A scarf. Isn't it a beautiful color?" she said softly. She tied the scarf around her neck loosely, knotting it at the corner. She fussed with it, patting it.

Haven stood stunned. *Oh, no…* He berated himself, *it's just a scarf, nothing immodest.*

Rachel noticed Haven's lack of response. "Haven? What's wrong? And what happened to your face?"

He croaked, cleared his throat, "Nothing to worry about." *Change the subject.* "Your scarf is a stunning color." Haven turned toward Jared. "Where did you buy this?"

Jared waved his hand dismissively, "They are for sale here and there now…the newest thing to amuse our girls." He smiled at Rachel fondly, obviously pleased that she was, if not happy, at least less unhappy for the first time in weeks. "The recipe for the color dyes came from the mountain dwellers. They are an industrious lot, probably with beautifully clothed women back home, I would say."

Guardian knowledge. Of course. Haven shook his head slightly. "Rachel, should we head back now?"

She stood on tiptoe and gave Jared a quick kiss on the cheek.

They headed home.

PART TWO

11

(A Few Weeks Later)

Leah lay in bed with Briysh, exhausted and bruised from his coupling with her. He was brutal and used her like an empty, unfeeling vessel. She suspected he cared nothing for her. She doubted he cared for anyone. He had never been gentle with her, but in the beginning at least he gave her gifts or coins in exchange for her *favors*. Now she only received threats from him if she didn't immediately comply with his demands. And his passions ruled his behavior.

Leah sighed, looking up at the ceiling of her room. Briysh snored next to her. She rubbed her hand against her belly gently in a small circle. She was pregnant, and the child was probably his. She feared telling him. She feared *not* telling him. Would he hate her for it? Would he come to care for her? She smiled at that possibility. Maybe a child would forge the path to a connection between them. Not love, surely. But maybe some form of affection. He could protect her and provide for her. Maybe he would even stop feeling the need to couple with all of her friends, and for that matter, any woman whose path he crossed that got his attention.

At first, she had enjoyed the freedom and fun of dressing up in beautiful clothes and cosmetics and perfumes, playing the temptress to men. She found she was a natural at it, and the men were oh so susceptible. She was flattered by them falling at her feet and paying her to sleep with them. And it was a definite improvement over the constant gnawing belly of her youth.

But it began to feel hollow. Loneliness creeped into her soul when she rested alone in the dark from her flirtations. And now that Briysh demanded so much of her time and energy, without compensation, she barely could support herself. This baby could be, no, *would* be, her way out of this situation.

Decided now on her course of action, she rolled over to Briysh and laid her head on his shoulder. She gently stroked her fingers through the mat of black fur covering his chest. His snoring stopped and his hand clamped down on top of hers.

"What are you doing?" He growled.

"I thought we could talk." She pulled her hand free and twirled her finger through a chunk of hair above his navel.

He grunted. "What do you want from me?"

She chewed on her bottom lip. She dragged her finger up and circled his nipple. "I'm going to have a baby......we're going to have a baby."

He said nothing.

She pushed on, propping herself up on her elbow to look into his eyes. "You are going to be a father, Briysh"

Briysh shoved her back, swung his legs over, and sat on the edge of the bed, feet on the floor. He said over his shoulder, "You are a whore. This is not my problem."

What? Wait...no. Her plan was derailing quickly. "But Briysh, don't you want a child?" A small smile tried to form on her quivering lips.

Briysh snorted. He stood, silently pulled on his pants and shirt, and left the room without a backward glance.

12

Three men sat around a table, consuming a vast quantity of food. They had been mostly silent as they ate, but one by one, as their plates emptied, they sat back. An alert waiter brought the wine that would lubricate their after-dinner conversation. After filling all the glasses, he left the bottle and hurried off.

Kharshea leaned forward and picked up his glass, then leaned back again, stretching long legs under the table. "So gentlemen, is it well with you?"

The fireplace behind him snapped and popped, radiating heat and backlighting him, so his features were slightly obscured, his eyes completely swallowed in dark hollows. A candle on each of the half dozen tables throughout the room cast small pools of light, lending an intimacy to the setting. The inn's dining area was mostly empty now as it was late.

Rhyima lifted his glass, swirled the contents, and took a healthy swallow. "My wife is expecting." He took another deep drink. "Again." He set the glass down, folding his hands on his belly. "With luck, she will successfully carry this time."

The third man, Marahka, grunted and turned toward Rhyima. "How many has she lost?"

"Two. But she is three months in now…the longest she's ever carried," said Rhyima.

Kharshea reached over and slapped Rhyima affectionately on the shoulder. "Have no fear, brother. You will have a son soon. Then he can raise hell with my son." Kharshea laughed.

Rhyima nodded and chuckled, too.

"Speaking of your son, Kharshea, you need to reign that boy in. Briysh is raising hell around the village, causing trouble for the people," Marahka said.

Kharshea crossed his arms over his chest and pressed his lips together tightly. After a pause, he waved his hand and said, "Briysh does what he wants. What is it to you?"

"Some look to us with ill will because of his brutish behavior."

"Is he any worse than the rest of us?" Kharshea shrugged. "He takes what he wants."

"Granted. But he is more, how shall I say it, *obvious* about it than we are. We have come in peace to settle with the people, improve their lives—"

"And slake our lust." Rhyima snickered.

Marahka sighed.

"Well, he'll be joining us soon. Then you can mention to him directly about his **brutish** behavior." Kharshea turned back to Rhyima. "So she is three months in. Dassah's pregnancy took about six months..."

"Yes, my first wife's was about the same," Rhyima said. Both the other men nodded.

Kharshea was pleased Rhyima would soon have a son since the disastrous event of his father-in-law killing his first child. The younger sister, his new wife, had finally become fertile. "Our sons develop faster than the humans'. Superior seed, of course!"

"Speaking of superior seed. Whatever happened to our esteemed leader, Aarkaos? He began all this, yet I have not seen him in the valley, nor heard of his exploits," Marahka said.

Kharshea chuckled. "Maybe he is busy plowing as many women as possible and fathering many brats. It occupies all of his time so he has none left for his faithful underlings." His smile faltered a bit. "But you're right. I've heard nothing of him since we arrived here."

"Maybe he discovered a preference for the valley fauna over the squawkings of the human women, as I noticed some of our brethren have. We could search the woods and lairs for him." Rhyima smirked at the possibility.

Kharshea shrugged. "Fair point. There is little difference between the bleating of a goat and the whining of a woman."

Their conversation fell silent as the waiter returned, delivering another bottle of wine.

Briysh strode up to the table then. He turned to the waiter. "Get me a chair."

The waiter quickly retrieved another chair and set it at the table by Kharshea who had moved over a bit to make room. "Son, sit and tell us how you have been!"

Briysh flopped into the chair gracelessly. "Father. *Gentle-men.*" Sarcasm dripped from his voice. Rhyima and Marahka warily nodded to him.

Briysh chuckled. "How have I been? Good, I'd say. I eat well,"—he patted his stomach—"and grow stronger every day!" Then he raised his voice and called over his shoulder, "But I *am* quite thirsty."

The waiter, face ashen at his slip, delivered another glass to the table. His hand trembled slightly as he placed it in front of Briysh. "Here you are, sir."

"You're useless. Leave us." Briysh reached for the wine bottle and filled his glass, then sagged back into his chair.

"You are taller every time I see you, Briysh," said Rhyima. "As tall as a man now."

"Taller than that. I am almost your height and I will soon exceed it. I will tower over all of you." He tossed his wine back with one gulp. He wiped the back of his hand across his mouth. "Apparently there is another thing at which I exceed." He reached for the bottle again, refilling his glass.

Briysh waited for one of them to ask what that thing was. But the Guardians just stared at him.

Kharshea finally spoke, "Please, share your accomplishments with us." He smiled and gestured to the group around the table.

"I…" He belched. "…exceed at breeding." Then he smirked. "I just learned this day that I have impregnated a girl."

Rhyima said, "Are you convinced of this? Surely, you are too young."

"I vow to you that my manhood is perfectly functional." He laughed harshly at this. "I have four summers now, and that is clearly old enough to prove myself a man."

Marahka said under his breath, "Superior seed, indeed…"

Kharshea spoke up then, "You will marry the girl? A child is a proud achievement. I will speak with her father and ease the way…"

Briysh cut him off. "Shall I marry all the whores who birth my babies?" He tapped the table. "I think not. They are a needy bunch, these harlots, whining for attention, for money." He turned and spit on the floor.

13

Briysh and his two companions, Araza and Semqat, shoved and jostled each other as they jogged out of the village into the countryside. Briysh, the oldest and tallest of the three standing at over seven feet, kept his black hair in a braid that reached to his shoulders. He wore leather pants and heavy black boots. His broad, muscular chest and back were bare, tanned deeply from the sun.

Araza plowed into Briysh. "Come on. Run!"

And the three were off, long legs taking immense strides. They crossed a field and darted toward a stone wall that stood waist high. Araza and Briysh leapt and sailed over it. Semqat, the youngest, had fallen behind and had to stop and climb the wall. The other two boys pulled up and turned around to watch him.

"You run and climb like a rosy-cheeked maiden, Semqat." Briysh said, not even slightly winded from the exertion. "I don't think you are man enough to run with us." He turned his back to Semqat and began to walk away with Araza shadowing him.

Semqat's face flamed with humiliation, nearly matching the fiery red hair that curled riotously around his head and down his neck. Sweat dripped from his hair, soaking the collar of his linen shirt. He trotted to catch up with them. He shoved himself between Briysh and Araza and took a few deep breaths. Then he looked up at Briysh and spat, "I am man enough, and you are pig dung."

Araza chuckled. "Pig dung, huh? Briysh, why don't we let Semqat prove himself to us. What do you think?"

Briysh sighed, sounding annoyed. "Fine. I'm hungry. Bring us something to eat."

"All right..." Semqat knew there would be more to come. Whatever Briysh had in mind wouldn't be easy. "What do you want?"

"What are you hungry for, Araza?" Briysh smirked. "Mutton?"

"Yes, that sounds like a nice light midday meal." Araza grinned back at Briysh, starting to catch on to what he was planning.

The three continued to hike on, headed toward a dead tree silhouetted in the distance with twisted limbs that snaked toward the sky. It perched on the bank of a steadily flowing stream, gnarled roots reaching around to grip the stream bank.

"Here's what you do. Go to that flock over there." Briysh pointed toward a group of a dozen sheep in the next field over. "Grab a sheep and bring it to us by the tree." He indicated the dead tree. "Araza and I will get a fire going and will be ready for you."

Semqat thought this sounded easy enough. They had poached and slaughtered animals many times. But as he looked at the flock in the distance, he realized the sheep weren't unattended. He frowned. "There's a shepherd with them. Let's look for a different flock."

Briysh spun on him and gripped him around the throat. "No, you maggot, I want a sheep from that flock."

Son of a whore... Semqat didn't have any qualms about stealing a sheep from under a shepherd's nose. But he was smaller than the other two boys and could be smaller than the shepherd. He didn't really want a fight. He gritted his teeth and gave a quick nod.

Briysh released his throat. "Be at the tree in a quarter of an hour." With that Araza and Briysh strode off.

Semqat took off toward the flock. His bare feet handled the uneven terrain with no problem. As he got closer to the pasture, he realized the shepherd was actually a shepherdess, and she stared directly at him. He slowed his pace so as not to startle the sheep. A young ram stood close to the stone wall he was approaching. He angled toward it.

He glanced over at the woman. She was really just a girl. Not a threat at all, he decided. She stood with her hands on her hips, glaring at him. She wore a simple brown smock dress with a hem to her shins that fluttered in the breeze. He ignored her.

He came up alongside the wall. The sheep, completely oblivious to his presence, had its head buried in the lush grass, tearing and chewing at it. Semqat reached over the wall and grabbed it by one of its curling horns.

"Hey, what are you doing?" the girl hollered at him.

He grabbed the sheep's jaw with his free hand and jerked its head up, instantly snapping its neck.

"STOP!" The girl ran toward him.

He dragged the limp, wooly body over the stone wall, just as the girl arrived.

"What have you done?" She reached for the sheep and Semqat saw tears pooling in her eyes. A heavy swath of freckles bridged her nose and cheeks. She really was young, but he felt no pity, only disgust at her weakness.

She sank her fingers into the dead sheep's wool and tried tugging it back from him over the wall. He reached around and shoved her, knocking her backward onto the grass. He hefted the limp sheep, tucking it under his arm and began loping off to where his companions waited under the tree.

Semqat felt good as he jogged across the field. The wind had picked up a bit and blew through his sweaty red hair, cooling him. He smiled knowing that he had held up to Briysh's challenge. As he approached the tree, both Araza and Briysh stood up from where they had been reclining and looked toward him. No, they looked past him. As he dropped the sheep at their feet, he turned around to see what they were looking at. He was amazed to see the shepherdess running toward them. Her sandaled feet pounded the ground, braids bouncing against her back, and her breath huffed in and out.

"What on earth…" Semqat frowned. She certainly was a plucky one, coming after him.

Briysh smiled. Under his breath he said, "Kill her."

"No, I'm done wasting my time. She's nothing—just a girl." Semqat turned away to ignore both Briysh and the girl. He looked for a sharp stone to gut the sheep.

"No, you're just a girl," Briysh snarled. Then he bent over the sheep, and with one hand he anchored the sheep down by the shoulder against the ground, and with the other he began to twist its head around. The muscles in his arm bulged and flexed with effort. The bones in the sheep's neck grinded and crunched as he twisted, until they finally snapped on the third revolution. Briysh yanked hard, severing the head from the body. He held up the white wooly head leaking blood on the ground to Semqat. "Kill her now." His voice rumbled, dark and deadly.

Semqat angrily snatched the head by a horn and turned toward the girl. She had fallen on her knees and sobbed over the bloody, headless carcass. Her fingers sank deep into the wool and she pressed her face into its side. Her thin shoulders shook.

Semqat glanced up at Briysh. Briysh looked directly at him and raised an eyebrow, then nodded toward the girl. Semqat looked over at Araza, who just shrugged. Semqat took a deep breath, raised the sheep head up and smashed it down onto the girls head. Her sobbing ceased and she fell to one side, rolling onto her back. She stared up at Semqat, her eyes slowly blinking while blood pooled under her head.

Semqat's hand dropped to his side, the sheep head bouncing against his thigh, as he watched the girl with fascination. Then he turned back toward Briysh. "There. I did it."

"You're not done. She still lives."

Semqat had enough of Briysh's bullying. "I'm done. If you want her dead, you do it." He spit at Briysh's feet.

Briysh calmly turned his back on Semqat and spoke to Araza. "Let's leave this maggot. His manhood must have shriveled off. He has no business with us." They both laughed.

Semqat's face began to flush. He could feel the sweat dripping down his back and blood thumping in his head. Without consciously realizing what he was doing, he lifted the sheep head that he still clutched in his hand. He raised it high over his head and took two steps toward Briysh's back. Then he brought it crashing down onto Briysh's skull much harder than he had hit the girl. Briysh crumpled to the ground at the foot of the dead tree, his head smacking hard against a protruding root.

Utter blackness enveloped Briysh. His mind swam through the murky thickness for an eternity, for a minute. No sense of time existed, no light penetrated, no understanding existed.

A need began to build deep within him. He couldn't identify it, but he could feel it pulsing, pushing up from his core and spreading out along his limbs. It felt like pressure at first, but then it began to burn and sizzle along his nerve endings. The need became an intense craving, a raging compulsion. A ravening greed boiled in his gut and his mind.

He thirsted.

Briysh blinked his eyes as light flooded back in. Time-lessness evaporated into the bondage of uniform progression. Clarity slowly seeped under the edges of his consciousness. At first his awareness was only of the voracious hunger that receded a bit, back to the center of his being.

As he swiveled his eyes, he recognized Araza standing near him, leaning against the cadaverous tree. He had his arms folded across his chest and laughed deeply. Briysh noticed that Araza's eyes crinkled at the corners and they shone brightly. His irises were green, flecked with shards of gold. His pupils dilated in pleasure, seeming to swirl.

Briysh shook his head, trying to focus on something other than these details he never usually noticed.

"I think you can stop now, Semqat." Araza chuckled as he pushed off from the tree.

Briysh swung his head in the direction Araza was looking. He saw Semqat for the first time. Semqat kneeled on the grass, swinging the sheep head and smashing it down over and over on something pulverized and chunky between tree roots in front of him. Semqat's fingers poked deeply into the sheep's eye sockets, tightly gripping the skull. Strings of bloody gore hung from his face and plastered the front of his clothing. His arm dropped by his side, the head sliding off his slack fingers and clunking onto the ground. He looked down, his lungs pumping from the exertion.

Briysh looked on with curiosity, his foggy mind still trying to clear and make sense of his surroundings. Glancing farther over, he saw the shepherdess lying still in the grass, her head haloed in a bloody puddle. Her eyes blinked slowly, but remained blank and uncomprehending.

Memory and lucidity slammed back into Briysh. His eyes whirled back to the shattered object of Semqat's wrath. Below the bloody pulp at Semqat's knees, Briysh saw the bare torso, arms, and leather-clad legs and booted feet of a man.

What's going on? He realized that he was observing the scene from overhead, as if he hung from the tree. He twisted his body and spun through the air. Nothing held him. He hovered below twisted black branches, just over Araza's head. He looked back toward the prone body.

It was his… His own dead, pulverized body!

A new emotion blasted through his being, temporarily subduing the thrumming of the consuming thirst. Fury. Hot and scalding it overwhelmed his senses, as he watched Araza lean over and ruffle Semqat's hair almost affectionately.

The blackness seeped over his consciousness, freeing him once again to its curdled, unmeasured depths.

14

Kharshea mourned the death of his son. His hope for immortality now lay with the prostitute Leah. He didn't know much about her; Briysh had told him only her name. But he was determined to search the areas of the village that Briysh had been known to frequent to find this woman who carried his grandson.

Briysh hadn't cared for her, but Kharshea had determined that he would help her. He'd bring her home and allow Dassah's mother to tend Leah through the pregnancy and birth. If Leah survived, then he would take her for himself to breed more sons.

Leah slowly swept the floor of the small room she called hers. The bed was neatly made and her few possessions were tidy in the single tall cabinet in the room. She concentrated on the rhythmic swishing of the broom and the pull of her shoulder muscles as she tried to keep the terror at bay.

Her belly bulged with the growing child. It had only been about five months by her best reckoning, but the baby had grown much too fast. Either she would give birth soon, or she would burst. That accounted for her fear in part.

The other part that haunted her was the fact that she had no one. No friends visited her, they had all been pushed away by Briysh's uncivilized behavior, and Briysh had simply disappeared several months back. Not that he had been particularly helpful or sympathetic to her plight, but she kept hoping he would come around, that his paternal instinct would kick in at some point and he'd claim the child and help her. But her room stood empty, her life empty, her spirit empty.

She couldn't work while heavy with child, so she could earn nothing. As she stowed the broom in a cabinet, she saw her brightly dyed dress hanging there. The brilliant blues and greens mocked her. What good did it do her now? Where would her next meal come from? Who would help her deliver the child? She fell slowly to her knees and sobbed, completely broken.

Leah eventually got up and moved to her bed, allowing depression and sleep to engulf her.

She startled awake some time later to an insistent pounding on the door. A quick look through the window told her that night had fallen. It was dangerous to open the door this late to an unexpected visitor. She walked to the door in complete darkness and placed her hands on the rough wood and leaned her ear against it. "Who's there?"

A deep voice boomed through the thin wood door. "My name is Kharshea. I am looking for Leah."

Leah frowned. The name didn't sound familiar. Maybe she had been recommended to him. "I don't know you. What is your business here? Who sent you?"

"Leah? I am Briysh's father. Please open the door so we can talk."

Leah gasped. She squeezed her eyes shut and fisted her hands against the door.

"You aren't going to hurt me, are you?" she said just barely above a whisper.

Kharshea heard her. "Leah, I'm here to help you. Open the door."

She slid the wooden bar back, took a deep breath, and opened the door. Light flooded into the room from a lantern Kharshea held aloft. She stepped back and looked up. "I see where Briysh got his height from." She attempted a small smile.

Kharshea just nodded, his lips pressed tightly together. He ducked under the lintel and stepped into the room.

Leah thought it felt like he took up most of the space in the room. He may have been of a height with Briysh, but this man was definitely broader, more filled out. She looked up his body to his face and noticed his eyes. The pupils appeared to be solid black, but it may have been a trick of the flickering lantern in the otherwise dark room.

"Would you like to take a seat, sir?" She motioned to the bed, the only surface available in the room to sit on.

He nodded and sat on the edge of the bed near the head of it. His eyes flicked around the room immediately taking in the poverty that Leah lived in. Then he looked at Leah's bulging belly. "Please sit with me." Kharshea patted the bed next to him.

Leah carefully perched at the foot of the bed, putting as much distance between them as possible, though he took up much of the bed.

"Is that Briysh's son that you carry?" He nodded toward her belly and folded his hands on his lap.

He gets right to the point. "I don't know if it is a son, but I do believe that Briysh is the father. But I haven't seen him…"

He cut her off. "How many months along are you?"

She wondered if he would leave when she told him, believing her to be a liar. "Five months…" she whispered.

He paused and then a wide grin spread across his face. His teeth flashed in the candlelight. "Then it is my grandson growing inside you. Pack your things." He stood and slapped his hands along his thighs. "I'm taking you home now."

"What?"

"Come, woman. You will deliver soon. I am going to provide for you—midwife, food, home…family."

Leah just stared up at Kharshea, tears leaking down her face. *Could it be this easy?* "Thank you, sir." She swiped at her eyes. "But I don't think Briysh will want me around."

"Briysh is dead." Kharshea's voice was flat.

Leah swallowed loudly. "What? What happened?"

"It doesn't matter. You're with me now."

Even though Briysh had been harsh, even brutal, to her, she felt a bond with him. Maybe because of the child. Maybe because she found him so beautiful, even in his cruelty. She didn't know but she keenly felt the loss of him.

Leah nodded, then quickly gathered her few items, folding her nice dress carefully, and wrapped it all in a shawl. "I'm ready."

15

Kharshea strode with purpose along the lane toward a section of forest that lined the base of the mountain. When he got to the tree line, he surreptitiously glanced up and back down the road to confirm no one watched him. Then he stepped off the path and through the trees.

When Kharshea got deep enough into the leaves to be obscured from view, he stood still and bowed his head, concentrating. Within a few moments, his body simply disappeared from the realm of man. He lifted his head—his view remained the same, though any man observing him would have seen him simply blink out. Men had the notion that those in his realm were somehow wisps of wind or some other vaporous nonsense. He had just as solid of a body now as in the realm of men, but it obeyed the laws of the universe differently, interacted with nature differently, not to mention the eyes of men were veiled and could not see it. Leave it to man to believe if he couldn't see it, it must not be. So childlike.

With the power of his mind alone, he propelled himself through the woods, slightly aloft, at high speed. At the base of the mountain, he veered up, skimming the sheer cliff face to the summit within seconds.

Kharshea stepped onto the rocky surface of the mountain top and turned around. He faced the opposite rim of the mountain range, the green valley cupped far beneath him. A heavy mist surrounded the mountain top, obscuring the view from below. But he could see the dense mist and see through it, as if it weren't there at all. Such were the abilities of those of the mountain realm. In order to be seen by men—and to interact with them seamlessly—Kharshea and his brethren assumed the confines of a terrestrial body, shackling their strength and abilities to a great degree.

But Kharshea didn't shed his human skin today for the feeling of liberation it gave, but for a more serious purpose.

He inhaled deeply and bellowed across the expanse of the valley. "Briysh!" The single word echoed back from the far mountains, rebounding several times before fading completely. Anyone in the mountain kingdom would have heard the desperate call. Men in the valley were incapable of hearing it though.

Unlike men and their wonderings, Kharshea understood death was not an end, rather it was simply a transition. But Briysh represented a new type of creature in existence, part man and part Guardian, so Kharshea was unsure *where* Briysh would transition to, nor did he know what lay in Briysh's future. He prayed that Shalliyt's curse would not extend to his son. Kharshea's knowledge had been severely limited during his time in the valley. He badly wanted to find his son.

"Brother, Briysh is not here."

Kharshea turned and saw a fellow Guardian he'd not seen in years.

"Dahka, it is good to see you, brother!" They embraced, then Kharshea stepped back.

"And you, Kharshea." He paused and crossed his arms across his chest. "We've been watching you in the valley. Are you happy with your life there? With your women?" Disapproval leaked through the questions.

Kharshea knew what Dahka was really asking—Was it worth it? Losing his immortality due to his uncontrolled lust.

Kharshea looked off to the side, for the first time feeling fear and shame. He licked his lips and spoke quietly. "Dahka, you know if I had known the penalty ahead of time, I would have chosen differently. It seemed Shalliyt had deserted us."

"Kharshea, you knew we were not abandoned. You allowed your lust to rule your mind and your reason. You became rebellious." Dahka paused and tapped his chin, thinking. "You have a son now. Do you love him?"

"More than anything."

"You are the son of Shalliyt. Do you think he loves you any less?"

"No." Kharshea's voice cracked and he started to understand the enormity of his disobedience.

"No. His love for us is greater than anything we are capable of. But he also loves the men of earth, his other sons and daughters. And you, and those with you, have unleashed a horrid plague among men. A darkness spreads across the valley even now and will ultimately claim most, if not all of them. Your rebellion may have eternally destroyed Shalliyt's precious children."

"There will be no mercy for me," Kharshea said dully.

Dahka shook his head. "Mercy is Shalliyt's to extend, but your offense is grave. Soon you will not be permitted to return here to your home."

"What about Briysh? Is there clemency for him?" Panic began to grip Kharshea.

Dahka ignored the question. "He is not here. He and his kind will never be permitted in the realm of the mountain."

"Where is he?"

Dahka turned around, putting his back to the valley. He motioned in front of him. Kharshea looked where Dahka pointed. His sight zoomed past the layers of mountains to its end…and to the land that lay outside the valley.

"He's in the wilderness?" Kharshea asked.

"Yes. He is consumed with a thirst he does not understand. He will search and wander endlessly." Dahka's mouth drew down into a frown.

"What does he search for?"

"His body…"

Kharshea didn't understand.

Dahka continued. "Kharshea, you created a being who was never intended to exist. Shalliyt created us and he created mankind. He did not create your son or those like him. No future awaits him in the mountain kingdom—his human half prevents him from even entering here, nor can he get his body back to rejoin the realm of man, as it rots in the ground. He will wander till Shalliyt puts everything right again. In those days, men will receive regenerate bodies. But not Briysh's kind—they will be no more. He is one of the *afflicted*."

"There must be a mistake," Kharshea whispered.

"We learned this through the Teller. He is the mouth of Shalliyt in these days. He tells the truth." Dahka reached toward Kharshea. "I'm sorry, brother."

But Kharshea fled. He headed straight for the wilderness that lay on the far side of the mountains. There just had to be a mistake. Kharshea had lost his immortality and had set all his hope in his son. Shalliyt's rejection of his son would be disastrous.

In that moment, some of Kharshea's reasoning and clarity began to slip. Desperation led him further along the dark path that lust and rebellion had already started him on.

16

Leah sat at a small kitchen table in Kharshea's home. Well, it was actually his dead wife's parents' home. She had finally figured out who was who in the family. Hannah, Briysh's grandmother, sat next to her at the table, snapping green beans into a wooden bowl.

Hannah had been welcoming toward Leah. Leah had no idea if Hannah knew she had been a prostitute, but she had no plans to enlighten her. Hannah had to know, at best, that Leah was Briysh's unmarried girlfriend—shameful enough by itself. So Leah was thankful to be accepted anyway. Hannah was friendly but reserved.

"Hannah, can you tell me about Briysh when he was little?" Leah worked on some much-needed mending of her clothes. She immediately saw Hannah tense and shudder. A long moment stretched out.

"Leah, were you in love with him?" Hannah stopped her snapping and set her hands over the bowl while she gazed at the younger woman.

Leah ducked her head a bit under the scrutiny. "Yes, I think so. He could be difficult at times, but under it all I think he cared for me, too." She looked back at the mending folded into her lap, with a smile spreading across her face.

Hannah just stared at her. She started to say something but stopped and closed her mouth. Her eyes cast around the kitchen walls. Leah wasn't sure how to interpret Hannah's reaction. Finally, Hannah looked back at Leah.

"Leah..." Hannah pushed the bowl away and folded her hands in front of her on the table. "You have to know that Briysh wasn't...right..." She sighed and dragged her clasped hands into her lap. "Something was very wrong with him."

"What do you mean? He was strong and handsome and..."

Hannah cut her off. "He was four summers old!"

"What happened when he was four?" Leah was having a tough time following the conversation.

"He…died."

"I know he died." Leah thought maybe Hannah was the one that wasn't right.

"He died when he was four!"

"Hannah, you aren't making any sense." Leah's mending lay forgotten in her lap.

"He was born four summers ago to my beloved Dassah, here in this house. My little girl died four summers ago giving birth to that…to him." Hannah rushed on, knowing how ridiculous she sounded. "He grew quickly. It was unnatural. Everything about him was perverse. And I can't say how he felt about you, but I never saw him care about any other soul. Not me or his grandfather, not his father. He lied to people. He manipulated every situation. He abused others for no particular reason. As he grew, the evil within him grew."

"Evil!" Leah stood. "I'm sorry, Hannah, but you are speaking foolishness." She turned to walk away.

Hannah leapt up and grabbed her arm to spin her around. "Don't you wonder how you could be so heavily pregnant already?"

Leah was silent. Of course that thought plagued her. "Yes." She whispered. "The midwife said I would deliver any day now. How is this all possible?" Her eyes glistened with unshed tears.

Hannah drew Leah into an embrace. "I don't know. Kharshea is from the mountains and he has introduced this… this, whatever it is, into our family. I have heard of other families having the same issues when their daughters married these foreign men. Some even say they aren't just foreign…that they aren't even human." She paused here and pushed Leah away from her a bit, holding her at arm's length.

"But you, Leah, are the first to carry the next generation. We have no idea what to expect." Hannah pulled her in again and wrapped her tightly in her arms. "I promise to do everything to get you through this," she whispered. "I failed my daughter. I won't fail you too."

17

"And now, the offspring, who are produced
from the spirits and flesh, shall be called the
afflicted upon the earth, and in the wilderness
shall be their dwelling. Evil spirits have
proceeded from their bodies; because they are
born from men, and from the holy Guardians
is their beginning and primal origin;they
shall be evil spirits on earth, and the afflicted
shall they be called. And the spirits of the
offspring oppress, destroy, attack, do battle,
and work destruction on the earth, and cause
trouble: they take no food, but nevertheless
hunger and thirst, and cause offenses. And
these spirits shall rise up against the children
of men and against the women, because they
have proceeded from them." —The Teller.

Briysh writhed and twisted, in his body or his mind, he
didn't know. He only occasionally seemed to surface from some
mindless depth of brutish sensation into awareness and clearer
thinking. During a period of cognizance, he found himself drifting around the great wilderness that lay sprawled out from the
valley in all directions.

A hot, dry wind blew in swirls, lifting dust and debris in
skittering circles. Briysh's throat was scorched and cracked. He
had thrown himself into a stream at one point to assuage his
burning thirst, but the cool, wet water flowed through him and
over him as if he weren't really there. He could feel the coldness
of the water and the wetness of it, but he had no way to gulp it
or absorb it, no way to quench or refresh himself.

His hunger drove him, too. He had seen a wandering
hyena nearby and salivated at the thought of catching one
and tearing it to pieces with his teeth. He imagined gulping
down the chunks of raw flesh to settle his rioting stomach. But

that had proven as frustrating as the stream; as he wrapped his hands around the neck of the hyena, who hadn't noticed him approaching, it simply loped off, fiercely shaking its scruffy mane. Briysh could not maintain any grip on it, though, like the water, he could feel the bristly fur between his fingers and the flexing cords of its neck tendons.

As if that wasn't enough, Briysh also had a monstrous hunger in his loins, lust shooting through his veins, pulsing at the back of his head. As with his hunger and thirst, nothing relieved the pressure that roared within him.

It was in the late afternoon that Briysh came 'awake' this day. The heat of the sun beat down on him as he hovered slightly above the cracked, parched ground. His continual needs coalesced in his mind like an unceasing fire.

In the distance he heard a noise. He gravitated toward it, seeking anything to distract from the hunger and the unending anguish that was his existence. The sound began to take form as someone calling out. It almost sounded like…it was! His name!

"Briysh!"

In a rush he slid through the thick air toward the caller, who appeared to be standing at the base of the mountain outside the valley. As Briysh moved closer he could make out the figure of his father. His father looked much smaller surrounded on three sides by the vast plains of the wilderness and behind him the soaring cliff face of the smooth mountain side. In an instant he stood—or hovered—by his father's side.

"Father?" Briysh whooshed out.

"Briysh, my son." Kharshea immediately gathered him into his arms.

Briysh felt some immediate relief at the contact. "Father, you can see me."

"Oh my son, my son." Kharshea just rocked back and forth holding him.

Briysh pulled away, uncomfortable with the emotion his father showed. "Father, tell me what has happened to me. I thirst terribly."

Kharshea motioned Briysh to follow him to the relative cool in the shade of the mountain. Kharshea folded his lengthy frame down to sit on the ground and lean against a boulder. Briysh sat on a nearby rocky outcropping. At least he felt like he might be sitting. He glanced over at his father, who he noticed had tears welling in his deep black eyes. Silence swelled between them. Insects buzzed lazily in the heat but didn't come near them.

Briysh glanced away, then looked back at Kharshea. "Father, just tell me. What am I?"

Kharshea took a deep breath and pinned Briysh with his eyes. "As you may have gathered, your terrestrial body was destroyed. You were violently attacked, though I don't know who did it."

"I do," Briysh sneered. "But continue. So I'm dead?"

"Just your body. Your soul perseveres. Souls cannot be killed by man or Guardian. Only Shalliyt has power over the soul."

Briysh spit into the dirt at the mention of Shalliyt. Or tried to—nothing actually came out of his mouth or hit the ground.

If Kharshea was perturbed by Briysh's blasphemy, he didn't mention it. "You thirst because you are caught in this realm of the soul, a realm you were not meant for. Your soul is craving a body to house it and will only find relief then. Only in a terrestrial body can it once again feed itself and quench its thirst."

"What do you mean by a realm I'm not meant for?" Briysh rubbed at his temples, trying to think through the fires burning within him.

"Your…existence…was never condoned by Shalliyt. No realm is adequate to house you properly. But because you were formed from me, you have some rudimentary access to this world." Kharshea vaguely waved his hands around to encompass what "this world" might be. "But you are somewhat shackled. And because you were also formed from your human mother, you require a body for your soul to be at peace with itself."

Briysh leapt up. "What am I to do? I exist in misery here!"

"I'm going to help you, Son. I need to speak with some of my brothers who are knowledgeable in the ancient dark arts. There must be a way to reunite you with a human body once again. Though I don't think it can be your original one—that one was thoroughly destroyed and, according to my brother Dahka, Shalliyt isn't inclined to resurrect it at this time."

Briysh detected a dip in his father's voice, like he might be lying, but he had no idea about which part.

"Father, why can you see me, but the animals around here see nothing when I approach. Why can you touch me, but I cannot grab my food or cup my hand to catch water?"

"Those are things of the terrestrial realm that you no longer have access to. If I were transformed as an earthly man, I would also not be able to see you. I shed that for now to come find you." Kharshea spoke with something that sounded like longing or love.

Briysh shook his head. He felt himself beginning to be sucked back into the void with its yawning jaws, the void that awaited him to wash him in sensation and senselessness. He began to panic. "Father, take me to the mountain top. Surely it would be better there while you resolve how to return me to a body."

"As I said, your access in this realm is fettered. You cannot go to the mountain top. The wilderness is where you are destined to roam for now. But I will return..."

That was the last Briysh heard before his mind shut down and was overtaken by the thirst, hunger, and lust that now tormented him.

18

Kharshea leaned back against a tree trunk, exhaling loudly. He had just finished telling Rhyima the entire situation with Briysh. Rhyima looked off to the side, deep in thought. They stood in a thick copse of old trees, in the quickening darkness of late afternoon. The upper leaves of the trees were dappled in the remnants of pale sunshine, but none penetrated to where the two men stood, facing each other in the shadows.

"So, you are asking me how to get Briysh back into a body?" Rhyima folded his arms across his chest.

"Yes. I believe that is the only way to relieve his torment."

"I don't know. He can't go into his own body. It is decaying in the ground, inhabitable only by worms.

Kharshea flinched at the blunt assessment of his son's corpse.

"Resurrection is Shalliyt's alone to perform." Rhyima tapped his chin absently, clearly still mulling through the possibilities.

"Brother, you've done this before!" Kharshea was desperate not to lose hope.

"I've done it with animals—not self-aware beings who are independent thinkers and created in the likeness of Shalliyt!" Rhyima's voice rose in frustration. "What you are asking, if it even is possible, would be unequivocally forbidden."

"According to Dahka, our offspring would not be considered creations of Shalliyt. He called them *the afflicted*. So what would Shalliyt care what we did with them?"

"Hmmm." Rhyima scrubbed his hands through his hair. "Okay, I'll teach you how to get him into a terrestrial object, but putting Briysh into a human body is a darker art than I possess. The object should still provide him with some relief with its terrestrial confines. But I won't actually do this, and I suggest you don't either. Find an ignorant man to carry it out. You and I have already accrued enough curses and punishments."

Kharshea reached out to Rhyima then, grasping his shoulders. "Thank you, Brother. Thank you."

Rhyima just shook his head.

19

Leah lay exhausted and sweaty in her bed. She could hear her baby wailing in the other room, but so far she hadn't seen him. As soon as he had been born, the midwife, Maddie, wrapped him in a thick cloth, saying it was a boy and he needed to be washed up. Then she rushed out of the room with him tucked against her breast.

Hannah sat on the edge of the bed, stroking Leah's damp hair from her forehead. "You did well, Leah." Hannah offered her a smile. "There is no bleeding. After you rest, you will be well enough again."

"When can I see him?" She hoped he would look like his handsome father. "I need to hold my baby."

"Very soon. Have you thought of a name for him?" Hannah pushed a sweaty lock of hair behind Leah's ear.

"Do you think Kharshea will allow me to name him?"

Hannah sighed. "I don't know. He named Briysh, but since he was the father and Dassah was dead, we didn't interfere. I think you should choose a name. Even if Kharshea overrules you, you can call him what you want when it is just the two of you." She took Leah's hand in her own and gently stroked the back of it with her thumb.

"I think I would like to call him Lucas."

"Lucas is a good name. Let me go see what is keeping Maddie." Hannah set Leah's hand gently back on the bed and left the room, closing the door softly behind her.

Hannah followed the sound of the baby's whimpers to the kitchen. She walked through the doorway and was perplexed to hear the baby's cries coming from a basket, while Maddie sat on the floor on the other side of the room. Her knees were pulled up to her chest and her head buried in the folds of her skirt.

"Maddie! What are you doing?" Hannah strode over toward the basket to pick up the mewling child.

"No! Miss Hannah, don't touch him." Maddie reached an arm toward Hannah but made no move to rise.

"What is the problem? Why have you abandoned this child?" Hannah was torn between retrieving the baby and making sure Maddie was all right, because she could not understand why she crouched on the floor.

Maddie mumbled something.

"What did you say?"

"It's evil," Maddie hissed barely above a whisper.

Hannah would normally dismiss such as nonsense. But she was more aware than maybe anyone else the changes that were now flowing in her family's blood. Maddie was a seasoned midwife. She had seen all types of births and babies, whether dead, alive, or very ill. Something had clearly shaken her. She walked the last few steps to the basket, slower now.

"No, Mistress," Maddie sobbed softly.

"It does not matter, Maddie. A baby, any baby, must be cared for." Hannah peered into the basket. The cloth still enfolded most of the baby. His two little arms stuck out the side and waved around slightly, fists clenching and unclenching. The baby had mostly stopped crying, maybe from hearing the voices in the kitchen, and hiccupped a little while making wet noises with his mouth. Hannah reached down and grasped the corner of the cloth between two of her fingers. She slowly drew back the cloth to reveal her great-grandson Lucas.

◦⤙〜〰️⤚◦

Leah drifted off to sleep. She was anxious to meet her baby, but exhaustion overtook her. When she awoke some time later, her room was dark and the house was silent. Her breasts were uncomfortable, filled with milk as she had yet to nurse. Why hadn't they brought her Lucas? The physical pressure was enough to give her the motivation to sit up. She swung her legs over the edge of the bed and reached for the bedside table to help her stand. She accidentally knocked something off the table that clattered to the floor.

Her door immediately opened and Hannah stepped into the room. "You're awake." She remained by the door, illuminated from light on the other side of the door.

"Yes." Leah's voice came out with a croak. She cleared her throat. "Please bring me Lucas. He needs to feed."

"Of course." Hannah's hands twisted around each other. "Lie back down and I will bring him in."

"Bring a candle, too, please, so that I may see my son!" Leah's voice raised in excitement, though she noticed Hannah's nervousness and wondered about it. Was something wrong?

Hannah returned with a bundle in her arm and a small candle. She set the candle on the windowsill opposite from the bed and walked toward Leah.

"Bring the candle closer, Hannah. I won't be able to see him." Leah laughed lightly.

"It's close enough." Hannah reached down to pull Leah forward a bit with her free arm and arrange her pillows behind Leah's back so she could sit comfortably.

Leah just stared at Hannah. "What's wrong with my baby, Hannah?"

Hannah just shook her head. Her face was completely enshrouded in darkness so Leah couldn't read any expression on it. Hannah sat on the edge of the bed and waited for Leah to rearrange her nightclothes so she could nurse. Then Leah reached for Lucas.

Hannah set the swaddled bundle in Leah's arms. Leah immediately brought her wriggling baby close to her breast. Then she reached down to pull back the blanket. She stared at the little face that looked toward her. It was difficult to see much at all, it was so dark, but the first thing Leah noticed was that his head wasn't shaped right. It seemed narrow, almost pointed at the top. She stroked across his head and felt a thick pelt of hair covering his skull, which indeed was misshapen. She continued to stare at his face, attempting to make out his features in the dark room. She could see one of his eyes glittering just a bit in the low light.

Lucas reached up and clutched at a hank of Leah's hair that hung along her face. She smiled at him, then ran her hand along his face. If she couldn't see his features, she would learn them with her fingers.

Hannah sat stone-like, silent, next to her.

Leah's fingers gently searched out her boy's features. She traced his lips first. He immediately opened his mouth to suckle at the touch. She ghosted her fingers up to his nose. Something was definitely wrong here. She found two holes where his nostrils should be and she felt air whooshing in and out of them,

99

but there was only a slight ridge above them—no nose to speak of. A tear trickled down Leah's cheek.

She cooed to Lucas as she brushed her fingers lightly over his cheeks now. She imagined them as rosy and glowing. "Little Lucas, baby," she whispered. Then she continued her exploration with her questing fingers. He remained quiet in her embrace, occasionally tugging on the lock of hair he hadn't released yet.

She slid her finger up from his huffing nostrils seeking his eyes. Her finger suddenly encountered an eye just above his nose. Lucas slammed his eyelid shut. Leah's breath hitched. She quickly swept her fingers across his upper face from side to side.

"Oh, no!" she cried out. "No." She began to sob. Her son, beautiful Briysh's child, had only one eye and it sat just above his nonexistent nose. Leah quickly pushed down the welling panic and sadness. She pulled him up to her face and kissed him gently on his huge sloping forehead. "I love you Lucas. I love you my baby boy."

Hannah sat silently with tears coursing down her cheeks. She watched Leah lovingly tuck Lucas down to her breast to nurse, which he did greedily, still yanking on the hair he was clutching. Hannah was amazed at Leah's acceptance of her fiercely deformed child. What Leah hadn't seen yet was that her boy also had disproportionate arms and legs. They were much too long for his torso. Hannah reclined gently alongside Leah, while the younger woman nursed her child.

20

Kharshea sat in the grass, back against the stone wall of his cottage. Next to him, the garden Dassah had so faithfully tended flourished in a profusion of blooms, humming with bees. When Dassah died, her mother, Hannah, took over the growing of flowers and herbs.

Lucas ran around the yard howling in delight like a wild animal. Leah chased him, pretending to be a ferocious lion hunting him down. Lucas squealed when his mother finally caught him. They tumbled into the grass, Leah laughing and Lucas cackling.

The boy was only a few months old, but like Briysh, he grew inhumanly fast. Unlike Briysh, the boy was hideous and mentally slow.

Kharshea admired how loyal Leah was to her monstrosity of a child, though he knew that loyalty was transferred from her love of Briysh. And it was this devotion that Kharshea planned to exploit.

Kharshea had changed his mind about taking Leah for himself to breed—his dream of his heritage surviving through this lineage had been destroyed. It was unknown if Lucas was just a singular anomalous offspring, or whether he was a model for what the second generation would look like. If they were all born deformed and moronic—as Kharshea suspected would be the case—then there was no heritage to be had for the Guardians in this way of man. Regaining his beloved Briysh now became even more important.

"Leah, come here." Kharshea motioned to her to sit next to him.

She pulled herself up from the grass and smoothed her skirt as she walked toward him. Lucas barreled toward Kharshea and leapt into his grandfather's lap. Kharshea tolerated the boy's presence for the most part. Drool slithered down one side of the boy's chin.

Leah settled onto the grass next to Kharshea and waited for him to speak.

Kharshea banded his huge arm around Lucas's waist to settle him down. He calmed immediately and sucked noisily on his bottom lip.

"Leah." Kharshea paused.

She turned toward him and waited. Lucas reached for Leah; she grasped his spit-slimy hand and squeezed it gently.

"I thought you might be interested in a proposal I have." Kharshea found himself hedging, not sure how to bring up the topic. He decided he just needed to say it. "I think I know how to bring back Briysh."

She stared at him. Her mouth opened, then closed. Finally, she choked out "What?"

Kharshea absently rubbed Lucas's furry head. "There may be a way to bring him back. We—my family—where I come from…we have knowledge of the ancient arts. It might work. But you would have to do it."

Leah continued to stare at him. Kharshea could see hope widening her eyes. "I don't…don't understand," she said.

"There are rituals that can be performed, but they must be done by someone who was closest to him. That would be you." This was a lie, both the necessity of that element and the statement that she and he had been close. He knew his son hadn't cared for her at all. He had barely noticed her. But this invention served its purpose, feeding into the hope that she had never given up and the story that she had convinced herself about their past together.

Her reply was breathy. "I'll do anything, Kharshea. Anything."

He nodded. He felt relief that she was willing, and only a twinge of guilt pinged his conscience, that he was tricking her into doing something that would probably bring the wrath of Shalliyt upon her. But he rationalized that even if he explained the possible consequences, she still wouldn't hesitate.

Like so many of the people in the valley, Leah questioned the existence of her creator. The lack of belief among men had stunned Kharshea at first: he himself had been in the presence of Shalliyt in the divine council many times. His problem had never been one of belief but one of obedience. But he wasn't interested in the failings of man, so he never bothered to argue the point or convince them otherwise.

"What must I do?"

"You'll need to gather certain plants from the forest." He paused, realizing that Leah never left the cottage because, though it was left unspoken, she was hiding Lucas, protecting him from the ridicule of the neighbors. "Hannah can gather them," he amended. "These will be made into a tonic, which when consumed by the loved one gives them the sight temporarily."

"The sight?"

"The ability to see and communicate with the other realm. The realm where Briysh has gone to. You will be the seer and will communicate with him."

Joy surged through Leah. "Yes…" she whispered. "You said we could bring him back?"

"We'll work through that, but you making contact with him is the first step." Kharshea grabbed his now-wiggling grandson on his lap and tossed him into the air, easily catching him again. Lucas shrieked his delight.

Kharshea gave Hannah the specific instructions for collecting the plants and tree bark that was needed to create the tonic. It would have been easier for him to just go do it, but he wanted to distance himself from the process as much as possible. Hannah shivered visibly as he spoke with her. Kharshea suspected Hannah had some idea of the blatant evil he was orchestrating.

"I'll just let Seth know where I am off to." Hannah's eyes would not meet Kharshea's.

He stepped closer to her, dominating her height by almost two feet. He spoke quietly. "No. You will go now. I'll let your husband know where you have gone."

She didn't look up to meet his gaze.

Kharshea noticed at some point over the last few years she had stopped looking into his eyes altogether. Some, but only a very few, could see his otherness in the blackness of his eyes. Hannah was becoming aware, but as long as Seth remained blinded, Hannah would do nothing about it. He watched her fetch a basket and a stone cutting tool, then set off for the base of the mountain where the ancient tree stands held the required elements.

Kharshea turned the other way and headed through the village to the far side. He had a wood worker to talk to.

"You want a statue of a what?" Jared was incredulous.

"A serpent. Coiled at the base, rearing up with mouth open. The mouth must be open. And it should stand about this high." Kharshea motioned indicating the height should be to about his chest. "And then be placed on a platform."

"What are you going to do with it?" Jared walked over to a table and picked up a chunk of charcoal, holding it still, waiting for Kharshea to answer.

"What business is that of yours? I'll pay your fee—whatever you name." He flicked his hand in a careless gesture.

Jared leaned over the table, slightly shaking his head, and dragged the charcoal across it in quick strokes, sketching out his best rendition of a serpent. The tall man was right, it really wasn't his business—it was just such an odd request. But as time went by, everything about these mountain dwellers seemed somewhat odd.

"Does this look like what you want?" Jared felt a little excitement. As a carpenter by trade, he rarely got to work on something as frivolous as a sculpture. His normal fare was utilitarian pieces. This, to say the least, was not in that category.

Kharshea smiled for the first time since he'd entered Jared's shop. "Yes, that looks good. Make the neck arch a bit here before dipping down to the head." He scratched his fingernail along the drawing to indicate what he wanted.

"Very well. Do you have a preference for wood type? Or stain to protect it?"

"The wood must be that of the ash tree, but no stain—the wood must be raw."

Jared quirked an eyebrow but held his tongue on that issue. "I'll need a fortnight to complete it." Then he quoted Kharshea a high fee.

"No. I need it in half that time. And I'll double your price."

Jared smiled broadly. "I'll make it happen." He reached out to shake Kharshea's hand. "Good day to you, sir."

21

They sacrificed to evil spirits that were no
gods, to gods they had never known, to new
gods that had come recently, whom their
fathers had never dreaded.—The Teller

(Six Months Later)

Leah wended her way through the saplings, clutching her shawl at the base of her neck, with a woven willow basket slung over her arm. Her other hand kept the saplings from snapping back at her. The forest air felt cool against her face which had flushed with the exertion of her walk. The saplings gave way to larger-trunked trees spaced farther apart. She easily followed the path that had become pressed into the leaf mold of the forest floor. Picking up her pace a bit, she thought through the list of preparations required before the others arrived for the ritual.

Leah stepped into a clearing. A ring of woods surrounded a small hut situated among springy grass and ferns. Its thatched roof was derelict and covered thickly in moss. Weak sunlight filtered through the leafy canopy overhead illuminating the green roof. A set of shuttered windows flanked the door and were pulled tightly shut, as they always were.

She gently knocked on the door. "Lucas, sweetie. It's Mama. Open the door for me."

A grating sound indicated Lucas was sliding back the plank, then the door groaned as it dragged across the floor. Lucas stood in the doorway, in the dimness, blinking at his mother with his single eye. Leah knew it took a bit for him to focus once he came into the sunlight.

Leah stepped forward to run her hand through her son's hair that tumbled down his forehead. He grunted and huffed, making warbling noises with his lips. He surged forward and wrapped his arms around her. She was amazed that just in the last few weeks, he had noticeably grown. He rested his head against her chest.

She kissed the top of his head. "Come on Lucas, I brought you food." She disengaged herself gently and taking him by the hand, led him back inside the darkness leaving the door open for light.

The hut contained only a single room. It was small but sufficient to hold a dozen people in close quarters. The room was mostly bare, excepting a cabinet along one side that held some supplies and a straw pallet in the back corner that Lucas slept on. The main feature of the room loomed in the center—a wooden sculpture of a serpent mounted on a pedestal. It stood a few heads taller than Leah. She walked toward it now with Lucas still in tow.

Leah reached up with her free hand and softly stroked the smooth wood of the serpent's lower jaw. She turned to Lucas. "You have done a good job keeping this polished and lovely."

He gurgled in response.

Lucas lived in the hut now. It was the best Leah could do to keep him out of sight of people. The few friends and neighbors who had seen Lucas hadn't reacted well. They considered him more animal than child. The general consensus being the boy should be returned to his maker, for his own good of course. Even worse were the reactions of some of Briysh's kind when they spotted him. Thankfully, Kharshea had been with Lucas and Leah at that time and sent the ruffians packing.

Lucas did well with his small responsibilities. He was in charge of keeping the hut swept of debris that filtered through from the roof onto the rough wood floor, he polished the serpent with a scrap of wool, and he opened the front door once a day to air out the hut. He had also learned to feed himself from the baskets Leah brought every few days. During her visits she would sometimes bathe him in the cold stream that ran along the back of the hut along the wood line.

Leah didn't like being separated from Lucas, but Kharshea kept her busy at home now with producing the various tonics that Dassah had once made. Hannah helped with growing the herbs that could be grown and foraging from the meadows and forest those that couldn't. Unlike Dassah, Leah had no talent with a garden, so she mainly collected what was needed from the gardens and did the brewing and steeping. Seth and

106

Hannah took the tonics to sell at market, along with his onions and potatoes. As of yet, they had not begun selling the particular concoction that Leah had in her basket today.

Leah led Lucas to his pallet, still holding the basket. She sat down, leaning against the cool stone wall and pulled Lucas down next to her. He clambered into her lap. She settled him and reached into the basket, drawing out a small loaf of bread. As she tore a piece off to hand him, he reached up and began to trace her face with his fingers. This was a familiar ritual; he outlined her nose then her eyes. With his other hand he reached up to his misshapen face and traced his own features—holes with no nose and a single owl-like eye. When his fingers reached her lips, Leah growled and sucked them into her mouth, playfully tugging them. Lucas's face lit up and he made an attempt to growl back. Leah took advantage of his open mouth and popped a piece of bread into it. Then she tossed him onto his back and tickled him till he shrieked.

She stood up, removed his smaller food basket from within the larger one she carried and set it next to him. "I have to get ready for the women, Lucas."

He went exploring in his basket.

Leah went to the cabinet and removed all the candles. Carefully she reached into her basket and drew out a small wooden box. She removed the lid and gingerly unwrapped the tobacco leaf that contained a smoldering coal. Taking some dried moss, also from her supplies, she dropped it on the coal and blew gently. A small flame erupted that she used to light the wick of a candle. The moss quickly disintegrated and she tightly folded up the coal in the leaf again and replaced it in the box. She lit the other candles one by one, then placed them around the pedestal surrounding the serpent. She walked over and closed the door so the candles provided the only light. The room took on a brighter glow with all the candles burning. It gave the effect that the serpent was rising from the fire. The flames flickering shadows against the smooth coils of its body made it look like it was undulating, breathing, alive.

She fell to her knees and watched the dancing shadows. A strong sense of longing came over her. She leaned forward and placed her hand on one of the massive smooth coils. "Oh, Briysh, I miss you." A single tear ran down her cheek.

Swiping it away, she got to her feet. She needed to get ready. Returning to the basket, she reached in and withdrew a small sealed crock and a cloth bundle, and set the items on the pedestal.

The crock, sealed in beeswax, contained the tonic that allowed her to push back the veil that separated the seen from the unseen, to see and speak with Briysh.

She unrolled the bundle and carefully laid out half a dozen sharp-edged stones. This was a new feature to their ritual. Leah didn't know what the stones were to be used for yet; Briysh would tell her when it was time. She ran her thumb along the edge of one stone, hissing when a red line appeared along her thumb, welling up with blood.

A sharp rap sounded on the door. Leah stuck the edge of her thumb in her mouth to suck off the blood and hurriedly came to her feet. She walked over and knelt down by her son. Lucas had discovered a chunk of cheese and was sucking it. When Leah got close, he offered the gooey end that had been in his mouth to her. She laughed. "It's all for you." She gently pushed his hand back toward his mouth.

"It is time, Lucas," she whispered.

Lucas sucked down the piece of cheese and scrambled to the far end of his pallet against the corner. He reached under it and pulled out a dark woolen cloak. He wrapped it around his shoulders and pulled the hood over his head. All of his features were obscured except his mouth. He leaned forward to pull the basket toward himself then huddled with it in the corner, in the shadow.

"Good boy." Lucas had no recognizable language and wasn't intelligent like his father, but he understood and obeyed.

Leah opened the door and stood back, motioning the four women who stood silently into the hut. They dressed somewhat like Lucas, heads covered by hoods of cloaks that fell to their feet. The women moved quietly to their positions surrounding the serpent. Leah closed the door, sinking the room back into the sacred light of the candles. Though the women's identities were hidden, she knew them well.

All of them had been prostitutes like Leah. They still were. When she had approached them about joining her in the rituals, it had stirred their curiosity. At first the women were hesitant, but what started off as merely a distraction from the crippling grind of their existence soon became addictive. Especially Leah's closest friend, Abigail, who absorbed all she could of the experience. She was intelligent and inquisitive. Leah could not have been any more thankful for the rallying around her of the women in her quest to regain Briysh in some way.

Leah, head uncovered, took her position at the front of the serpent. She reached up and unbound her hair, letting it fall in dark, slightly curling waves, onto her shoulders and down her back. She removed her shawl and draped it over head. She looked around the circle at the women, who looked back at her, eyes glittering in the candlelight. They knelt as one, heads down.

The women began a soft, low-pitched hum. The droning drifted and began to quaver a little, matching the flickering undulations of the serpent's coils. Leah reached forward, plucking up the crock that sat on the pedestal. She removed the wax seal and lid, then passed it to the woman on her left. The woman tilted back her head taking a swallow of the bitter liquid, then passed it on to her left.

Leah would drink last. Her eyes flickered over the smooth serpent and she felt her eyes drawn to the statue's glass eyes. Everything in the room began to recede, her vision tunneling then going black. She squeezed her eyes shut in surprise that she was passing through without the help of the brewed mixture. With her eyes still tightly shut she was now able to see clearly around the room.

"Briysh," she whispered. The other women immediately picked up his name and began to softly recite it. Over and over they said his name. It swelled and filled the room.

Lucas pulled his hood down further, tucking his bony knees under his chin. He wedged himself as far as he could into his dark corner.

◦⟞⟀⟜◦

Briysh felt the oily darkness sliding past him faster and faster, thrusting him into the wicked heat and light of the parched wilderness, out from the sludge that was his existence. Awareness and longing slammed into him. His body twitched and throbbed with unrelenting need.

Within a few moments he sensed it through the turmoil of his affliction: he was being summoned.

With simply a thought he tunneled effortlessly through air, then mountain, then forest, as the chanting echoed louder and louder in his mind. He paused as he arrived at the hut, then passed through the wall, finally slamming into the serpent that stood at the center.

It felt good. Inhabiting the wooden body gave him some mitigation from the unrelenting hungers that plagued his mind and body. He wiggled and slithered his essence throughout the long coils of the body, stretching and glorying in the relief.

He finally turned his attention to the handful of women who worshiped him. The women were utterly foolish for doing this, but the worship was a balm, and they could be useful in spreading it to others. Briysh assumed the more that fell at his feet, the greater would be the relief that washed through him. He also experienced an empowering while the women groveled before him. He could imagine that with enough followers he could begin to feel even…godlike. He smiled.

When Leah first summoned him, she had been alone. He had filled the serpent but had no ability to manipulate it. He had spoken with her through the unyielding wooden mouth. But Leah followed his instructions and found more women, and she gained in power as the priestess of this small cult. It was a beneficial situation all around. More women gave him increasing power, and in turn, he gave them power. And for humans, he knew, power was addictive and not easily turned away from.

Now he was able to subtly move the wooden body, causing it to ripple and surge slightly. The movement felt rapturous to his tortured senses.

He turned his attention back to the women. They knelt with hands palms-down on their thighs, chanting his name, all with eyes closed and hooded heads bowed, though each looked directly at him in their altered state. He slowly swung the serpent's head around to look at each woman individually. The chanting faltered as the women stared in astonishment at the wooden serpent moving on its own.

Briysh saw the boy in the back corner. He knew it was his son, but he felt nothing for him. The boy was completely covered and trembling. Briysh could feel the fear radiating from him. The boy seemed to sense Briysh's stare and shuddered and whimpered. Lucas hadn't taken the mind-changing drug, so couldn't see Briysh in the way the others could, but he could see the wooden serpent writhing. He would not be able to hear Briysh, either.

"Leah." The serpent head swung toward Leah, the mouth moving slightly as Briysh spoke.

"Yes, my lord." She reached out and with the tip of her finger touched the pulsing warm coil in front of her.

In a burst, the serpent snapped his head down, striking at Leah's hand. Not her physical hand, which remained inert on her thigh, but the spiritual one that had been freed in her vision state. Leah pulled her hand back.

"What gives you the right to touch me without permission?" The Briysh serpent hissed.

"I'm sorry, my lord. I couldn't help myself. You are so beautiful—"

"Enough!" He cut her off. "Did you bring the sharpened stones?" The candle light flickered in his eyes making them glitter and flash.

"Yes, my lord." She pointed toward the stones lined up on the pedestal.

"Pass them around."

Leah's inert hands came forward this time and picked the stones up one by one and passed them to the left, keeping the last one for herself.

Kharshea had continued to visit Briysh in the wilderness, and the two had discussed how to bring Briysh back closer to the terrestrial existence he craved. This was all new, so they didn't know exactly what would work the best. But Leah was the perfect submissive follower to try out different methods to appease Briysh. Kharshea had gotten her started with instructions from Rhyima, but Briysh now communicated directly with her. Kharshea told Briysh they needed to try blood. The life was in the blood.

Speaking to all the women, the Briysh serpent said, "Extend your left arm. Hold the stone in your right hand."

They obeyed.

"Open a vein with the stone. Slant your arm down and cup the running blood in your hand."

Without questioning, the women sliced deeply into their left forearms, watching the blood first well up, then trickle down their arms.

"Rub the blood onto my coils."

As one they stood and approached the serpent. They rubbed the blood lovingly along the smooth wooden surface. The blood soaked through the wood.

The effect on Briysh was immediate. Relief and even pleasure seeped into his being. Exhilaration coursed through him.

"Stop the flow with your cloaks." He realized it would never do to have his followers expire from blood loss, though they seemed oblivious to it.

The women wrapped their cut arms in their cloaks and resumed their position on their knees.

The Briysh serpent, for the first time, uncoiled. The wood became completely pliable to his thoughts. He writhed toward the ceiling, his body unfurling into the space of the room. Joy spread throughout his body.

Lucas yelped and scrambled to get under his pallet, pulling it over his head.

The women just stared in drugged awe. When they came back to themselves, they would wonder if they had really seen this.

22

Aarkaos scanned the horizon. He saw nothing but dirt, scrubby brush, and the occasional jutting rock. He slowly walked to one of these rocks and mounted it.

The view didn't change from his low perch. Just blasted heat and desolation spanned as far as he could see. He flexed his shoulders, and splashes of light winked off his jeweled scales in the searing sun. He was obviously the most beautiful thing out here in this barrenness.

Aarkaos glanced behind him at the mountain range in the distance. His mountains. His mountains that ringed his valley. A noise somewhere between a growl and a hiss escaped his throat from his escalating anger. His humiliation.

Just the day before he had sat proudly upon his throne in those mountains. His throne throbbing with the energy of lightning, surrounded by stones pulsing in full glory.

His plan had unfolded with perfect precision. Of course it was perfect—he was the source of it! Wisdom of the ages pumped through his being. He had no equal in mind or body.

He didn't care about having sex with the women of the valley. Lust was a baser, thoroughly human condition, beneath the notice of a Guardian. Or it should have been. Aarkaos chuckled. But then, the fool Guardians had fallen to the temptation with hardly a second thought. They traded their immortality to experience a soft body and a pretty face.

Of course, Aarkaos hadn't outright warned them of the consequences. But it really didn't take much thought to figure that out ahead of time. Imagine, Shalliyt condemning those preying upon the ones they were to guard. But, ah well, that was how lust blocked intelligence and wisdom. And that was why he had no use for it.

Over the years he had watched his scheme unfurl. Increased knowledge and power given to the people with no idea how to properly utilize it; increased violence, greed, and envy; and the birth of abominations, both in the animal and human realms. All for the glorious climax: the irreparable pollution of the human lineage.

A broad smile filled Aarkaos's face. Until he remembered.

Everything proceeded according to plan, until yesterday. One moment he sat upon his throne. The next, he had found himself face down on cold rock in a dripping, stinking cave.

Aarkaos could only assume Shalliyt had returned and been displeased at the occupation of the throne by another. How childish. What had he expected after such a long absence?

Aarkaos had pushed himself up from the damp floor and brushed his hands off. Only then did he look around in the dimness.

A single light radiated from a candle flickering next to the seated form of an ancient, haggard, sightless man.

The Teller. Shalliyt had sent him to the Teller's cave.

Aarkaos looked directly at the Teller who, unflinchingly, stared straight back at him. Aarkaos understood the Teller had ways of seeing not related to his eyes. He was a prophet gifted by Shalliyt.

"I've got nothing to say to you or hear from you, old man." Aarkaos turned on his heel to leave.

"You will listen." The croaking voice stopped him at once. The Teller sighed. "You will not hear, but you will listen."

Aarkaos, enraged, spun back toward him. He would kill him, then he would not have to listen.

But he stepped back as he saw the Teller now surrounded by a dozen warrior Guardians. They were well armed.

They could not kill Aarkaos, for he was not a creature capable of dying, nor were any of the Guardians. But they could inflict a damaging, debilitating pain with their swords.

Aarkaos's tongue flicked out and in repeatedly. Fury boiled through his veins.

"Sit and listen." The Teller remained calm, almost bored.

"Fine, get on with it." But Aarkaos refused to sit.

"This is what Shalliyt says, and what he ordains for you:

'You were the seal of perfection, full of wisdom and beauty.

'You ruled the mountains, the paradise of Shalliyt.

'Every precious stone adorned you, your settings and mountings were made of gold.

114

'You were anointed the principal among Guardians, for so I ordained you.

'You were on the holy mount of Shalliyt, you walked among the fiery stones.

'You were blameless in your ways.'

'Then in the pride of your heart you said, "I am god. I will sit on the throne of god in the heart of the mountain."

'You sinned, so I drove you in disgrace from the mount of Shalliyt. I expelled you, principal among Guardians, from among the fiery stones.

'Your heart became proud on account of your beauty and you corrupted your wisdom because of your splendor.

'So I threw you to the wilderness, the realm of the dead, the depths of the pit.

'Maggots are spread out beneath you and worms cover you, for you will come to a horrible end and will be no more.

'Then you will know that I am the Lord.'"

After the prophecy was spoken, Aarkaos once again found himself face down. Instead of cold stone against his face, hot dirt filled his nostrils. He snorted out the dirt, flexed his spine, and stood up.

He knew immediately that he was in the forsaken wilderness. He had marched over to the nearest pass through the mountains into the valley, murder and rage hot on his mind. But the pass, all the passes, had been guarded. Protected by Guardians who had never taken up his cause.

Aarkaos stood on his lowly rock, reassessing his plan. It now appeared he was no longer Lord of the Mountain, but rather Lord of the Dirt. Shalliyt had blocked the access to his human children.

But Aarkaos chuckled, then began to laugh louder and louder till it echoed off the mountains. Shalliyt was a fool. Aarkaos knew there was one who roamed the wilderness, one with access to the valley, albeit in a limited fashion. His laugh died down to a satisfied grin as he imagined the new plan. Yes, he was still lord. Lord of the Dead.

23

"Ah, there you are, my tasty worm fare."Aarkaos brushed his hands down his glittering scales. Then he swiveled his eyes back to Briysh."Stop disappearing on me so I can instruct you. Am I correct in presuming you want this?"

"Yes, of course."Briysh fluctuated between outraged and offended. This new interloper to his wilderness had styled himself as lord over Briysh. When Briysh had dared to argue against the tyranny, Aarkaos had swung his thick tail smacking Briysh right back into his mindless torment. He had only just now managed to struggle back out of his oily timelessness into the searing desert.

"Hmm?"

"Yes, of course…my lord," Briysh gritted out between clenched teeth.

"Yes, then."Aarkaos sat on a rock, motioning for Briysh to settle on the ground by his feet. He obeyed."Don't worry. I'm not like the god of the humans searching for harmony and respect."Aarkaos sniggered.

Briysh spat in the dust.

"I will teach you the way to manipulation, power, and pleasure."He smiled down at his pupil.

Briysh looked up at the patronizing serpentine figure promising him the key to his relief. He had the appearance similar to the Guardians like his father, some familial resemblance. But he looked different, too, especially with his jewel-encrusted body and flickering tongue. Not to mention that blasted tail.

Maybe he had been some sort of ruler of the Guardians. He was certainly conceited enough and constantly running his hands over the glittering gems. But then what was he doing in this soul-less wilderness?

Briysh had utterly nothing to lose. Kharshea's instructions from Rhyima had gotten him into the wooden serpent, But he craved more—and Aarkaos was making claims. In exchange for his obeisance, Aarkaos would teach him how to take full control of a living, breathing, warm body—a huge improvement over the stiff, lifeless statue.

Aarkaos began his instruction. "Rhyima is quite right. The power is in the blood. But even his understanding is limited."

Briysh sat staring, fully engaged now.

"The shed blood of the women gives you the ability to manipulate the serpent statue. But you are 'sharing' their blood with them—since they walk away afterward, they are clearly still using it. They hold back from you, limiting the power."

Briysh thought he might know where this was headed.

"I know, it's impractical to take all of their blood, because you need them functional to serve you, to worship you, to help you with the process. And obviously, when you eventually inhabit their bodies, you want them still alive, even healthy."

Briysh groaned at the thought of inhabiting Leah so completely.

Aarkaos continued. "So you must have them bring you other living things to give you all of the life, which then gives you the ability to slide into a still-breathing human. Are you following this?"

"Yes, my lord."

"The type of life exchanged in sacrifice will determine the amount of power and the length of time it will be effective. An animal will work, but a human sacrifice is more powerful. An innocent's life infinitely more so. I leave it to you to experiment." Aarkaos smiled indulgently.

Briysh smiled back.

24

"Renny, you have nothing to lose." Abigail took the other woman's hand in hers and squeezed it gently.

Renny fiddled with some blonde strands of hair that had escaped her bun and looked off to the side of the courtyard where her daughter, Marah, lay curled up on a mat.

The courtyard was formed by homes on three sides, which lent their stone walls to the enclosure. The ground of the yard was also lined with smooth river stones. Speckled shade provided a lovely retreat from the busyness of the village, its shape also keeping it quieter than on the street that ran by the fourth side. Planters lined the space, brimming with a riotous profusion of blooming flowers that filled the air with languorous scents. This was the wealthy section of the village.

Abigail knew it would normally be shocking to see herself, a former prostitute, calmly sitting and talking with a resident of this area amongst the affluence and seductive fragrance. But Abigail and Renny had been friends since girlhood.

Renny had captured the notice of a wealthy man who had fallen in love with her. They had married, and soon after, Renny gave birth to a beautiful little girl. Her life was amazing and complete. She had always welcomed Abigail into her home.

Renny watched her daughter twisting on the mat, dragging herself around by her hands and arms. She had soiled herself.

"Abigail, I'll be right back."

Several years after Marah had been born, tragedy struck, devastating Renny's idyllic life. Marah, blonde and sunny like her mother, had fallen from a tree she'd been climbing and broke her back. Her legs now hung useless and atrophied. Renny's stunning baby girl was a cripple.

Renny's husband spared no expense taking Marah to every known healer, trying any liniment or ritual, anything to heal his girl. But it was not to be.

Abigail watched Renny go to the doorway to her home. She leaned in—the door was open because the day was so pleasant—and called to her servant. Renny gave instructions to the older woman and returned to her seat by Abigail. They both watched the older woman heft up Marah and take her inside. Abigail wondered how long the woman would be able to do that. Marah was still a growing girl.

"Renny, she could walk again!"

"Abigail, that is a false path I have traveled down too many times."

"I promise you, this really could work."

"How does Leah suddenly have the ability to heal people who can't be healed?" Renny knew Leah from their childhood, too. She remembered Leah as pleasant, but not with any particular ability to fix incurable cripples.

"She has access to ancient wisdom that our people have forgotten."

"Access to? How?"

"Through a divine guide who helps her."

"Divine…Shalliyt?"

"Uh, no. But he is a messenger of Shalliyt."

"Aren't we forbidden from seeking spiritual help from other than Shalliyt?"

"Have you asked him for help for your daughter?"

"Of course."

"And did you receive it?"

"No, not yet."

"One of Shalliyt's holy emissaries is interested in helping our people, in Shalliyt's stead. What could possibly be wrong with that? Isn't healing an act of love?"

Renny sighed. "Is it very expensive?"

Abigail quickly looked away. "How much is too much to heal your beloved Marah?"

Renny nodded. "I'll speak with my husband."

"The healing ceremony will be at the end of the week. Tell me if you will be going. I can take you."

Abigail and Renny hugged. Abigail kissed her cheek, tucking another stray lock of hair behind Renny's ear. "She can be healed. Just trust this one last time," she whispered. Abigail turned and walked away.

25

Briysh rested inside the wooden serpent in Leah's forest hut. He was gaining much better control of himself in his new state of being. At times the mindless eternal darkness still sucked him in and then eventually spit him back out into the wilderness, but this occurred with less frequency. However, the burning hungers of his body had not abated. He continued to find some relief when he inhabited his serpent.

Leah walked toward him, her skirt swishing along her ankles as her hips swayed. She reached up and stroked along the serpent's smooth wooden head. "Ah, Briysh, my love. Are you here with me yet?"

Her hand coasted down the arc of its neck. The wood starting here and going lower was deeply stained a reddish-brown. The repeated administration of the women's blood had soaked into the raw wood unevenly, giving it a mottled appearance. Lucas kept it polished to a shine.

Briysh thrived on that blood. But it had to be fresh to affect him. "Leah." His voice came through the serpent's mouth in a hissing sound.

She sighed with a smile stretching across her face.

Briysh watched her turn and walk toward the back dark corner that concealed Lucas in the deep shadow. She leaned over and ruffled the boy's hair. Lucas kept looking around his mother toward the serpent, mistrust clear in his eye. She whispered something to him and he jumped up and bolted out through the open front door, giving as wide a berth as possible to the statue. Leah moved over to the cabinet and removed some supplies. She turned to the Briysh serpent. "Everything is ready."

He hissed again and settled down to wait.

The full moon was high enough to cast its silver shine into the small clearing in front of the decrepit hut. A few torches on stakes driven into the grass outlined the small throng of people huddled quietly outside. They peered toward the open door to the hut, but with no illumination within, the people saw only a gaping black hole. Briysh, looking through his serpent glass eyes, could see them clearly through the narrow door, outside in the flickering torchlight. This was a gathering of the hopeless. And the hopeless were the easiest to work with. They would desperately believe anything that could improve their situation. They would easily be swayed by deception and subterfuge. They would quickly offer their praise and worship. They would serve his purposes perfectly.

He could see Leah's back now as she addressed the group. She gesticulated with wide arms. A long robe flowed around her bare feet as she moved, walking a few steps back and forth, engaging her audience. Briysh couldn't hear her—she spoke quietly in a way to make people lean in to catch everything she said. The people looked at her enraptured. She stopped, bowed her head down, while she lowered her hands slowly to her sides. Dead quiet settled.

Her four fellow devotees stepped forward from the group, all wearing similar robes. Leah silently turned toward the hut and walked through the door, the others following her lead. Their audience would see them simply disappearing into a yawning darkness. Abigail was at the rear of the line. She picked up a small candle that flickered at the entrance, stepped through, and shut the door behind her. The women, still silent, surrounded the Briysh serpent. Abigail leaned forward to put their only source of light on the pedestal directly under the serpent mouth. She removed a pinch of dried herb that had been placed there earlier and sprinkled it over the candle flame. A pungent herbal scent filled the room. She took her spot around back.

Briysh directed the ritual, beginning with their chanting and worship of him and culminating in the cutting of flesh. As the women rubbed their blood into the statue, Briysh flexed and stretched, the wooden coils becoming pliable again through the sorcery. The Briysh serpent uncoiled, his tongue loosening and flicking in and out of his mouth. His scales became more prominent, shifting, the sputtering candle glow delineating each

122

individual one. The serpent's neck arched toward the ceiling, head swiveling. The chanting echoed loudly through the small room, and Briysh had no doubt the others could hear outside and probably stared gape-mouthed at the hut. Immense pleasure trickled through his veins and soothed his aching desires. His mind was stimulated, invigorated by the feeling of power.

When the transformation was complete, Briysh stopped his flexing and shifted his attention to Lucas.

"Boy, step forward," he commanded. His power had grown enough that anyone could hear him speak, not just the entranced women.

A soft shuffling could be heard in the corner. Lucas stumbled forward out of the darkness, into the small flickering circle of light, to stand by his mother. His eye stared at the ground, and a furred lump was tucked under his arm. The Briysh serpent head descended toward the boy. Leah clamped her hands on the boy's shoulders to keep him still as he stood in front of her. The head came face to face with Lucas, its whip-like tongue snapping in and out. Its jaws began to stretch wide, wooden teeth now visible toward the back. A fetid smell issued forth causing Lucas to recoil.

Leah held Lucas firmly and kissed him on the top of his head. "Now, Lucas," she whispered into his hair.

Lucas grabbed the object that was clasped tightly against his armpit. It was a brown and white rabbit that he had caught earlier in the day, unconscious but breathing. He shoved it into the gaping jaws. The wooden jaw snapped shut on the rabbit, while the serpent head flung itself toward the ceiling and began swinging around. Blood, gore, and puffs of downy fur flew everywhere.

Leah released Lucas, who scampered back to his dark corner, and she raised her arms in the sprinkling of blood that now dripped from the ceiling, her head tilted up in ecstasy.

Briysh felt a huge surge of power bolt through his body from the sacrifice, and in that moment, he left the wooden statue and instantly slid into Leah. The wooden serpent became lifeless, coiled up in its original state. The possession of Leah caused her self to go…away. She would be dormant, unaware of what went on around her. It was time to begin.

Briysh opened the door and stepped out toward the small gathering. It seemed no one had spoken as silence lay thick across the meadow. Even the usual night noises of crickets and owls were absent. The people would see Leah's form standing before them, not his, but he didn't care. He felt wonderful, alive, in command. He looked across the dozen or so faces expectantly turned toward him. His four other women spread out behind and to his sides. They would manage the people while he worked. The meadow shimmered in the silvery moonlight, lending an ethereal mood to the setting.

"I will heal your sick," Briysh said, as he sat down in the dewy grass. "And in your gratitude, you will show reverence to Briysh who waits within." He indicated behind him toward the door.

It was difficult to determine if the shocked looks flitting across the faces of the people were due to his audacious proclamation or rather the fact that it was a man's voice, not Leah's, coming from her mouth.

An elderly woman at the back turned around and stumbled toward the forest. She used a thick crooked branch as support and dragged a crippled foot behind her, shaking her head. Everyone watched her go, listening as her shuffling noise disappeared into the darkness, but no comment was spoken aloud.

Briysh watched them carefully as they turned back toward him. He looked each one directly in the eye before moving to the next. "Does anyone else wish to leave and forfeit their healing?"

Silence.

"Good. Let's begin."

The four robed women moved toward the people then. They each took a person or family to speak with, receiving their payment before they could approach the healer. Abigail went directly toward her friend Renny, who had come with her husband and daughter. The husband held Marah in his arms. Her head lay against his shoulder, strands of her blonde hair, looking silver in the moonlight, fanned against his cheek. Her legs dangled uselessly down his side.

"I'm glad you came," Abigail spoke quietly to them. "You will be amazed with the healing."

"Are you sure about this?" Renny's arms were folded in front of her and she rubbed her hands back and forth over them.

124

"I'm sure you should give it a try," Abigail said. "She has the power to help Marah."

Renny glanced up at her husband then back to Abigail. "I don't doubt the power. It is the source of it that concerns me. She requires us to worship...whatever's in that hovel!"

Renny's husband spoke for the first time then. "Keep your voice down, Renny. Can't you be thankful for a healing no matter who does it? What matter is it who gets credit for it as long as it helps Marah? Would you seriously deny your daughter the chance to walk again because you can't pretend to be grateful to who or whatever heals her?"

"I don't want to offend Shalliyt," Renny whispered. Tears gathered in her eyes as she contemplated how far she would go to help her daughter.

"Nonsense, Renny." Abigail reached over and wiped a tear off her friend's cheek. "When Marah's healed, go inside and kneel down in front of the statue and offer your praises to Shalliyt!"

Renny smiled a little. Her husband looked at her, raising an eyebrow. Renny nodded. He shifted Marah a bit on his hip and held out his hand filled with coins and gave them to Abigail. She slipped them into a pocket of her robe and led them to Leah.

"Don't speak to her. Just listen," Abigail whispered to the couple before walking away.

"Lay Marah here in front of me," said Leah's man voice.

Renny felt a skittering up her spine. She had known Leah well when she was younger and nothing about the person in front of her reminded her of the young girl. Renny's husband leaned over and carefully laid Marah lengthwise in front of Leah.

Briysh stared at Renny, clearly sensing her distress. Addressing his comments to her directly, he said, "I shall heal your daughter in the name of Shalliyt." Briysh kept Leah's face impassive, but he laughed to himself. It made no difference what words were spoken. *He* was doing the healing and *he* would receive the power from Renny's devotion. Shalliyt was nowhere to be found. It made no difference if he healed in the name of the village idiot. The glory and power would all be his.

"Thank you," Renny said, tears streaming down her face. She came to her knees and cradled Marah's head in her lap.

Briysh switched his focus to the child. His preference would be to strangle her pathetic, thin neck. But he was working toward a greater purpose. If he could convince Leah to love him despite the festering disgust he felt for her, then he could convince anyone of anything. He stroked the child's forehead, smoothing the silky hair away from her face. Her eyes were huge and stared unblinking into his. Briysh moved his hand down over her chest. It rose and fell as her lungs pumped in air betraying how scared she was. He continued on, then stilled his hand over her lower stomach. He laid his hand, Leah's hand, flat on the spot directly above the injured back. Then with his own hand, invisible to the onlookers, he reached into Marah's body. In the same way he tunneled through mountains, he split through the young girl's flesh and wrapped his fingers around her spine, squeezing and smoothing it, infusing it with power that would temporarily allow it to function properly.

Marah gasped at the sudden surge of heat and current in her spine. Her parents simply saw Leah's hand resting quietly on their daughter's belly.

Briysh withdrew his hand. "She is healed," the too-deep voice said. "Stand her up and she will walk. But carry her home till she builds strength. Now go inside and pay your respects to Briysh, on your knees, as you praise Shalliyt." Briysh realized the end of that sounded a bit sarcastic. He offered Renny a small smile to cover up the slip.

Renny and her husband stared at Marah, clearly disbelieving that anything had changed with their broken daughter.

Marah's father leaned over and offered his hand to her. "Can you stand, dear?" He gently pulled and she indeed began to move her legs.

Renny gasped, her hands flying to her mouth. Her husband gently wrapped Marah in his arms and stood up, then slowly lowered her to her feet. She wobbled. She stood.

Murmuring spread among the people who had gathered around to watch. The tension broke and the people seemed anxious for their turn with the healer, instead of wary. Briysh motioned the next person to present themselves, as Abigail assisted her friend and family into the hut to offer their devotion and reverence to the healer sent from the divine, Briysh.

Renny barely noticed the statue she and her husband knelt before. She couldn't take her eyes off Marah who had done

126

her best to get on her knees with her parents, laughter bubbling up from her little body, her eyes dancing in the candle light.

They worshiped at the altar of the serpent as a family.

26

As Briysh grew more powerful among men through the rituals he learned from Aarkaos, he also stepped into a new role among his own kind. He became their leader. Aarkaos dealt with him exclusively, allowing Briysh to be next in line, leading the dead Offspring as they trickled into the wilderness. He was suited to the position because he had more experience in this new state of being and had some mastery over himself. This had only gotten better thanks to the rituals and sacrifices that cooled his blood and cleared his mind.

Kharshea had explained to him that violence was escalating in the valley, most notably among the Offspring. They got in plenty of fights with men as they plundered and stole from them, but it was the senseless power struggles amongst their own kind that had been primarily leading to the sharp increase in deaths.

So these newly dead Offspring arrived into Briysh's wilderness, disoriented and writhing in torment. He gladly took on the task of organizing these freshly disembodied. He formed them into a coalition of sorts. It was no friendship, as loyalty had never existed among them, but rather a means to achieving a common goal. Well, several goals.

Briysh first helped them gain some semblance of control over themselves by sharing the rituals to a small degree with them. Not that he cared one shred about their personal misery, but he needed them thinking clearly for the greater goal.

Kharshea had told Briysh that they were known, in this realm, as the Afflicted. He had also indicated that any easing of the affliction had to be done on their own. No other help or future was available to them. Briysh had put together from what Kharshea did and, maybe more importantly, did not tell him that the completely pathetic creatures known as man had the potential of a blessed eternity with their creator. However, he and his brethren had none, and were in fact not even claimed by this creator, who would one day simply dispose of him and his kind, like one shovels dung from a barn.

His fury exploded and his resolve formed. The humans of the valley he once felt indifference toward, were now objects of his hatred and wrath. The purpose of his existence crystallized. And this mission was embraced by all the Afflicted.

They had no means to make direct war on this god who was not their father. But they could go after the stupid creatures this god called his children and seemed to love.

Man would now serve Briysh in two ways: the use of their human bodies would give the Afflicted relief and even pleasure, and manipulation of their weak minds would turn them against their god. It was a delicious plan.

Briysh taught his brethren how to gain access to the human bodies they craved through the use of herbs and blood, and how to demand devotion and adulation from the owners of those bodies. Leah had been very accommodating in offering her acolytes for their use. As they experimented, they discovered that different members of the Afflicted had different strengths and abilities in impacting the humans. The variety kept things quite entertaining.

Briysh also took it upon himself to institute new names for the Afflicted. They chose monikers that aptly represented their character. Briysh became Lust. In life, he lusted for women, and in death he lusted for worship and power. His new cohorts included Liar, Fear, and Agony.

Briysh continued with his new healing "ministry," gathering for himself many followers who would kneel before his serpent self, some of whom would spill their blood for him. He grew increasingly powerful. His priestess, Leah, became well known through the valley. She was considered a gifted healer. People wanted to believe in the healings so strongly that they overlooked the occasional case where the sick person reverted to their former condition a short time later, some even ending up worse than they were originally. But this did not trouble Briysh at all, as they would return for a second healing, giving Leah more coins and Briysh more power. And then there were some conditions in which Briysh had no ability to effect a change at all. He made it clear to these people that their lack of faith in him was the issue, not his healing abilities.

27

Leah's main disciple, Abigail, had been claimed by Liar. She was now able to earn a decent living as a diviner of sorts. Abigail set up a small booth in the market. A scarlet-dyed wool curtain hung over the door offering some privacy. A young girl called Naomi would supervise at the curtain while Abigail was with a customer, while lining up the next client to go in.

On one particular day the market teemed with people, but the mood of the crowd was agitated—a more frequently occurring event in recent months. People seemed to be more prone to fighting, and theft from market stalls was common now.

Abigail sighed. She didn't care for the feeling roiling around her this particular morning, but she had to admit it was good for business. Contented people didn't seek out fortune tellers. She sat alone behind her red curtain that glowed with the afternoon sun as she relaxed and emptied her mind of any busyness that could block her connection to the Sacred Counselor. She felt so fortunate to be visited by this spiritual friend who came to her and helped her help others. He didn't take over her body in the way that Leah's spiritual friend did. It felt as if the Sacred Counselor sat upon her shoulder and whispered the information she needed for the divining into her ear.

She checked that her long sleeves were pulled down, hiding the series of scars that had formed from the bloodletting with the serpent.

"I'm ready, Naomi," Abigail said softly. She distantly heard some jostling from the other side of the curtain as her customers vied for a spot or shoved their coins into Naomi's hand, but she tuned it out and focused on her blank mind.

The curtain edged open and a middle-aged woman pushed in. Abigail pointed to the opposite side of the rug for her to be seated. The woman, in hushed awe, went to the spot and squatted down on her heavy thighs. Between the women sat a small pot of tea and several cups.

Abigail poured the woman a cup and passed it to her. "Drink this." The tea contained an herb that relaxed the person and loosened their thoughts, the Sacred Counselor had said, to aid in understanding the customer's true wishes.

The woman drank it down and looked at Abigail expectantly. "Do you want to know my name?" Her voice had a screechy quality, even as a whisper. Her fingers fidgeted along the edge of the cup.

"No, that won't be necessary." Abigail drank some of the tea also. "What is it you would like to know?"

The woman looked around, unsure suddenly. Her eyes began to well up with unshed tears.

Abigail reached for her hand. She clasped it firmly—the woman's was slippery with perspiration. "Go ahead and tell me what troubles your heart," Abigail said gently.

The woman nodded. "Yes. All right. Yes." She looked around one more time, then her eyes finally settled on Abigail. "It's my husband. I think he has… I think there may be another…" She couldn't finish.

"You want to know if he is being unfaithful to you?" Abigail squeezed the woman's fingers in sympathy.

"Yes, that." The woman exhaled and seemed to deflate. "I know I am older now and my body has changed since we married…" She rubbed at her bare arms as she hugged herself. "Do you want to know his name?"

"No, that won't be necessary either. Please just be comfortable and quiet for a bit and we will know soon." Abigail closed her eyes. She felt the familiar brush of something against her ear and knew her Sacred Counselor had departed to find the truth.

Liar took leave of Abigail after hearing the question. These people were pathetic, he thought, as he alighted on the customer's shoulder. He easily reached into her mind with his, thanks to the herbal concoction opening the way, and found the information he needed to find her husband. Then he tunneled through the air at high speed directly to the location of the man in question.

He arrived in moments at the back room of a butcher shop that sold a variety of meats to its customers. The husband stood against a waist-high counter wearing a red-stained apron. His sleeves were pushed up past his elbows and his large hands deftly wrapped some cut meat in a cloth. A swatch of his hair had fallen forward onto his sweaty forehead and he pushed it back with his upper arm.

"Ada, please bring me some twine," he called out to someone not present in the room.

A young, attractive girl, presumably Ada, came into the room holding the ball of twine. She had thick, black hair that was pulled back and tied but still hung nearly to her waist. Her complexion was creamy and flawless. She was barely old enough to be a woman, likely the age of the butcher's daughter if he had one. "Here you are, sir." She smiled as she handed the twine to him, and Liar saw two large dimples form in her cheeks. She turned and left the room.

In that moment, Liar reached out and placed his hand on the man's head. He couldn't read the husband's mind like he had the wife's, but he could sense the man's emotions. Pulsing through from the man's head to Liar's hand were feelings of fondness and protectiveness toward the girl. Liar also sensed some concerns related to the business, but he ignored these. Liar leaned over and brushed his lips over the man's ear. The man would only "hear" Liar's words as thoughts in his own mind—as if he had thought the words himself.

"Ada is beautiful. I wonder what she would look like unclothed?" Liar smirked and licked his lips.

The butcher stopped his wrapping and stared forward, frowning.

"I think her naked skin would be soft and smooth. And so much better than the hide of the cow I'm married to." Liar rubbed his hands together, getting warmed up now.

The butcher's expression filled with horror. He shook his head as if he could shake his thoughts away. Liar could feel waves of uncertainty, dismay, and just the smallest hint of lust rolling off the butcher. These emotions fed Liar. Empowered him.

This dolt must actually be fond of that cow of a wife! Liar was laughing now.

Liar leaned back in to continue whispering the filth into the husband's ear. "Just one touch...what would that hurt? Her hair is like fine silk and would feel so good slipping through my fingers. Her young body would quiver under my touch. Ada finds me virile and attractive!"

The butcher's face flushed and he rushed out of the room, out the back door.

The negative energy left in the wake of the butcher was a healing balm to Liar's mind and body, such as it was. Pleasure shot through his veins. He drifted through the building to where Ada had just finished helping a customer in the front room, unaware of the turmoil with her employer in the back. He perched on Ada's shoulder and gave her ear a long lick before he began whispering into her mind. "My boss is a strong, healthy man. But he is lonely. He needs me to touch him."

Liar felt confusion emanating from Ada. That emotion would work just fine, too.

Ada tucked a lock of hair behind her ear then rubbed the ear as if she felt Liar there.

Liar decided she may be too perceptive so he needed to finish quickly. "I must go to him now. He needs me, and my body aches for him." Then Liar left before he saw her reaction and flew back, newly energized, to Abigail in her market stall.

Abigail felt the rush of the return of the Sacred Counselor.

"My adviser is here, now we can answer your question." Abigail closed her eyes and awaited the counselor's wisdom.

The distraught woman startled out of the lethargy she had sunk into for the few minutes that they awaited an answer. "I'm ready," she said hesitantly.

Liar sat on Abigail's shoulder and whispered to her. "Your husband is a butcher. His shop is on the main thoroughfare near the center of the village."

"Your husband is a butcher. His shop is on the main thoroughfare near the center of the village," Abigail repeated aloud for the woman to hear.

The woman perked up. Abigail knew this would be what convinced her. The woman had not given her name nor her husband's name earlier, so now she would trust everything Abigail said to her. The woman smiled in obvious relief, all hesitation about her decision to come here lifted.

"A beauty named Ada works for him," Liar spoke, and Abigail repeated.

"Yes!" the woman brightened. "She is a lovely young woman that is also our neighbor. She is a delightful cook and makes us the best desserts and brings them to us! She is our daughter's closest friend and has been nothing but a joy to us."

"Your husband is sporting with her right now in the courtyard behind his store. He is holding her long black hair wrapped in his fist while he pulls up her skirt and grinds into her." Abigail felt nauseous as she repeated the vulgar words.

The woman's face fell. "What?...Ada?"

Liar felt first confusion and disbelief radiating from the woman.

Abigail reached for her hand again. "I'm sorry. The truth is not always a pleasant thing."

The woman's face crumpled. She buried it in her hands as sobs began to bubble up from deep within her.

Liar's blood zinged and thrummed through his system as the woman's distress and anguish multiplied nearly instantly, bathing him in her luscious emotions. He felt his power surging making him nearly euphoric.

"Naomi? We're done," Abigail called out.

Naomi parted the curtain and drew the woman out, gently patting her on the back as she sent her off into the crowd. The people waiting in line turned and watched as she stumbled away, still weeping. Her reaction seemed to signal an authenticity to the divining they awaited. Naomi ducked her head back into the booth. "Do you need a minute to gather yourself?

"Yes, thank you."

Liar had carefully moved away from Abigail to the opposite side of the tent before he let the laughter consume him. He needed Abigail to take him seriously and she couldn't hear him unless he touched her. This had been the best one yet!

28

His face itched. Without opening his eye, Lucas rubbed his cheek on the scratchy mat. It still itched.

He huffed and sat up, scrubbing short fingers against the stubborn spot. That was better. Opening his eye in the gloomy hut, he searched out the crack around the door and saw light. He stared at the brilliant glowing strip. He put up one hand blocking his side view. Now he could stare at the light and not see the shadow of the wooden statue. The serpent was very scary. His mother tried to make him feel better by explaining that the statue somehow held his father. His father was pain and fear to Lucas. It felt confusing that his mother loved the statue. Lucas quickly looked away realizing he had turned to stare at the very thing he tried so hard to not to look at.

A flicker in the glare at the bottom of the door grabbed his attention. Was somebody out there? Yes. A soft rapping on the door made him jump to his feet. It wasn't his mother's special knock. So he would just peek. He carefully folded his blanket and laid it at the bottom of his pallet. He scratched at his face again. He thought it might be a bug bite. Yesterday he fished in the stream behind the hut and small black flies bothered him. Maybe they could bite. But that didn't stop him—he caught three fish with his line and bone hook! He ate two fish last night. He probably should have only had one. But he felt extra hungry because he was a big boy and he ate two. The third one he carefully wrapped. He stowed it in a small hole he dug under the side of the hut. He put a heavy rock over the hole so the night creatures wouldn't steal it from him. He was a little hungry now. He could eat…

"Lucas!" The rapping was a little louder now. "Are you in there?" It was a harsh whisper. Maybe the visitor was trying to be quiet so as not to wake him up. But they wanted to wake him up, too.

Lucas clumped over to the door, carefully skirting the statue. He peered out the side crack in the door. "Who are you?" He harsh-whispered back. "I'm not supposed to answer the door." He could see a woman. She looked a bit like his mother. Her brown hair piled on top of her head in a bun. Freckles flecked across her cheeks. She held a bundle. "My mother made a rule and I have to obey." He said these words but he knew that the other person would not hear them like that. Mean boys said he sounded like a growling animal when he talked. They growled back at him and laughed.

This woman clutched her bundle tightly to her chest as her eyes searched out the location of Lucas's warbling voice. Facing his direction, she harsh-whispered more. "Lucas! This is for your mother." She held the bundle out from her chest. It moved a bit. Then it began to holler. She quickly clamped it back to her chest, smothering the noise a little.

"Oh." He didn't know what to do. He rubbed his palm across his eye. Then he turned around. Sometimes if he didn't look, then his worry went away. He stopped rubbing, and now he was looking at the father-serpent lurking in the darkness. It stared at him with dead eyes. He needed to wipe it with oil today. It was okay and not scary then because it made his mother so happy when he did a good job. And dead eyes meant it wouldn't move or scare him. He would scrub it especially hard today because the blood on it was very thick. The oil and blood mixed together and made a nice, smooth layer that bumped out and around its scales.

A screech ripped through his thoughts. Lucas spun around and looked out the bright crack. The woman was gone. The bundle lay on the ground, wriggling. It made so much noise. He didn't want anyone else to hear. He was supposed to be quiet. He was supposed to 'not attract attention' his mother would say, to keep him safe. He liked being safe. Making a big decision, he opened the door, ducked his tall frame through the opening, and bent over, grabbing up the bundle, which quieted immediately.

He left the door open a bit so the light would shine in. It made a long bright path across the floor. He laid the bundle in the light path and began to unwrap it. It was sheepskin. He fingered the soft material. He could put this on his bed. He could rest his itchy face against it. Lucas liked that idea, and his mother would like it too. She would say he was 'clever.' He smiled.

Drawing back the sheepskin, he laid bare the…what? An animal or a baby? A baby, he thought. Lucas drew his finger over the baby's face. It had two eyes like everyone else. Everyone except him. The baby's lips latched onto his fingers and began sucking and slurping. Its face was cute. But below the face was not so cute. A long body twisted strangely. Then it ended. No arms and no legs. Lucas knew this baby was different. Like he was different. But in a different way. Lucas loved the baby.

Later that night, Leah arrived at the hut to find Lucas feeding bits of cheese and fish to his new friend. She hung her cloak on a peg, lit several candles from Lucas's candle, and placed them about the room. Then she approached Lucas where he was stretched out on his pallet, feet hanging over the too-short bed, his arm cradling the baby, and she knelt down next to him.

"What do we have here?" She stroked a finger from the springy hair on the baby's head down the length of his contorted body. Lucas smiled up at his mother. "Oh, Lucas," she said. "This is a very special baby."

Lucas beamed. He already knew that. They were friends. He didn't have any friends, and he thought it would be nice to have a friend. And this baby would be his friend.

"I spoke with his mother earlier. He has a daddy like you do."

A wooden father? A serpent father? Lucas wasn't sure.

"This baby will have the highest honor." She sighed and lay down next to Lucas and his bundle on the pallet. "Your father will be so pleased."

Lucas reached over and took his mother's hand. A warm feeling bubbled in his tummy. He drifted off to sleep touching his mother and his friend.

Lucas awoke to the familiar sound of chanting. It felt very late at night. He kept his eye closed, as he liked to do, and let his other senses take over. He smelled incense. Incense and chanting meant his father would soon be here. He pulled his blanket up over his head. The blanket was rough, but under his cheek on the pallet was soft. Why wasn't it scratchy? He moved his cheek a bit thinking about it. Oh yes! The sheepskin—it did make a fine pillow. Then he suddenly remembered the baby. He jolted up and found his arms still encircled his new friend. Sometimes he had dreams about good things, but when he woke up, the good things were gone. But this time, it was still here. He hugged the baby close. But he was very careful. He knew inside him that one had to be gentle with babies. He pushed the blanket off his head because he also knew babies needed air. He laughed quietly to himself.

"Lucas. Come here, Son." His mother used her strange chanty-voice. He didn't really like that voice. Well, the voice was okay, but he knew she would have her far-away eyes, too, and he didn't like them so much. "Bring the baby. It is time for him to meet your father."

Lucas leaned over and kissed the baby's forehead and gurgled to him, "It will be fine. You are special, like me!" He scooped him up with the sheepskin and tucked it around him. He walked around the women kneeling at the base of the serpent statue, which had begun to writhe. His father was here. Lucas kept his eyes on his mother. Her head was bowed and her hands rested on her knees.

"Present your sacrifice, woman."

Lucas cringed. His father had a loud, angry voice always. Lucas didn't know what a 'sacrifice' was, but it must be the highest honor his mother told him about.

Leah stood and slowly looked toward Lucas. She had far-away eyes. "Stand in front of your father and face him. You've done this before." She stepped back.

He had done this before. But those were rabbits he had trapped. They weren't special. They didn't have the highest honor. A trickle of horror began to slip down Lucas's spine.

Lucas looked up into the face of the serpent. Its neck dripped with blood from the women cutting their arms. He could smell the blood. He forgot to polish the statue today. Because of his new friend he just forgot. He hoped his mother wouldn't get angry with him. The serpent, his father, didn't have dead eyes anymore. They were alive and looked like they were on fire, like tiny flames burned inside them. His father wouldn't hurt his friend, because he wasn't a rabbit. He felt sweat break out all over his body.

"Show me the child, Lucas." His voice was a little less angry now, and had a hiss sound. Like a snake.

Lucas gently peeled back the sheepskin exposing the infant. "Be brave little one," he warbled and kissed him once again. The baby gurgled back. Lucas raised both arms presenting his friend to his father.

He saw the serpent jaws begin to stretch open. They were opening so wide. Much wider tonight than before. He could see down the serpent's throat. He could see the throat pulsing. He didn't realize the throat was so wide, like a deep cave.

Lucas stared mesmerized by the serpent's undulating, constricting throat. He didn't notice quickly enough that he was in danger as the serpent's head descended rapidly, the jaws engulfing him and the baby. He didn't hear his mother's gasp of ecstasy as she called out Briysh's name. His final thought was that the teeth hurt as they tore through his skin, not at all nice like the sheepskin.

PART THREE

29

Under the shroud of deepest night, the young goat lay on her side panting. She had hidden herself behind a reedy knoll tufted with yellow-green grasses and scraggly brambles. The depression she lay in was slimed in her own blood, the vegetation sweat-slicked and matted under her writhing body.

Her legs kicked out stiff and straight, and her lips pulled back from her teeth as she grunted. Neck muscles stretched and tautened with exertion. Her small tail flicked uselessly from side to side in the grass. Bulging eyes reflected back the slivered moon as they rolled in agony. She bore down hard, breath held, gut tensed. The spasm slowly faded.

Labor had wrenched her body for several hours now, but progressed little. As she settled into the brief oblivion of exhaustion between contractions, crickets trilled loudly around her, unaware of the aberration unfolding in their midst.

A line of trees edged the pasture near where the doe was prostrate with fatigue. An owl with brown-masked face perched, leathery toes curled around a thick branch, and looked down at the wretched scene, head slightly cocked. He blinked a single eye and swiveled his head.

The doe jerked out of her lethargy as another wave of constriction gripped her. The movement rocked her onto her distended milk bag, swollen and hard, adding another layer to a pain she could not fathom. She lurched away from the extra pressure and felt another splash of birth fluids escape her heaving body. But this time there was movement at the opening. Two soft-shelled hooves, wrapped in a film, now protruded from her back end. If a goatherd had attended her, he would have noted immediately that the hooves were presenting upside down—a breach.

The goat felt a renewed strength to push harder. For several cycles the twin hooves advanced and receded along their slippery passage. Coarse bleats scraped past her vocal chords in a sudden frenzy of effort. The hooves emerged fully again, followed at once by thickly furred hocks and hips and tail. The doe flopped still, just her lungs heaving, the back half of her kid out of her body. The newborn's hind legs scissored slightly in the drenched grass. Its mother gave one final heave and the rest of the kid's body slithered out, thumping into the world.

The doe struggled to her feet. As she turned around, the placenta—attached to the baby by a pulpy, curling cord—slipped from her body, hitting the ground with a wet smack. Compelled by instinct, she began to lick the mouth and nose of her baby to clear the clinging birth membranes and to allow the first gasp of breath. The distinctive scent of the kid branded itself into the doe's brain, so she would always be able to identify her offspring. As her tongue laved nose, cheeks, eyes, and ears, the child lifted its hands, human-like fingers furling and unfurling, toward the doe's hairy cheek. Its pink lips worked silently, face scrunching at the tonguing assault. Small whimpers grew into the indignant wail of the newly born.

The owl, lone observer of the anomalous birth, blinked a single eye again, stretched clamped toes, spread massive wings, and took flight. He soared low over the tableau then ascended silently into the night.

30

"The Guardians are not men, though they take the form of man. They can assume the shape of any being they wish, to defile all of creation if it is their desire. They have whored after our women and begat monsters. But now, because of their insatiable lust and greed, they have turned to the beasts and the birds, and all that moves and walks through the valley. Iniquity and bloodshed will inhabit our midst, all flesh corrupted. The imagination of men will be filled with vanity, their thoughts continually evil…"

After the Telling ended, Haven sat on his bench in the dim cave, unmoving. His elbows were braced on his knees and his head hung in his hands, his hair flopping over his forehead. People filed past him silently to head to the emotional safety of their homes.

"Haven. Come here, son."

Haven's head shot up to see the Teller, still seated on the platform, casting his milky blue eyes toward him. "Yes, sir." Haven's voice came out with a croak. He stood, walked to the Teller, and half knelt, half sat, awkwardly before him.

"You still worry for Rachel." As usual, it wasn't a question.

"She is in danger. I don't know how to make her understand." Haven rubbed both his hands against his thighs. "I've explained it to her for months now, reasoned with her—"

"Tonight, take her and follow him discreetly. Watch. Shalliyt will shield you from view." The Teller stood, his motions surprisingly fluid for a man of his age.

Haven wrinkled his brow. "Follow who?" But the Teller walked away without another word.

Haven kicked a stone as he meandered on the path home after the Telling. The Teller's words had shocked him to the core, again. He had known that the Guardians were not men, and he'd been telling this to anyone who would listen to him. But he realized, in his mind, he still considered them *man-like* in

147

some way. But that was false. They could become whatever creature they wanted, enabling them to fornicate with any creature in the valley. Though the physical connection of the act was possible through their sorcery, the resulting progeny, though viable, was deformed and cursed. Haven knew Shalliyt ordained creation to reproduce after its own kind. Horses produce only horses, and ash trees produce only ash trees. The offspring of the Guardian and woman, or Guardian and animal, did not follow kind reproducing after its own kind and therefore was an abomination to Shalliyt. The Teller said the offspring proceeded from their mothers soulless. Haven couldn't even fathom the consequence of the existence of soulless beings. A shudder ran through his body.

He needed to speak to Rachel. Even after their encounter with Eli months ago, she hadn't been convinced of the inherent evil of the Guardians. She had insisted that the *gentleman* who courted her was different. Since then, Haven suspected she had been spending more time with the man. He hadn't seen her around, and certainly not at the Tellings.

Haven pulled himself from his thoughts, still kicking the stone on the path, as he came alongside the hedgerow bordering Rachel's yard. He was about to round the end when he heard Rachel's voice. He quickly pulled back, remaining hidden from sight.

"...oh sir, you are being so forward." Rachel giggled.

Haven heard a lower voice speak, but could not make out the words. Rachel shrieked. Haven had to look. He peered around the edge of the bush and saw the Guardian, Ashteala she'd called him. He grabbed her around the waist and hauled her into an embrace. Haven heard himself growl and began flexing his fingers. He would not hesitate to take on this man—no, this *creature*—to protect Rachel. Even if he was a foot taller than Haven and imbued with who-knew-what kind of power. Haven's fingers curled into fists and he was about to sprint out.

But Rachel laughingly slapped the man's hands away, and the man took a step back.

"Soon, my dear. Soon and you will deny me no longer." Ashteala lifted an eyebrow and smirked at Rachel.

She furiously blushed, but her smile showed she clearly relished the attention. "Be gone with you now, you rogue." She made shooing motions with her hands.

148

The Guardian grasped her hand, bowed slightly to her and kissed the back of her hand. Haven could see he wore the same smile from the first night he had seen him. The smile that did not reach his flat, black eyes.

Haven rounded the corner just as the other man turned and walked away. He realized his hands were still fisted. He took a deep breath and stretched out his fingers, heading toward Rachel. Rachel watched Ashteala leave, oblivious to Haven's approach behind her.

He laid a hand on her shoulder.

"Oh!" She jumped, spinning around to face him. "Haven, you startled me!" She put her hands on her hips. Her eyes were dilated and her face flushed. She turned and looked back over her shoulder to see the tall man disappearing in a bend in the path away from her house. She chewed on her bottom lip.

"So he is your suitor now, is he?" Haven's comment brought her attention back to him.

Rachel flinched a bit at Haven's tone. "It is Father's wish…"

Haven knew she was deflecting, probably because she felt bad for him. Or maybe Jared had put some pressure on her. It didn't really matter. Rachel was in danger and Haven didn't have time to get angry or mired in self-pity. He was about to launch into another of his lectures that drove Rachel crazy, but suddenly the words of the Teller came to him: "*Take her…follow him…watch.*" It made some sense now.

Haven slid his hand down from her shoulder across the silky material covering her arm and grasped her hand. "Come with me," was all he said.

A smile spread across her face. "Are we going on another grand adventure? Maybe one less emotionally taxing than our last?" She laughed lightly.

He squeezed her hand but didn't answer. He tried to keep his face from reflecting the turmoil churning deep inside himself. He had no idea what was soon to happen, but he suspected tonight would not be her idea of fun.

Rachel seemed giddy, with a bounce in her step. Haven knew he wasn't the source of her good mood and he pushed down the pain that thought caused.

Suddenly she paused, her steps faltering. Confusion crossed her face as she realized they were headed down the same path Ashteala had just taken.

Haven adjusted his hand to interlace his fingers with hers. Rachel looked down at their hands, then back up to his face. He looked into her green eyes. He could get lost in those eyes. He reached over with his free hand and touched one of the springy black curls that framed her face. *I love you.* But he remained silent.

He looked forward and tugged her along a little faster. He needed to catch sight of the Guardian again. Dusk was upon them, the sun having just dipped behind the western mountains, leaving a drenching red glow on the sky above, turning the ever-present mist covering the peaks a brilliant scarlet. *A bloody shroud covering the home of the Guardians, how fitting.* Haven thought perhaps he was getting a little too morbid in his thoughts.

The path wound into a wooded copse; it was much darker in the dense growth. The path narrowed a bit, but was still easily navigable. Flocks of sheep and goats took this route from time to time. All the leaves up to waist-high were stripped from the underbrush, courtesy of long, twining goat tongues browsing while walking.

After a few minutes in the cooler tree cover, Haven and Rachel emerged from the other side into the quickly darkening evening. They had their first glimpse of Ashteala. He was across a field from them, just walking into a small animal shed. Before he crossed the threshold, he looked around, as if to see if anyone watched him. Haven stopped abruptly. They stood in the deep shadow of the tree line, and the Guardian's eyes swept right past them. He pulled the door closed behind himself and Haven heard the thunk of the cross board locking into place from within.

Rachel looked back and forth between Ashteala and Haven, a frown spreading across her pale face. She and Haven had barely spoken on their walk. Haven gave her hand a small squeeze, then stepped into the clearing. "Run," he said in a low, gruff voice.

They ran across the field hand in hand. Haven led her around the back of the shed, both breathing heavily from the sprint. He knew the Guardian had locked himself inside so there had to be another way for them to watch, since the Teller had specifically commanded him to watch. A perfect spot awaited them in back. The shed had one window, an opening high on the wall with wooden slats across it. Below the window, two stacked bales of hay provided a seat. Before walking over to the bales, Haven placed his hand over Rachel's still-huffing mouth. "Shh. We must be silent," he whispered.

She nodded, and Haven removed his hand. She took a deep breath and pressed her lips together, breathing through her nose. Haven guided her over to the bales with a hand on the small of her back. He helped Rachel clamber onto the bale. She had to sit up on her knees to raise her high enough to peer through the bottom opening of the window. Haven scrambled up behind her. He wrapped an arm around Rachel, pulling her toward himself—her back pressed against his front, so they both comfortably fit on the bale.

They directed their attention to inside the shed, Haven looking over Rachel's shoulder. Ashteala had lit a lamp, though it was burning very low, casting wavering shadows against the wall. It sat on a wooden stool off to one side. The shed appeared to house only a pair of splotched brown and white dairy cows. One was just below their window, and the other occupied an adjacent stall. The stalls were open-ended at the far side, the cows tethered with rope to the wall next to their feed box. Long tongues lazily stretched out and curled around clumps of hay, bringing it to their mouths for a leisurely chew.

Haven felt Rachel jerk a little, so he pulled his attention from the masticating cow and back to the Guardian. He disrobed, carefully folding his garments and setting them on a table. Rachel had turned to look at Haven, her eyes wide with horror.

Haven stroked the side of her face while giving her a gentle squeeze with the arm embracing her. He spoke softly into her ear. "Rachel, I need you to watch. It will be okay, little one," he whispered.

Haven could imagine how completely scandalized Rachel felt spying on the man who was courting her, as he removed his clothes. She may flirt with danger, but she was innocent to the core. Haven did not know what was going to happen, but he sensed it would probably be distressing for Rachel. But if it would save her life, maybe even her soul, then it had to be done.

Rachel could see the seriousness in Haven's gaze. She swallowed visibly and wet her bottom lip with her tongue, nodded, and turned back to the window.

The Guardian stood still, completely naked, his back to his covert audience. He lowered his chin to his chest…and simply faded. Rachel gasped. The air where he had been standing had the vibrating quality of a road radiating heat on a warm day. Haven held his breath, his heart pounding hard.

The shimmering air throbbed with increasing intensity, causing the lamp to flicker. Haven wiped sweat out of his eyes, and he realized Rachel was shaking in his arms. With a loud *whump*, the two found themselves staring at a monstrous, snarling bull where Ashteala had been standing. Rachel spun in Haven's arms and buried her head in his chest. Both dairy cows startled and began grunting in rising panic. The bull scraped the ground with his hoof, tossed his head, massive horns slicing through the air, and stalked toward the cow tied just under the window, right in front of them. The Ashteala/bull creature was mere feet away from them, and Haven could smell the musky stench of the creature. Haven physically turned Rachel back around toward the window and whispered harshly, "Watch!"

She did, her head pushed back against Haven's chest. Her eyes widened in terror, and tears ran down her cheeks. Her hands were clenched into fists in her lap.

The cow in front of them bawled, her eyes rolling wildly, trying to see the monster bull behind her. She seemed to echo Rachel's fear. The cow yanked hard at the rope tying her halter to the shed wall. It did not give. The bull lowered his head, snorting into the dirt. Then he threw his head up, spittle flying in all directions. He sniffed the air and let out a roaring bellow of his own. He reared up, hooves flailing in the air. Haven could see the bull's testicles in a sac the size of a man's head, swinging between his back legs. The bull lunged, falling forward, and covered the cow from behind, brutally sating his lust.

Tremendous noise filled the shed, but Haven realized Rachel was screaming into her fist. She'd clearly had enough. Haven leapt off the bale and grabbed Rachel. He cradled her under her back and behind her knees. With her arms flung around his neck and clamped down, she sobbed into his neck. He hugged her to his chest and fled into the night.

31

Seth looked over at his wife. Hannah bent over and neatly arranged the ceramic pots and bottles of tonics they were selling. She looked old. Much older than she should. Seth sighed. And he felt old.

Seth rarely allowed himself to indulge in ruminating over the past, or worse, over regrets, but today they were forefront in his mind. He had met Kharshea at this booth in the marketplace years ago. He had been instantly intrigued by the mountain dweller's offer to show them how to make the unique healing tonics using ingredients that grew in the valley all around them but had never been put together in such a way as to have such a beneficial effect on people. Seth's coin purse bulged with the profits that had poured in. His life should be perfect.

Except now his daughter Dassah, with a face that glowed like the sun itself, was dead. His grandson, whose birth killed Dassah, turned out to be an antisocial aberration of nature who had no use for his grandparents, or anyone but himself. And he was dead—Seth was humiliated to realize what a relief this had been. But that brought another woman carrying his great-grandson into his home. Leah was pleasant enough— once he could overlook the fact that he had a prostitute living under his roof—but then she gave birth to a grotesque child they had to keep hidden from the neighbors: dull, one-eyed, rapidly growing... Thankfully, she had gotten him out of the house for good. Come to think of it, he hadn't seen it...him... for a few months now.

Seth shook his head. Now that Leah had gone on to be a highly sought-out priestess of some kind—he had no idea what that was about—his Hannah was left with the work of making the tonics. Seth told her she no longer needed to do it—they had plenty of coin to support themselves—but she seemed to need to keep busy.

Kharshea still lived with them but wasn't around often. His only demand on them now was for Hannah to keep making a particular concoction that Leah required for her rituals. He just wasn't the sort of man one said 'no' to.

Hannah stood up straight, stretching her back. "That should do it. I think we will have enough this week." She smiled at Seth.

He smiled back. Even with her lined forehead, graying hair, and tired eyes, she was beautiful to him. He realized in that moment that he had never really appreciated her the way he should have. He quickly turned away and fussed with the bins of potatoes he'd brought. Demand for food was huge, so he always sold all that he brought along.

"Good day, fine folk!" A raspy voice boomed out, getting both Hannah's and Seth's attention.

"Benjamin, you old goat." Hannah propped her hands on her hips and smiled fondly at the man.

"Never seen such a mean crowd as is wanderin' the aisles today." The older man coughed into his fist. His eyes leaked a bit, and he leaned against the frame of the booth.

Hannah's smile faltered. "What's wrong with you? I thought that cough was finally gone?"

"Bah!" Benjamin waved a hand in the air. "It was. Now it's back—all the cursed smoke fillin' the air." He bent over coughing harder now. When he was done, he pulled a cloth from his pants' pocket and wiped at his mouth and eyes. "I been to see your girl. Twice now, actually."

"Leah?" Hannah asked.

"She's not our girl. Just the mother of—" Seth stalled out, trying to figure out how to quantify his relationship with a prostitute and her deformed child, but Benjamin saved him the trouble.

"She sure has a freakish voice. But she touched me and I felt better right away." He hocked into his cloth.

"But the smoke brought it back?" Hannah sorted through her bottles, looking for one to assist Benjamin.

"Yeah. I went to see her a second time and said about the smoke to her. She said my faith was weak 'cause the smoke shouldn't matter."

"That makes no sense, Benji." Seth had suspected whatever Leah was up to might be a con game. "And the smoke…

why do these fields keep catching fire? Heard some more cottages burned, too. What is wrong with this place? The whole world is going crazy." Seth turned to the back of his booth, suddenly overwhelmed again by everything.

Benjamin leaned in a bit. "So, Hannah, I thought you might have one of them amazing tonics that would help an old fella a bit while he worked on his weak faith." He shot her a cock-eyed grin.

She handed him an amber bottle stoppered with a cork. "Here. This will loosen up that congestion so you can breathe more easily. Don't know that it'll help with your faith." She winked at him.

Benjamin reached into his pocket. "Whadda I owe you?"

"Nothing, since you're my favorite old goat."

"Thanks, Hannah. You are an angel!" He called over to Seth. "Ya know that right? That you're married to an angel?"

"Yes, of course." Seth came forward again, in control of himself for the moment. "Stay away from Leah. I don't know what she's up to, but I wouldn't trust her."

"Nah, she's fine. Pretty gal and she *can* heal." Benjamin wiped at his mouth again, and glanced over his shoulder. "Her voice is odd, and the bowing to the snake statue is a little strange…"

Seth and Hannah glanced at each other.

"Anyway, I must be on my way, my fine friends. Thanks for the drink, Hannah." He lifted the dark bottle toward her in salute and turned and melted into the swelling crowds.

Immediately a woman came to the booth, inquiring after Seth's potatoes. He dealt with her, and the customer after her, and soon forgot about Leah, and bowing before snake statues, and smoky air.

155

32

"We can multiply the harvest yield. This isn't a problem."
Rhyima's long legs ate up the path as he strode alongside Marahka. They took the main route as it wandered alongside the sheer rock face on one side and a wooded area on the other. The shade from the trees gave some pleasant relief from the midday sun and the heat radiating from the sun-warmed rocks. The acrid smoke wasn't as bad today, but somehow the air seemed thinner, hotter.

"It *is* a problem, and it's our problem, Rhyima."

Rhyima snorted. "Not really. I don't need to eat. Do you?"

Marahka came slamming to a halt. "No, I don't. But your son might want to, and that should make it your problem."

Rhyima rolled his eyes and started forward again. "Keep walking. We're late." He refused to acknowledge Marahka glaring at him. "Fine. It's our problem. And, as I said, we'll boost production."

After a brief time of a huge bounty of crops in the valley thanks to the Guardian's intervention, the trend reversed. The increasing number of Offspring consumed much more food than the men of the valley, to fuel their phenomenal growth. With their rude behavior, the sons took what they needed without the niceties of payment or labor for compensation. Their bullying of men to hand over the crops and livestock was causing great strife among the population. To avoid the annoying confrontations, the Offspring mostly resorted to thievery.

But now, several areas in the valley were short of crops and food. People going hungry in the valley was historically unheard of. Marahka felt strongly that this needed to be dealt with immediately to prevent any further deterioration in the relationship between the Offspring (and by extension, the Guardians) and the people. He clenched his jaw to bite back a response to Rhyima's cavalier attitude.

"We gave them metal to facilitate farming practices…" Rhyima put up one finger. "We gave them formulas for embellishing their standard manure-based compost." Two fingers up. "The mysteries of understanding the position of the stars in relation to their agriculture." Three. His voice rose. "Recipes to substantially augment animal fertility." Four. "Tonics to make themselves healthy and strong." Five. "Not to mention the women have had the privilege of birthing powerful, strong boys never known before." He closed his open hand into a fist and punched the air in emphasis.

"Hmm. Except the strong boys are the problem, not the solution in the agricultural complication. They eat and don't work." Marahka's comment went unheard by Rhyima as he got heated up in his own logic.

"The men of this valley should be grateful to us. They should want to work harder to feed the children of their daughters and sisters. They should sing our praises." Marahka glanced over at him. A smile split Rhyima's lips, and he clasped his hands behind his back. He murmured, "They should worship us as the gods we are."

Rhyima's words hung in the air as the two Guardians continued walking, each man lost in his own thoughts.

A piercing scream sliced through their contemplations, bringing them both to a halt. The scream stopped abruptly and a roar filled the air.

Marahka was the first to act and leapt from the path into the woods, shoving through the underbrush toward the disturbance. Rhyima followed on his heels. They were none too quiet, cracking through small trees and large branches that got in the way, birds and squirrels scattered before them. But the noise didn't matter as they came upon the opening to a smallish meadow, where a perplexing scene unfolded before them.

Soft, springy grass carpeted the area, stippled throughout by a profusion of wildflowers. A mill pond off to one side sparkled in the sun. The pleasant areas throughout the valley had been gradually changing; many lay burned to the ground, some torn up from rough use, others simply chewed down as new pastures had needed to be found to graze the sheep and goats. But this tree-encompassed meadow had escaped the transformations, remaining bucolic and peaceful, except for the macabre picnic transpiring in its midst.

Marahka recognized the Offspring Araza, Semqat, and Shet-Tsebeh (so named for he was the first born with six fingers on each hand), sitting in a circle around a large sheet of bloodied white linen. The three were grunting as they chewed on gristled bones, tearing off chunks of flesh with their teeth.

"Boys!" Marahka called out to them. "What do you have there?"

Rhyima hissed at him under his breath. "Let them be. It's surely just a goat. It won't be missed."

Araza spun around to see the Guardians standing at the edge of the meadow behind him. His face dripped gore and he waved toward the men. "Come join us!"

Shet-Tsebeh jumped to his feet, glaring at Araza. Marahka was surprised to see the boy had gotten much taller since he'd last seen him around town. He now stood at least a head higher than Marahka, probably close to eight feet tall. And he was thin.

"No. Go away. There is only enough for us." Shet-Tsebeh's bloodshot eyes flashed back and forth between the Guardians. He kicked out at Araza, landing a heel to his ribs.

Araza threw down the bone he was gnawing on and surged to his feet. He shoved at Shet-Tsebeh with both hands. The boys were the same height, though Araza was clearly in stronger form. Semqat, still seated, quickly crawled away from his vulnerable position beneath the two angry giants. He grabbed up Araza's discarded bone as he scurried to the other side of the crumpled, white linen.

Marahka noticed several things in the few moments as the scene unfolded. First, Semqat, significantly smaller than the other two, had a beautiful head of fiery red hair with streaks of a darker russet winding through it. It curled wildly at the nape of his neck. Second, the orange-brown red of Semqat's hair clashed terribly with the bright bluish-red color soaking through much of the white linen spread across the grass. As Semqat cleared out to the other side of the impromptu picnic cloth, it revealed the dead-eyed face of a young boy staring up toward Marahka, his shattered and torn body collapsed beneath the folds of his linen shirt.

159

"Raqa,"Marahka swore under his breath. He stepped forward, but Rhyima reached forward and gripped his arm.

"Just leave it."

Araza and Shet-Tsebeh shoved each other, trading insults. Suddenly, Shet-Tsebeh launched himself at the stronger boy and brought his mouth down hard on Araza's neck. He tore the base of his neck open. Araza looked stunned before he crumpled to the ground, his blood springing out from his neck in a pulsing stream.

The Guardians hadn't moved, it had happened so quickly. Shet-Tsebeh looked up at them, perched on Araza's chest as the blood now trickled quietly to the ground. He growled at the men as he guarded his kill. Semqat skittered off into the woods on the far side, with several large bones clutched to his chest. Rhyima, still holding Marakha's arm, tugged at him. "Let's go."

"But—"

"There is nothing we can do here."

"We can't just leave this…"Marakha waved his hands in front of him vaguely, "here…like this."

"Yes, we can." Rhyima dragged Marahka back the way they had come through the woods, glancing over his shoulder once to see Shet-Tsebeh crawling back and forth between the dead boy and the dead Offspring, growling and pawing at them both like a feral animal.

33

Haven looked over at his friend Jonathan. The two sat in the small natural area that served as the central point of the village market. In the middle, a stone-lined pond had a thick crust of slimy green moss covering the water. The stench emanating from it indicated the elegant fish that once swam in circles had expired from the decline in environment. Five stone pathways spread out from the murky pond like spokes on a wheel, extending to form the backbone of the market. Grass filled the wedges between the radiating paths, with flowers and fruit trees placed throughout. The grass, flowers, and trees had fared as well as the fish in the pond—neglected and dying.

Truly, the only thriving element here was the vibrant slime on the water. That, and the prostitution.

Haven had been shocked at first as to how open the young women had become in flaunting themselves. They were all wearing the ridiculously bright clothing that made them look like carefree wildflowers or strutting birds with no propriety whatsoever. Body parts previously kept hidden were on full display—opulent flesh jiggled about freely now. Over the past weeks and months he had begun to notice it less, or rather was less surprised by it, and that bothered him even more. Jonathan was presently speaking to a girl they had known since childhood, Eva.

Jonathan rubbed his hand through his black wiry hair, which stuck straight out in every direction. His deep brown skin provided a stark contrast to Eva's milky pale flesh as she approached him and then brazenly nuzzled up against him. Haven could tell Jon was a bit nervous from his habit of rubbing his head. Next he would drag his fingers back and forth through the patchy scruff that covered his chin and jaws, then he'd return to his head. Haven would have chuckled at the predictability of his friend's mannerisms, as he proceeded to do exactly as anticipated, if he wasn't so disgusted by his behavior at the moment.

Eva sat next to Jon. "So, Haven." Eva's silky voice cut through the internal morality speech spinning through Haven's mind. "You and Rachel, huh?" She offered Haven a grin and a wink as she leaned around Jon to look Haven in the eye.

Haven frowned and looked down at his hands, clasped between his bent knees. "What about Rachel?"

"Are you two together yet?" She purred.

None of this was Eva's business. "No, we're friends." Haven looked up from his hands and out toward the dwindling crowds of people searching for end-of-day deals in the market. He sighed. He hoped they were still friends.

Haven and Rachel's evening voyeurism at the animal shed accomplished Haven's objective to a degree. Rachel completely spurned any further advances or visits from her courting Guardian.

Unfortunately, Rachel refused to see Haven, too.

It was difficult for Haven to know exactly what was going on since Rachel wouldn't speak to him. Haven had convinced his mother to pay Jared and Rachel a visit, ostensibly to get information about Rachel's new "suitor."

Tirzah had returned jubilant. "Haven, I spoke with Jared; Rachel wasn't feeling well. But he told me that because of Rachel's wishes he told the man to no longer return, that she did not wish to court him." Tirzah frowned. "Jared was perplexed by Rachel's rejection. She wouldn't give him a reason, but he said she was extremely upset. But no matter." She had patted Haven's arm. "I just know she will be yours one day."

Haven prayed this was true, but as the months had gone by he worried it never would be. Had he gone too far?

Eva faced Jonathan, throwing her leg over to straddle his lap, her hands on his shoulders. She leaned into him, putting her face very close to his.

Jon's breath hitched as his eyes went wide. He sat very still, finally removing his nervous hand from his hair and awkwardly holding it out at his side.

Looking straight into Jon's eyes, Eva continued to address Haven. "Bed her. Then she will agree to marry you." She giggled then leaned in the last few inches, planting a kiss on Jon's mouth, her eyes open and still looking into his.

The moment hung suspended: Jon didn't move, Haven stared at them, even the crowds seemed to quiet.

Then in a sudden flourish of reds, blues, and greens, Eva jumped up, her brilliant skirt flouncing. She leaned over, giving both men an eyeful of exposed cleavage, and whispered loudly to Jonathan. "You know where to find me." With a smile and a soft stroke down his cheek, she turned and pranced off.

Jonathan stared after her. Haven stared at Jonathan.

Haven smacked him in the chest. "Hey, close your mouth before an owl nests in there."

Jonathan snapped his mouth shut. He looked at Haven sheepishly. "She's just so…"

"Yes, I can see that."

Jon rubbed both hands vigorously through his hair, so it stood up even more wildly than before. Then he dropped his hands to his lap. "So what is going on with Rachel? She still ignoring you for the dangerous tall guy?"

Haven had shared with Jon his fears about the Guardian Rachel seemed fond of. Jon was not a deep thinker and didn't really understand Haven's fears about disobedience to Shalliyt and the dangers as prophesied by the Teller. But Jon was Haven's friend and supported him anyway. Haven hadn't told Jon about the incident at the shed. That was too personal and too painful to share.

Haven glossed over it. "No, she finally saw something about that man that scared her. I think she's done with him. I'm going to speak to Jared about courting her. I don't want to wait any longer." Haven rubbed the back of his neck. Of course, it would be a good idea if he and Rachel were on speaking terms before that conversation could happen.

"Ahh! You do want to bed her. Finally!" Jon laughed. "Gonna try and sneak her into your horse barn one night. Show her how you stack the hay? Hmm?"

Haven looked appalled. "No, I would do no such thing! I would never shame her that way. And…" Haven turned more fully toward his friend and poked his finger against Jon's chest pointedly, "if you care anything for Eva, you won't shame her either."

Jon groaned. "Haven, she's offering. I don't think she will feel any shame at all."

"That doesn't matter. You still need to protect her interests, even if she doesn't seem to want to. It's the right thing to do, Jon."

Jon rolled his eyes and Haven knew exactly what Jon was thinking. All their lives Haven had wanted to do good, make people proud, follow the rules. Jon preferred to have a good time and get away with what he could when he thought no one was looking. He would never knowingly harm someone, but his own pleasure usually came first. The two helped to balance one another. Jon forced Haven to have some fun occasionally and Haven provided a reminder of a moral plumb line for Jonathan.

A commotion interrupted their conversation. Jon and Haven stared as a gruff, older man walked near them attempting to corral an animal he had tethered. The animal seemed to be spinning in a circle at the end of its lead. Haven could not make out what it was.

"Damn you, curst creature. Walk forward!" The man pulled forward on the lead while smacking the animal presumably on the back end with his free hand, attempting to get it to walk straight. A pair of snapping jaws appeared out of the flurry of fur and began snarling at the insulting hand. The man yanked his hand back and kicked the animal instead. It lunged forward and did take a few straight steps then.

Haven's jaw dropped open. He was less than a stone's throw away from what looked like a three-headed wolf. It's thick, matted fur was tan with darker brown patches throughout. The body, legs, and tail all seemed normal, but three heads protruded from the shoulders. Two of the heads seemed to share a neck and the third had its own. It was this third head that seemed to have the flexibility to turn and snap at its controller.

"What is that, Haven?" Jon spoke very quietly.

"I don't know. But I would like to." Haven pushed himself up from the ground. "Sir! A moment please."

The older man turned toward Haven. He was dangerously red in the face from exertion, and sweat poured down his neck and soaked his shirt. "Yes, son. What can I do for you?"

As soon as he released the tension on the lead, the beast settled down at his feet. The two closely linked heads snapped and growled at each other. The third head, which bore the rope lead around its neck, lay down on one of its paws. Haven was entranced by this behavior.

"Uh, sir, what is this, and where did it come from?"

The man produced a handkerchief from his pocket and swabbed his face and neck. "It's a dog, I suppose. I found it wandering around my sheep. Luckily it is so uncoordinated with the heads, that it wasn't a threat to the flock."

"With respect, I've never seen nor heard of a dog with more than one head." Haven squatted down on his haunches to get a closer look. The animal seemed to be drifting off to sleep.

The man rubbed his chin. "Me neither. But here it is."

"What are you doing with it?"

"There's a fellow in the market over there…" He pointed down one of the stone paths. "That buys these kinds of deformed creatures."

Several other people gathered around, looking at the sleeping hound. Some looked curious, others terrified. One of the women in the group spoke up.

"I talked with that man. Yeah, he said these beasts was becoming more common. He had a handful for sale and each one's different." She lowered her voice to a loud whisper. "He told me, though I didn't see 'em, that some look part human."

A few gasps passed through the growing crowd. A heavy pressure built in Haven's gut. He thought back to the horrible night at the cow shed with Rachel months earlier and wondered if this was the result of some similar coupling.

The woman continued, delighted that she seemed to have a rapt audience. "Yeah, he said some was more beast like and some…" She paused for greater dramatic effect. The crowd complied by leaning toward her. "…some…could speak. Yeah, like people."

Another man laughed loudly. "That's ridiculous!"

The man with the three-headed dog pointed toward his leashed burden that had stretched full out on its side, tail slowly thwapping the stone path in its dream state, "What about this? Is this ridiculous?"

"Abnormal defect of nature. It happens. But the power of speech…I don't think so."

"Yeah, go visit the guy. You'll see…"

Jon yanked on Haven's arm. He leaned in to whisper, "Can we get out of here?"

Haven looked at him. Jon blinked rapidly and tucked his arms tightly into his armpits.

Haven grabbed his elbow. "Let's go."

34

Haven was harvesting in his south field, his mind occupied with strategies for reconciling with Rachel, when he had been interrupted by having to fix broken fence wrecked by vandals. Part of his crop had been destroyed in that section—not stolen, just beaten down for some reason he couldn't fathom.

Needing a break, he decided today was as good as any to approach her. He put on a fresh shirt and packed a basket. He loaded in some crocks of jams his mother had made and several loaves of bread. The few glimpses he'd had of Rachel from a distance showed she had not been eating well. Since her mother had died, Rachel had taken over the cooking for her father and herself. Haven wanted to make sure they had food to eat if she wasn't cooking.

Haven headed the short distance to Rachel's home. Chances were he would not see her, but giving up never crossed his mind. At the very least he could leave the basket on their doorstep. But ever determined, Haven hoped he would get a chance to speak to Rachel. This was the time of day when she might emerge from her self-imposed isolation to do the necessary farm chores.

As Haven crossed into Rachel's yard, he heard squawking coming from the small chicken shed next to the house. *She must already be in there.* He hiked himself up onto the stone wall by the shed doorway and sat to wait till she finished. He could hear her singing quietly, attempting to soothe the birds as she pilfered their eggs from beneath them. He turned his face up to the sun—eyes closed, sunlight glowing red through his lids and warming his face—and strained to listen to her melancholy tune weaving beneath the raucous noise of the chickens.

The heavy furred skin serving as a door pushed aside and Rachel stepped out into the bright sunshine, shaking her head to knock off the wispy feathers and dust that had settled into her hair. She abruptly ceased her soft singing, and Haven tilted his head forward and opened his eyes.

She stared at him. Her eyes were flat and weighted underneath with dark circles of exhaustion, her lips pressed tightly together. Her clothes hung on her body loosely, showing she had not been eating as Haven suspected. She clasped a small egg-mounded basket to her chest.

"Hello," Haven said softly. He wasn't sure if he should stand or remain seated where he was. He didn't want her to run off.

She nodded her head once, then looked off over to her side at the field. Her face was blank. She picked at the wicker basket absently.

Her lack of response twisted in Haven's gut. Rachel was normally so chatty and giggly, vivacious in all things. He could not stay away, so he carefully stood and walked over to her. He reached his hand out to touch her chin and turned her face to look at him. But she flinched at the contact, so he withdrew his hand.

"Rachel, I brought you and your father some food that my mother prepared." He motioned toward the basket sitting on the stone wall. He looked into her eyes for any sign of response. For a moment they remained blank, then she took in a deep shuddering breath. It was like she was waking up from a long sleep. Haven could see emotion playing over her face and her eyes suddenly filled with pain. They began to well up with tears as she finally looked directly at him.

"Thank you. That was very thoughtful of you." She swiped at her face, fighting the tears.

Haven pressed further. "It's a beautiful day. Would you like to take a walk?" He spoke quietly, like he would to a frightened animal. "We could go into the village. Maybe stop at your father's workshop? I think he would enjoy seeing you out and visiting."

He expected her to reject his suggestion outright. But she stood there quietly, one hand hugging the egg basket, the other fiddling with her skirt. "I think…I think that would be fine. I need to…" She chewed on her bottom lip. "I need to put these eggs away and…wash my face."

Haven couldn't stop the huge grin from spreading across his face. *All is NOT lost!* He turned and grabbed his basket off the stone wall and followed her to the doorstep of her house. He passed her his basket and sat down on the stone step to wait for her.

The path to town led them near to Haven's cottage, so he suggested they stop there first to see if his mother needed anything in the village. He thought it might help Rachel to see another friendly face, too. As they approached his home he saw his mother out on the front stoop speaking to Jonathan. They turned toward Rachel and Haven as they got closer.

"Jon!" Haven gave him a quick hug. "What brings you here?"

"Looking for you. I needed to pick up a few tools in the village and thought I'd see if you want to come along." Jon glanced over at Rachel, who had her eyes cast toward the ground. "...but it seems like you have other plans?"

"Actually, we're headed there, too. So let's go together." Haven lightly placed his hand on Rachel's back. He just couldn't keep his hands from touching her. She looked up at him and gave him a small smile and nodded. "Mother, why don't you join us?"

Tirzah had been looking at Rachel through the discussion so far. Haven knew she had to be curious about Rachel's demeanor. She seemed to be debating whether to come along.

"I would like it if you would join us," Rachel said.

That seemed to decide it for his mother. "Okay then," she said with a smile.

The men walked together on the path, with Tirzah and Rachel behind them a little ways. The women's heads were bowed together as they seemed to be discussing something intently.

After a bit of companionable silence, Haven spoke. "So did you go back to see Eva?"

"No. The guilt you loaded on me was enough to discourage *that* pursuit," Jon huffed and rolled his eyes.

Haven smiled. "Good for you."

"Don't be smug."

Haven sighed.

"Haven, what do you think is going on with the strange animals? After we saw that three-headed dog, I went over to the dealer's booth that the woman mentioned." Jon glanced over at Haven. "She was right. There were some odd-looking beasts there. One of them—"

"I don't want to hear about them, Jon." Haven shook his head to dispel the weight of dread that this topic brought to him. The vision of Ashteala and the screaming cow hadn't dimmed in his mind at all, and he was positive that was the type of behavior leading to the deformed animals.

"Why aren't you curious about them? I think it's fascinating."

"It's not fascinating. It's evil."

"Why is everything good and evil with you?" Exasperated, Jon kicked at a rock, sending it sailing into the tree line running alongside them. "Why can't it just be an oddity of nature? A mistake?"

"A goat born with an extra set of horns or an all-white deer is an 'oddity of nature.'" Haven said. "One with three heads? Or speaking like a man? I don't think so. And why so many all of a sudden?"

"So they are evil and invading us along with the Guardians? Is that what the Teller is filling your mind with now?" Jon's hostility was palpable.

"No." Haven took a deep breath. "The Teller said—"

"Yeah, I was right, it's the Teller. And you don't think he's an 'oddity of nature' too?"

Haven glared at Jon. "The Teller said the Guardians would begin turning their lust toward the animals eventually, begetting monsters with them."

Jon stopped walking abruptly and just stared at Haven. "The Guardians are sporting with wild animals? And these animals actually conceived? And…you…*believe* him?" Then Jon laughed.

"Boys, move over! Watch yourselves!" Haven's mother called out. She and Rachel had stepped off the path and motioned for them to also.

Barreling toward them from behind, a cart pulled by a panicking bay horse, rocked precariously from side to side on its wheels. The driver desperately gripped the reins in his leather-clad hands, yanking back.

Jon and Haven jumped off the path. Just as the horse passed them, it reared up, nearly upending the cart completely. The wild ride was over, but the agitated animal still danced in its harness, pawing at the ground and furiously switching its tail. The driver jumped off the cart, cursing his horse as he tied the reins tightly around the wheel spokes and cart frame, so the horse couldn't budge it.

Haven stepped forward. "Sir, are you alright?"

The man grunted and nodded as he began to inspect his cart.

Haven walked toward the horse, running his hand along her lathered flank, speaking to her in a low voice. Her ears kept twitching backward, but she settled as Haven gently rubbed up her neck. "What's got you so bothered, hmm?" He pulled her head down to his level and gently blew in her nostrils. She snorted back and relaxed into his touch. Haven glanced over to find Jon. He didn't see him at first, so he abandoned his stroking of the mare's velvety ears and walked around her.

Then he saw Rachel, Jon, and his mother standing at the back, mouths agape, looking at something in the bed of the cart. The driver was on the far side of the cart now, kicking at a loose board, still mumbling curses. Haven strode back to see what had captured their attention so completely. After rounding the edge of the cart, he turned and looked into the crimson eyes of a softly snarling beast. Haven retreated to stand with the others.

The creature had the sinewy body of a young boy. He sat against the back of the cart hugging his bent legs to his chest. On his knees sat an overlarge skull, with a bullish nose, sullen eyes, and pair of short horns. Long brown fur tufted at the base of the horns, around the ears and along his cheeks. A very fine, shorter fur coated the snout and chin. A strong stench of animal dung mixed with a sour odor saturated the air around them.

The muttering driver interrupted the frozen stand-off by smacking the side of the cart as he apparently finished his repairs. The creature jumped up at the sudden noise, but was yanked back by a heavy leather collar encircling his neck, connected by iron links to the cart. He slammed back down, hissing and snarling. The horse began prancing again, agitated by the strange, noisy burden she carried.

"Enough!" the driver shouted.

The creature cowered down, forward onto his chest, palms flat on the cart with elbows up, like he was ready to spring again. He continued to glare at his audience and growl deep in his throat. Then he plucked up a small stone from within the hay bedding and hurled it toward them. His aim was not good and missed them all. The man mounted back onto the cart with reins in hand and was off again toward town as if nothing strange had just happened.

Haven turned to Jon. "Just an 'oddity of nature'?"

"Yeah, well, I don't know what that was. But what the Teller said is absurd." Jon huffed. "I'll see you around…another time." He tilted his chin toward the women, then turned and jogged off toward town, following the path of the cart.

35

Despite the weird scene with the bull-headed boy in the back of the cart and the disheartening reaction from Jon, Haven felt optimistic for the first time in a long while after he returned from the village. Rachel was coming back to herself. She seemed comfortable chattering away with his mother. The two women enjoyed themselves looking in the shops that carried the new fashions for women—brightly colored clothes and make-up. Haven wisely kept his opinions to himself and instead focused on the two women he loved, having a good time together.

At one point, they had gotten to a section of town where a handful of men lined the walkway in their ratty clothing, begging for food. Beggars weren't unheard of, but there were so many. Rachel actually leaned into Haven for protection, and he put his arm around her shoulder, holding her against him. He was ashamed to realize he had been far more interested in how her hair smelled up close, than in why there were suddenly so many beggars.

They came to a part of the village where it looked like the buildings had been attacked by vandals—much like his field had been. He had finally pulled his thoughts away from Rachel's sweet-smelling hair and steered the women away. They went directly to Jared's shop, so Rachel could visit with her father. Then he walked them both home as the sun set in a hazy gloaming.

Haven had waited several days, but now he was determined to claim Rachel. She needed protection in this new world of theirs—the insidious dangers from the presence of the Guardians threatened body and soul. And he would be her protector.

Of course, Jared loved Rachel and did what he felt was for her own good as a parent. But Jared was blinded by much of what was going on. He had allowed that Guardian access to Rachel for months. Haven tried not to be overly judgmental, but if he were honest with himself, he was angry.

Haven's plan had always been to wait till she reached her seventeenth summer to ask for her, but waiting any longer wasn't safe. And she was only a few months shy of that. Over dinner he spoke with his mother of his intention toward Rachel. She had smiled and kissed him on the forehead. "Good luck, Son. It would be a delight to have Rachel as my daughter."

Haven headed up the footpath to Rachel and Jared's house. The sun had begun its descent, glowing orange in the muggy, gray haze. The surrounding brush and trees were eerily silent, as if the oppressive air had squelched the whirring and chirping of the usual creatures.

The door opened to Haven's knock. "Haven? What brings you out tonight?" Jared crossed his arms, mouth frowning slightly.

"Sir, good evening." Haven smiled, sweat breaking out on the back of his neck. "I hoped to speak with you—"

"Come in." Jared paused a moment, then stepped back to admit Haven. "Let's have a seat…" he motioned to the sitting area in the parlor. "Rachel! Come join us. Haven's here."

"Actually, sir, I came to speak with you…privately."

Jared's frown deepened, but he said nothing. He turned to Rachel who had just come from the kitchen, wiping her hands on her apron. "Haven and I are going to have a chat in my study. Could you make some tea, and we'll all visit together after."

"Yes, of course." She turned to Haven, smiling shyly. "Hi Haven. Are you well?"

"Yes, thank you." He leaned down and kissed her, her cheek soft and warm against his lips. "You look radiant tonight." And she did. The change over the last few days was amazing. Her face was still thinner than it should be, but her cheeks glowed and her eyes sparkled.

She blushed, smiling broadly, and looked down at her hands twisting in her apron.

"Haven," Jared interrupted. "This way."

In his study, Jared dragged a chair over to the table that appeared to be used as a work desk and motioned for Haven to take it. Various chunks of wood and metal covered the surface of the table. For as neat as his shop was, Haven was a little surprised at the clutter mounded here. He briefly wondered what

Jared was working on, but then he got back to the business of being nervous.

Jared took the chair opposite and leaned back a bit. He laced his fingers over his belly and looked at Haven over top the assortment of objects.

"So, Haven. What's on your mind?"

Haven took a deep breath. "I'd like your permission to court Rachel. I...I would eventually like to marry her." He rushed on. "Sir, I love her and want to—"

Jared waved his hand sharply, cutting him off. He laced his hands again, tapping his forefingers together. He stared at Haven.

Sunlight slanted through the window, creating a broad stripe of light on the floor and across the desk. Heavy silence hung like a thick curtain. Haven looked away from Jared's intense scrutiny and focused on the light slashing over the table, a chasm stretching between them.

Jared cleared his throat, drawing Haven's attention back. He leaned forward, his eyes hard. "What did you do to Ashteala?"

"I didn't do anything to—"

"Damn it, Haven." His fist pounded on the table. "You did something to him, or said something to Rachel to make her pull away from him."

Haven's mouth dropped open.

"He wanted to marry her very badly. He would have made her a fine husband. She'd never want for anything."

Haven sat back in reaction. Heat crawled up his neck.

Jared pointed at Haven, "But I know you interfered somehow. Petty jealousy and this boyhood infatuation you've carried for her for so long."

Haven was completely unprepared for this attack. And what could he say? Haven had interfered...but not from jealousy. He swallowed, his throat tight and dry. The truth. He needed to keep trying to make Jared see.

"Sir, I didn't do anything to Ashteala. I showed Rachel what he truly was." He licked his lips. "Not a man, but a very dangerous predator—"

"Enough!" Jared exploded. "Enough with the foolish talk of Guardians! And predator? Really Haven? This man promised to make me rich." He was practically growling now. "Your selfish coveting has destroyed both her and my future." He waved his hands over the wood and metal debris on the table. "And now you expect me to turn her over to you?" His eyes bulged under the strain of his fury.

Haven's stomach clenched. "Jared," he said, his voice coming out more as a croak. "This is about money?" He scraped his chair backward and stood. "Ashteala only wanted to breed her to make more of those soulless over-tall monsters destroying our valley. You would sell her for that?"

"Get out," Jared snarled.

Haven fisted his hands at his sides and turned to the door. He had never seen Jared this angry before, but he was angry himself and leaving was the best option, the only option for now. Haven opened the door and was startled to see Rachel standing a few feet away with her trembling hand covering her mouth, tears flowing freely down her cheeks.

"Haven?" She whispered.

Haven looked down into her eyes rimmed by damp lashes. He reached out to touch her face but pulled back his hand. He turned and walked away.

36

Rachel pushed her sleeves up further and kept digging in the vegetable bed, rooting out the last of the weeds growing intermixed with carrots and turnips. It was easy, mindless work—if a bit tough on the knees—that gave her lots of time to think. And today her mind was occupied with Haven.

She knew it was wrong listening at the door to Haven and her father's conversation. But she suspected, or at least hoped, that Haven would be asking for her. A thrill shot through her when he had uttered the words to that effect. She smiled remembering it. He was such a decent man, strong in body and mind. He had always been kind and protective toward her. And he was handsome enough. And very serious. Maybe too serious. So he wasn't perfect. He was too absorbed by his faith for her liking. Shalliyt was fine, but did everything need to revolve around him? Or at least the Teller's version of Shalliyt? Maybe the Teller had been right about Ashteala. But that unfortunate detour was firmly closed and would not be thought of again.

But then her excitement with her ear pressed against the door collapsed at her father's response. She had no idea he held Haven responsible for her rejection of Ashteala. She swiped at the perspiration beading on her forehead, leaving behind a smudge of dirt. She'd tried to speak to her father later, but he refused to discuss it with her. It bothered her that he mentioned the potential loss of income to Haven. What did that matter? They were doing fine as things were—

"Hello, my dear."

A tentacle of fear slithered up Rachel's spine at the sound of the voice behind her. Deep, resonant. Hideous. She slowly sat back on her heels and brushed off her dirt-crusted hands against her apron. She kept her eyes pinned to the loamy dirt lumped in front of her.

"Won't you even greet me, Rachel?" Ashteala stepped into the garden, his shoes sinking down into the soft soil.

Rachel took a deep, shuddering breath then squeezed her eyes shut. She was alone here with him. Her father had not returned from the village yet.

"You know, I have no idea why you shunned me." He leaned over and began to stroke Rachel's head. He squatted down and his voice was very close to her ear. "I've been exceedingly patient in waiting for you to come back to your senses." His hand tunneled under her hair and smoothed back and forth across her neck. "Don't you think?"

Rachel visibly shook. Her hands grasped her crossed forearms and her fingernails dug into her flesh. She would not look at him. In actuality, she could not move.

Ashteala's hand closed around the back of her neck, and he abruptly stood, lifting her, too. Rachel teetered now on her tiptoes, her head angled by force to look into the Guardian's face. Her nails pierced deeper into her own flesh and blood began to well beneath her fingers. Her breath came in raspy jerks and her eyes grew wide. In that moment, looking into this monster's face, she saw for the first time his black, flat eyes. His eyes clearly weren't human. Why hadn't she noticed that before? What was wrong with her?

A hand came crashing across her face in a brilliant flash of pain. Rachel still hung there, partially suspended, her cheek throbbing and her nose pouring blood.

"You are a spoilt brat." Ashteala's nostrils flared and a vein throbbed along the side of his face. "Answer me, girl."

Rachel took a deep breath. She couldn't remember what he had asked that required an answer. With one hand, she pulled up the edge of her apron and wiped her face. Ashteala set her firmly on her feet though he didn't release his grip on her neck.

Rachel whispered, "I saw you."

Ashteala stared at her and waited. "And...?"

"I saw you." It came out louder this time.

With his free hand, Ashteala grabbed Rachel's hair and yanked her head back. "Make sense, woman!"

Rachel summoned every bit of courage she had and looked directly into the Guardian's alien eyes and spoke with determination. "I saw you in the shed with the cows. I saw your perversion."

Ashteala's head jerked back. He stared at her. Neither spoke. Then Ashteala burst out laughing.

"So you saw me sporting with that cow." He leaned in closer to her and cocked an eyebrow. "Did you enjoy the demonstration? I have the same planned for you, but I suspect you will take a greater pleasure in it than that bawling heifer did. Maybe I won't even have to tie you up first!"

Rachel spit in Ashteala's face, a glob of bloody slime slapping onto his cheek. She never saw the lightning-fast fist that came up and punched her in the stomach.

"Ashteala!" Jared shouted out. He had missed what caused the altercation, but he saw his daughter being held by her neck and punched by the tall man with whom he had shared business ideas.

Ashteala let go of Rachel, and she dropped to the ground. "You have spoiled this girl, Jared." He brushed his hands off on his trousers.

Rachel got up on her hands and knees and began to painfully drag herself away. She could hear her father and the Guardian having a heated exchange. She prayed that no one was paying attention. She needed to get out of there. She needed to get help.

Rachel pulled herself to her feet and glanced over at the men. They were shouting at each other standing toe to toe. Ashteala towered over her father, and fear for him washed through her. She clutched at her stomach and began to run.

Haven and his mother sat down to dinner. He was offering thanks to Shalliyt for the bounty of the harvest that kept them well fed, when a noise at the door interrupted him.

Tirzah tilted her head. "Go see who that is."

Haven strode to the door and opened it. He barely reached out in time to catch Rachel as she fell into his arms.

"Rachel! What happened?"

Blood still leaked from her nose, and she was doubled over in pain. Haven lifted her up into his arms as his mother motioned for him to follow her. He took her into his mother's bedroom and laid her on the cot. His mother fetched a second pillow to help prop up Rachel's head.

"Rachel, please tell me who did this to you." He ran his hands over her shoulders and down her arms, encountering the bloody gouges she had put there.

"Haven, it's him…"

Haven looked blankly at her.

"Ashteala, the Guardian…the one we followed…the cows…" she sobbed.

"What about him? He did this to you?"

"You have to go help Father." Rachel grabbed onto Haven, trying to impart her growing panic for her father. "He and Ashteala were fighting, and I ran away to get to you."

Tirzah nudged him aside. "Go. Do what you need to. I'll take care of Rachel."

Haven leaned forward and pressed a kiss to Rachel's forehead, leaving his lips there for a moment. His gut clenched at the sight of her injuries and the pain she was in. "Mother, be sure to latch the door behind me. Don't let anyone in till I return." He kissed his mother, then took off at a run.

◦⋆◦ᗯ◦⋆◦

As Haven ran the short distance to Rachel's home he had time to think about whatever he was about to face. The Guardians were unnaturally strong and pure evil. Haven feared for Jared, but he also feared for himself. How could he stand up to a Guardian? Then he remembered Shalliyt, and a warm peace settled about him. Even in this world of intensifying chaos, Shalliyt was ultimately in control. Haven could trust that and knew that nothing would happen to him that was outside of Shalliyt's will.

Haven arrived at the front door of Rachel's house, his breath surging in and out. He threw open the door and ran into the house. "Jared?" Haven shouted into the house as he began to check through the few rooms of the cottage. "Jared? Where are you?" Silence.

Haven went back to the front door. There was no sign of commotion in the house at all. Rachel hadn't said where the men were. He quickly jogged down the steps and began to circle the cottage. And came to an abrupt halt.

There by the vegetable garden behind a stand of bushes, lay an inert form, a lump of tan clothing.

"Jared!" Haven rushed to the body. Plumes of blood spray arched across the grass and dripped from vegetable plant stems in the garden. Haven could now see Jared's body with his face crushed. As his eyes followed the sticky trail of blood, he saw that Jared's arms had been torn from his body and flung away. *What kind of animal would do this?* Haven stepped backward, then turned and vomited into the bushes.

180

37

Haven stood next to the kitchen table, staring out the window. His arms lay slack by his sides and his fingers flicked at his thighs with pent-up anger and frustration. He wanted nothing more than to go back into his mother's bedroom where Rachel lay sobbing and hold her and make everything all right for her.

He had told her as gently as he could that her father was gone. Trying to calm her fears, he assured her that she could stay with them, that he would always protect her. But she wasn't able to move beyond the news that her father had been killed, and she screeched in agony, clawing at everything near her. Tirzah gently pushed Haven from the room and attended to Rachel herself.

Haven suspected Rachel felt some guilt because she had been infatuated by her father's murderer. He had to make sure she understood this was not her fault. He angrily wiped away a tear escaping down his cheek, heaving in a sob that threatened to break free. A hand gently landed on his shoulder, and Haven turned to see his mother.

"Haven. Please sit." She turned and headed toward the kitchen fire. "I'm going to make Rachel some hot broth and try to get her to drink some. You should eat—you didn't get your dinner."

Haven sat. He pushed his plate away. "Mother, what are we going to do?"

"As you already told Rachel, she can live with us now. You two can marry soon—"

"Yes, I will take care of her, but that isn't what I meant." Haven placed his elbows on the table and leaned his head down to put his hands behind his neck, massaging the knotted tension growing there. "Our village, our valley is on the edge of collapse. Everything is becoming rotten. Evil is spreading!"

"Goodness, Haven. You are exaggerating, don't you think? I know this is horrible what has happened to poor Jared, but people die, people are even murdered. But that is life—not Shalliyt ready to charge in with his horde of Holy ones!"

Haven glanced up at Tirzah who had turned and was stirring the black pot that hung above the fire. "Mother, according to the Teller, that's precisely what is headed this way."

She spun around and put her hands on her hips, spoon jutting out. "Because of a murder. Haven, listen to yourself!"

Haven jumped up from the table. "Haven't you listened to anything I've been saying?"

"Watch your tone of voice with me." The spoon now pointed at Haven's chest.

He blew out a slow breath. "I'm sorry Mama. But please listen." When she didn't argue, he began to pace. If no one else would listen, surely his mother would. "The man that killed Jared isn't a man…"

"Of course he is. Go to the Teller and inform him of what has happened. He'll summon the elders and they will take care of the situation. The killer, *the man*, will be stoned or turned out to the wilderness—"

"*No, he's not!*" Haven scrubbed a hand over his face. "No, he's not," he said more quietly. "And the Teller will agree with me on this."

"So you are going to tell me this is one of the Guardians you have been fretting about." The spoon was safely back in the pot, scraping and stirring.

"Yes he is. Rachel can confirm this, too. She and I have both seen his sorcery. He will not be subject to man's law."

"Oh, Haven." Tirzah slowly shook her head.

Haven's frustration surged. How could he convince his mother of the truth and the danger? He knew she was faithful to Shalliyt…to a degree. She readily believed in his blessings, but seemed to glance over his teachings on judgment. Haven had her to thank for raising him with a knowledge of Shalliyt and the appreciation for his creation. But he couldn't understand how she separated what she would and would not accept from her creator's writings. If Haven could just devise an argument that was foolproof, she would see the logic and be forced…

Then a realization slammed into him. Haven couldn't force her. Moreover, it wasn't his place to convince her. The

182

Teller's words came back to him: "*Shalliyt will open her eyes. You are to simply remain faithful to him.*" And isn't that what happened with Rachel? Shalliyt directed him to follow Ashteala, and then Rachel's eyes were opened that evening at the cow shed in a way that no amount of sound reasoning on his part could have accomplished. Shalliyt *did* know exactly what was needed to reach her. His mother was no different, or Jon, or his neighbors, or anyone else. Haven exhaled and leaned against the wall. He brought his hands up and rubbed his eyes.

Tirzah, completely oblivious to Haven's earth-shaking revelation, nodded her head. "The Teller will help you. He is a kind man and has taken a real interest in you, Haven."

She brought the spoon to her lips and sampled it. "I think this is warm enough now." She got a bowl ready and ladled some broth into it. "He gives you wisdom about these things." She set the bowl on the table. "Would you like to take it to her?"

Haven pushed himself off the wall and took the bowl. As he walked toward the bedroom his emotions were all over the place. He was relieved as the responsibility to be good enough to convince everyone of the truth lifted from his shoulders, but depression and anger from everything that had gone on still boiled inside him. He paused at the door and laid a hand on it, collecting himself. He leaned an ear against the door; everything had gone quiet from within the room.

"Rachel?" Haven spoke softly as he pushed the door open.

He walked in and his heart broke at the sight of her. Rachel had fallen asleep from exhaustion. Her fingers clutched a thin blanket to her chest. Her breathing still hitched a bit from her bout of crying. Haven set the bowl of broth on a nearby windowsill and gently sat on the bed next to her. He stroked her hair back from her face. Wet lines from tears tracked down her cheeks and toward her ears and hairline. He rested his larger hand on top of hers clutching the blanket. "You are going to be okay." His throat tightened with emotion. "I love you, Rachel," he whispered.

38

Haven's feet dragged along the path as he headed to the Telling. Before he had been zealous, his blood zinging with passion, to spread the alarm about the Guardian's influence, but now he felt only suffocating dread. The rock wall of the mountain soared up on his right threatening to tumble down and crush him.

He shook his head to try and rid his mind of these unfamiliar feelings. That's when he noticed smoke in the distance near where he estimated the center of the village to be. The dark column ascended straight up in the wind-less calm of early evening.

Haven stopped to gape. It wasn't that fires never happened; they were a common fear in the tight quarters of the village where thatching could easily catch from a stray cinder, but the timing now was ominous. In Haven's mind, the smoke in conjunction with Jared's recent murder coalesced into a sinister portent.

The smoke had reached a height where a breeze aloft flattened it and drove it toward the western range. Haven turned away and continued trudging on toward his meeting.

Tonight wasn't a typical Telling: celebrating the grace and mercies of Shalliyt and hearing the prophecies communicated through the Teller.

Tonight was a special meeting for the purpose of discussing recent events, amongst the people and the elders, with the Teller acting as the superior adviser.

Haven had been saddened by the declining attendance of the Tellings; people were becoming complacent in their faith or outright forgetting their creator. But tonight, he suspected, would be a full house. The Teller's dire warnings may have been falling on deaf ears, but the people saw the destruction throughout their community clearly.

Haven arrived at the large door in the side of the mountain and ducked inside. Villagers, mostly men, filled the cavernous room; shoulder to shoulder they crowded on the benches with every available space gone. People stood along the back of the room and Haven didn't doubt the aisles would fill, too. Golden candle light flickered on the stands at the end of each bench and in sconces around the wall. He carefully wove through the throng to wedge himself back into a corner.

The front platform where the Teller normally presided was as yet vacant. The drone of the villagers' hushed conversations thrummed in the stone cave. Several more men stepped over the stone threshold, everyone shifting to make room. The temperature rose and beads of sweat formed at Haven's brow.

The Teller's door to the side of the platform opened slowly. Silence quickly overspread the room. Everyone stood as the elder made his way to his usual place in the center of the platform. He clutched his long robe with one hand, his cane with the other. His sightless eyes scanned the crowd.

"Will all the elders please step forward." His voice was husky with disuse.

Four men and one woman lined up in front of him, heads bowed in deference. These were the elders for the five districts of the valley: north, south, east, west, and center village. The silence stretched through the space again. It felt like it physically vibrated from the amount of tension in the cave. Haven shifted a bit leaning a hip against the damp wall. He crossed his arms and waited with the rest.

The Teller raised his hands and directed his eyes upward. "Bless Shalliyt from for ever and ever."

Haven recognized the beginning of one of the prayers from the ancient scrolls. The assembly automatically bowed their heads.

"Blessed be your glorious name, which is exalted above all blessing and praise." His voice rang out clear and strong now. "You, even you, are Lord alone; you have made the mountain tops, the land above the mist, with all its holy inhabitants, the valley and all that is in it, the wilderness and all that roams it, and you preserve them all. And the holy Guardians worship you."

The Teller lowered his hands and the people sat, except for those lining the wall and the elders at the front. Haven thought it was an odd place to end the prayer.

The Teller motioned to one of the men in front of him. "Elder of the South. What is your complaint?"

The man, tall and wiry with a bald head that reflected in the candlelight, stepped forward. "Sir, the southern district is suffering from youth who run wild. They steal possessions and food, burn property, rape women, kill livestock, and hurt children."

"You are in charge. Why have you not dealt with them appropriately?" The Teller pinned his milky-blue gaze to the man.

"I have tried. Sir, they grow quickly and are exceedingly large. Physically restraining them is difficult. They seem to have in common that their fathers are all men from the mountains. The fathers have become prominent in the community and have much influence when it comes to justice with their children."

Haven sighed. *What fools! The Teller has been warning about this very thing for years... why is this a surprise now?*

"Elder, the reason you have been placed over the people is to implement justice. You choose when the application of mercy should override justice and when punitive measures should be enacted. Do these fathers then wield influence over you?"

"No, of course not. I am impartial."

The Teller cocked his head, appearing to wait for the elder to see the error in his logic.

The elder licked his lips, clearly uncomfortable. "Witnesses fear speaking out, making the application of justice challenging."

"What do they fear?" The Teller shifted his gaze to the others in the crowd. "Does not Shalliyt always stand by the righteous?"

"The fathers control much of our commerce now. They could withdraw their support and improvement of the businesses, or sabotage them altogether."

The elder opened his mouth and then closed it without saying anything more. His adam's apple bobbed as he swallowed several times.

"Mmm..." the Teller finally responded. "Your possessions and food are stolen, property burned, and women, children and livestock harmed. And your 'witnesses' are afraid of declining profits?"

The elder clearly didn't care for this characterization of the situation and prepared to speak again. The Teller pointed to another.

"Eldress of the North. What is your complaint?"

"I have none, sir." The Eldress stood much shorter than the men around her, but she spoke fiercely. "The mountain dwellers, whom my colleague has slandered," she glanced at the Elder of the South as he made his way back to his seat, "have greatly enhanced our community. They have brought the northern village and outlying areas new medicines and tonics, and new metals to ease the labors of farming."

"You have grown rich, and life has become lazy for you?" The Teller quirked an eyebrow.

The Eldress looked offended but knew better than to argue. "We have no problems with the newcomers, sir," she stepped back.

"Elder of the West. What is your complaint?"

A broad, hairy man stepped forward. He cleared his throat. "Uh, yes. Uh, we have a problem… I mean I have heard rumor of a problem of a different nature." The man looked down at his feet, then darted a glance at the Teller and quickly away again.

"Yes? Continue." The Teller scowled at the man.

"Yes. Well, maybe it isn't all bad. But it doesn't feel right."

Silence stretched till it thrummed. Feet shuffled and someone coughed.

The elder took a deep breath. "In the western forest, I have heard talk of several groups engaging in worship…and other activities."

"They worship Shalliyt in the forest?" The Teller sounded distinctly sarcastic to Haven.

"Uh, yes, well no. I don't know. Reports vary. The oldest gathering meets at a derelict shack where a woman speaks with the voice of a man and heals. Reports are that she has healed many. Some praise Shalliyt for the healing."

"And the others?"

"I have heard that within the shack is situated a serpent of wood, and…" the man's voice dropped so low that Haven leaned forward to catch his words. "…some worship the serpent. There is also talk that within the shack resides a growing boy… a boy of unfortunate deformity. He has but a single eye and is dull of mind. They have begun to worship him also. But the people are generally pleased with the healings that have come to them. As we all know," he glanced around the crowd, "Shalliyt is the great healer." The crowd murmured its agreement.

The man finished with a slight smile and stepped back. Whether he condemned or condoned the behavior, Haven couldn't tell.

The Teller's reaction wasn't unclear. "The Afflicted are within your district. Fear greatly elder."

The broad man's smile died.

"Elder of the East. What is your complaint?"

The third man, his head covered in a riot of golden curls, stepped forward. "Yes, sir. My complaint is in relation to the livestock. Farmers have reported deformities amongst the newborn lambs, kids, and calves."

"What sort of deformities, elder?" the Teller asked.

"They are not the usual kind, sir." He paused and twisted his hands together nervously. "Some of these offspring appear to have human-like characteristics. Most of the farmers have killed the newborns out of fear and revulsion. A few were permitted to survive."

"And what has become of them?" asked the Teller.

"Sold in the village market as oddities, sir."

"Let me ask you something, elder." The Teller swiped his bottom lip with his tongue, then continued. "Do these offspring have the mind of a beast or of a man?"

"The ones I have witnessed were beast-like. I heard mention of one man who killed his because its childish cry unnerved him." The elder heaved a noisy sigh. "I've been told a dealer in the market has one on display that is more child than animal. But I have not seen this for myself."

The man stepped back, but then forward again.

"Oh, sir, one other matter. Just this week a man, esteemed in the community, was brutally murdered. There is one, a neighbor, who claims it was a mountain dweller who committed this crime. But it appears to me as if it had to have been more than one man by the extent of the…damage." He stepped back.

Haven's back went rigid. *How could Jared's murder be diminished that way? The man barely even remembered to bring it up.*

"The murderer is one and the same as the progenitor of some of the deformed animals," the Teller said.

"What?"

"Elder of the Center Village. What is your complaint?"

The final elder looked back and forth between the Elder of the East and the Teller. Haven saw they were trying to puzzle through the cryptic statement the Teller had laid out there. Haven, having witnessed the act itself that night with Rachel, knew exactly to what the Teller referred.

"Elder, your complaint!"

The man leapt forward. "Your pardon, sir. The village center has its share of problems, as is to be expected with many people living in close quarters. As for new issues, I have a mixed report. In many ways, commerce in the village is booming. I believe this is directly due to the influence of the men of the mountains. We have shops selling beautiful clothing for women and powders for facial enhancement. New metals have been developed to aid in farming, as the eldress mentioned, but also other items. Utensils for preparing food have been greatly strengthened with the metals, along with all sorts of other tools. Tonics are sold that seem to genuinely fortify the body and also livestock. A new shop that has just recently opened features instruments that produce beautiful music.

"But, with several of these great inventions, there is a darker side. Prostitution and promiscuity run rampant in our streets. These women seem to be the main, though certainly not the only, benefactors of the clothing and make-up. The metal has been fashioned as weapons. Crime with the use of deadly sharp knives and swords is now occurring. The tonics have been implicated in poisonings. As far as I know, the musical instruments have not been put to poor use, yet.

"Probably my biggest concern though, is the rise of sorcery, sir. Primarily women in the market place seem to have powers that have not been seen before. Divination, enchantment, and fortune telling flourish and often lead to disastrous situations. I fear these people offend Shalliyt." He stepped back.

"Indeed, they do. Your district, also, is infested with the Afflicted." The Teller clasped his hands in front of him and paused. "Elders. What do you propose as a solution?"

The eldress stepped forward first. "Sir, I must object. Why is it the women who are slandered amongst these elders— diviners, enchanters, prostitutes, and man-voiced healers?" She glared at her fellow elders. "Women have little power in our community yet all ills are solely their fault."

The Elder of the South stepped forward. His face began to redden. "You exaggerate, eldress, problems with both men and women have been brought forward. Should not women be held to account as well as men?"

"Enough. Step back. I asked for solutions, elders."

The eldress didn't move, but directed her address to the Teller. "The solution is to reward these innovators who have blessed our community. We need to encourage their work ethic and originality. We were stagnant without them—stuck in the old ways, old rituals..." at this she waved her hand vaguely as if to indicate this meeting, or maybe Tellings in general, Haven thought. "Now we have improved our economy, our health, and our wardrobes." She laughed at this.

The eldress stepped back, a smug look on her face.

"Indeed, Eldress of the North, those of whom we speak will one day receive suitable recompense, and you will be counted among their number for your loyalty to them."

"Thank you, sir!" She smiled fully now, clasping her hands behind her back. Haven shook his head. *She has no idea...*

"If I may, sir." The wiry Elder of the South stepped forward. "These huge men need to be ejected from our community, with their sons."

The Elder of the West stepped forward. "That's a bit strong. Maybe you could speak to the people, Teller, and explain to them about being careful. We shouldn't overreact and eject the good with the bad." He stepped back.

The Teller clasped his hands together. "Elder, you are aware that I am here every week speaking Shalliyt's will to the people?"

"Yes, sir, but if you really **stress** the **importance**..." He trailed off here and stopped speaking.

The Elder of the East took his turn now. "I think we need to be careful about prosecuting a whole group for the actions of a few. Clearly, offenders of our laws should be dealt with sternly. But we can't persecute a whole group. That's not fair. We need to find Jared's murderer and sentence him to death. As for the deformed offspring, I suspect the culprit must be a polluted stream coming from without into our valley. We could send some men to the edge of the wilderness to check the streams nearer the source."

Murmuring spread through the cave as people began to discuss the issue with each other in hushed tones. It continued for several minutes, the noise rising and falling. Haven looked around at the people. The elders appeared to be arguing amongst themselves. *Why didn't they understand the problem? Maybe* he *was the one who didn't understand, exaggerating the weight of the issue.* As his gaze swept the assembly, his eyes landed on the Teller, who seemed to be looking directly at him over the heads of the seated people.

The unerring focus of the Teller infused Haven with strength of conviction. He immediately felt guilty for wavering in his belief. Haven stood taller and nodded to the Teller, though he knew he couldn't see him.

The Teller thumped his cane twice on the platform. The whole assembly fell silent and turned their attention toward the Teller.

He addressed them all. "I will make known to you Shalliyt's will, then your elders will choose their course to address your concerns." He seated himself on the platform to prepare for the Telling:

"Repent. Your sin multiplies around you.

Turn away or it shall drag you under the weight of judgment.

You have turned your back on your Creator.

You have hated the Almighty."

The Teller paused and the tension in the cave throbbed. Even Haven was dismayed at the harsh words, but he knew the others would be completely confounded by them.

"Repent? What did *we* do wrong?" a man off to Haven's left spoke out. Several others grunted in agreement. The Eldress of the North glared at the Teller, her mouth pressed tight.

Another stood and pointed at the Teller. "Old man, you are a fool. These are not Shalliyt's words. I will not listen to such absurdity." He stood and walked toward the door. Several others followed. The murmuring spread across the space.

Haven was shocked at how disrespectful the people were being toward their Teller. He might not like the words that came from the Teller's lips, but they represented the truth. He looked at the Teller, who sat peacefully at the front, waiting, patient.

People continued to stand and leave, encouraging those around them to accompany them. The elders looked between each other, possibly wondering if they should step in and halt the exodus. The Elder of the Center Village shrugged and shook his head. In the end, they did nothing. About half of the assembly remained and quieted.

The Teller continued.

"The Holy Great One will come forth from his dwelling,
And Shalliyt will tread upon the valley and on the mountains,
And appear from his council
And appear in the strength of his might from the throne room.

"And all shall be smitten with fear
And the Guardians shall quake,
And great fear and trembling shall seize them to the edge of the valley.

"And the high mountains shall be shaken,
And the high hills shall be made low,
And shall melt like wax before the flame.

"And the valley shall be wholly rent asunder,
And all that is in it shall perish,
And there shall be judgment upon all.

"But with the righteous he will make peace.
And will protect the elect,
And mercy shall be upon them.

"And behold! Shalliyt comes with ten thousands of his holy Guardians
To execute judgment upon all,
And to destroy all the ungodly."

The Teller stopped speaking. His audience was stunned.

"I leave you to the leadership of your elders." The Teller stood and walked to his door by the platform, each tap of his cane echoed along the damp walls of the cave. The door closed quietly behind him.

39

Dampness seeped into Haven's pants as his knees sank into the dewy grass. He glanced around at the people kneeling around him in the small meadow. Everyone's attention focused on the wooden door of the shabby hut situated in front of the group. The humid night air sucked in and out of his lungs as he tried to remain calm and unobtrusive. A low pounding, like a heartbeat, thrummed through the space. The torches that encircled the meadow danced in the slight breeze, threatening the moths that flirted with their intense flames.

His eyes flicked over to the two beings standing to either side of the hut. Why no one else seemed alarmed by their presence made no sense to Haven. They could have been twins, they were so similar. Haven examined the one on the right, closest to him. The creature's face glinted in the torchlight smooth and hairless, like that of a boy on the verge of manhood. His head was thickly covered in a wiry red hair that snaked around his ears and onto his shoulders. Thick red eyebrows cast his eyes into shadow. A long nose led down to firmly drawn thick lips. He stood bare-chested with seemingly overdeveloped muscles for his youthfulness that bulged as he stood still, at attention. A chain hung suspended between his pierced nipples, like a harness across the chest. Haven's eyes dropped lower. The large chest tapered to a narrow abdomen, hips, and penis. Haven could not believe what he was seeing. The penis was immense, as thick as a forearm and hanging half way to the knees and nestled in a pelt of the same red wiry hair as on his head. His knees swooped backward...into hocks, and downward to very distinctly cloven hooves.

Both creatures held long wooden posts that were topped with a curving sharp blade made of the new metal, a spear.

Haven wanted to run or shout or do something. It wasn't normal for there to exist creatures that started off as a man up top and concluded with a hoof of a goat.

His head swung around searching out the source of the heavy pulsing beat. It wasn't loud, but it was incessant, and Haven felt it reverberating in his rib cage.

His eyes landed on a half-hidden figure along the tree line, another odd creature. This one stood much shorter, maybe waist high. Again, it had the face of a boy, but impossibly, the lower half looked like a huge bird. A falcon, maybe, with a swooping, feathered abdomen, stick legs, and talons gripping the ground.

Haven couldn't be sure because the creature nestled back among the trees, but something looking like folded wings protruded above its shoulders. Haven shook his head. This was too absurd.

Then he focused on what the creature held. In one arm it gripped a bowl with a tightly stretched animal skin across the opening. With its boy-hand, it hit the skin, making the rhythmic droning sound.

There had to be more of these hidden in the trees encircling the meadow, but Haven stopped searching.

He swallowed his fear and his panic, looked back down at the sodden grass beneath him, and reminded himself why he was here in the first place.

Haven had learned of these healing gatherings from the meeting with the Teller and the elders the week before. The elder of the west district had given a mixed report of the meetings but had claimed to not know firsthand. Did the people seek Shalliyt's will in their illnesses? Did they give glory to Shalliyt for the healings? If they did, then why would the Teller rebuke them, giving a message of repentance and destruction directed to the whole valley?

Haven came to see for himself. He also thought that if the activity seemed suspect, he could speak with the people and show them where they erred. It became clear during the end of the meeting with the elders that their leadership was deficient and that they ignored the prophecies. They would lead the people astray.

The old wooden door slowly opened, and all eyes fixed upon the priestess as she emerged. She wore a long robe, her face shadowed in the large hood. Four more robed women followed her out. They left the door wide open and lined up in front of the crowd, two on either side of the first woman. The low heartbeat sound accelerated.

Haven glimpsed a view into the hut between two of the women. The interior was barely lit, but it looked as if a statue stood just within the space. Of course, Haven had heard of the serpent statue, and he assumed that's what he was seeing. He had been completely incredulous when Rachel told him the statue had been carved by her father.

"Your father," Haven had sputtered, "Jared?" He stopped sweeping and just stared at Rachel. "…built the serpent statue that some say is now being worshiped in the forest?"

Rachel adjusted her apron nervously. "I don't know what they used it for. Father just said one of the men from the mountains specially requested the piece and told him exactly how he wanted it done. He asked the man what it was for and the man said it wasn't his concern. But he paid him very well for it!" Rachel grabbed the broom that Haven had abandoned as he stood there staring at Rachel with his mouth hanging open.

The plan had been to come to the village, to the wood shop, tidy it up, and find someone to take over Jared's business. They were planning to remove anything personal to Jared from the shop and contact the owners of commissioned pieces in progress. But instead, they arrived to find the windows smashed and anything of value missing. The thieves had been thorough. The door, with its shiny, new metal locking mechanism, had been left intact. Haven fit the key to the lock, his first time operating a metal device like this, and opened the door. So the lock held against the thieves; he had to admit it was impressive. But, regardless, the windows defeated the purpose. Haven and Rachel had begun sweeping up the mess, mostly shattered glass, splintered wood, and pottery shards. They still needed to clean up to try and sell the shop.

"I saw it, you know." Rachel kept her eyes fixed on her growing pile from the broom.

"The serpent?" Haven said.

"Yes. It was quite beautiful. Father made it graceful and swerving. He even notched scales into the wood. But…"

"But what?"

"It seemed a bit…" She stopped sweeping and tucked a stray curl behind her ear. Her green eyes looked out the open window, but Haven could tell she was lost in thought. Then she spoke more slowly. "It seemed almost menacing. The hairs on my arm stood poking up when I saw the thing." Then she laughed and waved her hand through the air, clearly embarrassed by her admission. "I know Father really enjoyed the opportunity to create something different from the usual commission."

Haven's attention returned back to the meadow where his wet knees began to ache from the position. The people on either side of him had fallen forward on their palms and faces at the presence of the priestess and her acolytes. This was not a good sign. He had only gotten on his knees since everyone else had done so when he arrived at the meadow. But he would not be falling on his face. He looked back to the priestess, her face obscured in the shadows of her hood. She hadn't spoken yet. She lifted her hands to the hood and pushed it back. The other women did the same. The pounding ceased abruptly, leaving an aching void.

Haven stared at her. Now that he could see her features somewhat in the flickering torchlight she looked familiar. He quickly glanced across to the other women, but he didn't recognize them at all. But the one in the middle—he knew her from somewhere.

And then she spoke.

"I will heal your sick," boomed out a deep, masculine voice from the very beautiful, very *feminine* woman's mouth.

Haven sat abruptly back on his heels he was so astonished at the voice. In his peripheral vision he saw more people fall forward in reverence.

The rich, baritone voice continued. "And in your gratitude, you will show reverence to Briysh who waits within." The priestess indicated behind her toward the door.

The name was all it took. Haven immediately recalled the incident outside Jared's shop where the prostitute had propositioned him—that was definitely her standing in front of the crowd in long robes—and where the feral offspring of a mountain dweller had punched him in the face. She had called him Briysh. And Eli, whose house and crops and face had been burned, had called him Briysh. Haven had no idea why Briysh would be in the hut, what his role was with the supposed healing, or how he may be connected to the serpent, but none of this was good. And why was the prostitute speaking with that voice. He remembered it being lyrical and silky and womanly when she had whispered in his ear.

People began swaying back and forth, moaning for help, praising the priestess. Haven couldn't stand it. Fear jolted through him, striking at the core of his being. Not fear for himself, but fear for the huge transgression the people were committing. He leapt to his feet.

"Stop!" he yelled. He spun around to see the dozens of people filling the meadow. He could see better now that not all kneeled—some were laying in the grass where they had been placed by hopeful loved ones for healing. Some clearly had deformities, amputations, skin diseases. He held his arms out to the people. "Don't do this thing. Only Shalliyt deserves your worship! Only Shalliyt can heal you if he wills, or comfort you."

A middle-aged man stood up near Haven and strode over to him. His nostrils flared and he pushed his index finger against Haven's chest. "Silence! You have no idea what you're talking about," he growled at Haven.

"This is an abomination. Do not do this!" Haven reached for the man's shoulder to plead with him.

The man knocked away Haven's hand and stepped very close to him. "My daughter was healed." He spoke loudly so all the people now watching this exchange could hear him clearly. His breath gusted directly into Haven's face. "She was nearly dead, and now she lives." Then he turned toward the hut and raised his hands. "Praise to the serpent," he shouted.

The people, on their knees in the grass, had a mixed reaction. Some looked distressed or confused. Many joined the man, and began a mantra. "Praise to the serpent!" they chanted over and over.

The people…were lost. They would be condemned. Why wouldn't they stop? He had to keep trying. As he raised his hands to try and get the people's attention back to him, away from the open door of the hut, with the serpent looming within, he felt a heavy hand settle on his shoulder.

"Haven," a deep voice growled behind him.

He spun around and found himself looking down at the prostitute in the priestess robe in front of him. The first thing he noticed were her eyes. They were unfocused and glassy— unseeing. He stepped back, startled, but her hand still rested on his shoulder. She clamped down on him painfully.

"Haven," she spoke again. "You don't belong here."

Haven couldn't control his breathing. The air sawed in and out of his lungs. He felt rooted to the spot. Pinned down by an immovable force. This just could not be the woman he had met. Who was she? *What* was she? He finally found his voice, though it barely came out above a whisper. "You are transgressing against Shalliyt."

The priestess immediately spit to the ground. Her hand squeezed harder on Haven's shoulder. She lifted her face to him again and spoke slowly. "He, too, does not belong here." Then quietly, so that no one else could hear, even in the dead silence of the meadow, she whispered. "Leave now, or I will kill you."

Haven nodded slightly. The pain in his shoulder was becoming unbearable. He thought she might be slowly breaking it, but he had no power to move.

She lifted her chin, getting the attention of the twin goat-like guards flanking the door of the hut. As one, they stepped forward and came toward them. "Escort this man of little faith from my presence." She released Haven's shoulder and stepped back.

Haven turned to leave, weaving his way through the people still kneeling. The guards shadowing him simply plowed through the people, stepping on them with their sharp hooves if they didn't scatter quickly enough.

Heading toward the mouth of the path that would lead through the woods and back into the village, Haven turned one last time and pled to the group, "Come with me, so that you may live. Only Shalliyt can save you!" Not a single person stood to follow. The guards leveled their spears at Haven. He glanced one last time at the priestess who had a hideous grin slashing across her face, and then he left, his heart bleeding for those who would not see.

40

Briysh hovered in the upper corner of Haven's horse stable. He could hear the early morning bird song so he knew it wouldn't be long till Haven appeared to feed the horses.

The horses pawed at the ground, snorting. They couldn't see him, but they clearly sensed his presence. The stable stank of warm hay and manure.

Briysh was unsure of what exactly he could do to Haven. Possession would be the most satisfying and give him the most power, but without the hallucinogenic herbs in Haven's body or blood shedding, Briysh didn't know how to gain access. Perhaps he would discuss it with Aarkaos later.

But he could scare him. Briysh had mastered the ability to briefly grab small objects and hurl them, he could drag his dagger-like nails down Haven's back and mark him, and now he realized, he could startle the horses enough to put Haven in danger.

Briysh wasn't choosy. He would do whatever it took to scare off this whelp of a man who dared to interfere with his ritual. This maggot's mouth would be no match for Briysh's growing power. No one else would hear his warnings.

The barn door opened, bringing Briysh out of his fantasy. Pleasure pulsed through his veins in anticipation.

"Whoa girls. What has you so worked up?" Haven spoke softly as he crossed over to the stalls housing Shiloh and Sheba.

Briysh floated down, intending to perch on the edge of Shiloh's stall. Shiloh's eyes rolled back into her head, then THWACK!

Briysh tumbled head over feet slamming into the far wall. He shook himself off and turned around to see what hit him.

Haven, oblivious to everything, stretched out his hand to Shiloh while softly clucking his tongue. And right behind him stood two huge Guardians glaring directly at Briysh.

Briysh noticed several things at once. Since the two looked right at him, they were in his realm, not Haven's. And Haven seemed unaware of them. Second, they were armed. The one closest to him withdrew a long, gleaming sword from a scabbard attached to a harness crisscrossing his chest. None of the Guardians in the valley were armed, and they didn't generally walk around in his realm, though they could.

"Briysh. Leave," said the Guardian now walking toward him, brandishing his sword. The second one stayed close to Haven.

Briysh glanced at Haven who poured grain into the horses' bucket, clearly confused as to what had the animals' attention as they ignored their breakfast.

"No, I won't leave. He is mine and I'm not done here." Briysh floated up higher to feel superior to the Guardian.

"You fool. You cannot touch him."

Briysh took the opportunity to fling himself toward Haven. A blinding white hot fire zipped down his back, and suddenly Briysh found himself back in the wilderness. He sat in the dirt and howled in agony.

The last thing he saw before he slipped into oblivion was Aarkaos off to the side laughing. Laughing at him. He hated Haven with a passion he had never felt before. Haven would die for this. Then the inky blackness claimed him.

41

Kharshea awoke to the jarring sound of shattering pottery and the feel of broken pieces raining down on his head. He plucked a shard from his hair and inspected it. He recognized the fragment of the design from a vase Dassah had made.

A chair slammed against the wall, the wood in it snapping.

"Briysh, enough! I'm awake now."

Kharshea no longer needed to go to the wilderness to summon his son. Briysh had gained much control and power, and would come to his father at will to get his attention. He was so proud of the progress Briysh had made.

Kharshea shook his head to dislodge the rest of the pottery remnants from his hair. He climbed out of bed and shifted into his incorporeal state. He could now see his son swirling and flashing around his room in a gyration of fury.

Briysh had advanced to interacting with physical substance, as in his rage he smacked at and hurled objects in the room, smashing some of them. If Seth or Hannah had walked in at that point to investigate the noise, they would have found a room empty of people, but with small things launching through the air.

Kharshea quickly settled Briysh enough to find out what the problem was.

"It is Haven, from the eastern edge," Briysh spat in disgust. "He is a true disciple of the Teller and his god."

"The Teller is old and Shalliyt is mostly absent," Kharshea shrugged. "What matter is it if this Haven follows them?"

Kharshea felt a niggling of fear in his spirit at his son's blatant disregard for, or even denial of the existence of, Shalliyt. Kharshea had rebelled against his god, but he surely did not deny his creator's existence. Or his undeniable power. Kharshea, though he stated Shalliyt had abandoned their world, knew through the curse he now lived under, that his god still watched and wielded that power—the power to determine one's eternity.

Kharshea remembered Dahka, one of the still-faithful Guardians, telling him that Briysh had no eternity because he was not created by the will of Shalliyt, rather by the will of man and Guardian. But Kharshea could not give up on his son so easily.

"Because Haven cannot control his mouth." Briysh groaned with what Kharshea knew was the fairly constant pain he endured. It could be dulled but never completely removed. Clearly Briysh's anxiety made it worse now. "I *need* the worship of the people, their sacrifice, their blood," he spat. "I will not lose that to some self-styled prophet ranting about what he does not know or understand."

"Does anyone listen to him? I've never heard of him."

"Not that I've seen. After he attempted to disrupt my healing ritual—"

"He showed up at your ritual?" Kharshea's brow quirked.

"Yes, he's a bold one. He spouted off to my true believers nonsense about dishonoring that god and bringing destruction upon themselves. I had him removed but who knows what doubt he may have planted in the minds of my faithful. I cannot risk this—he *must* be shut down." Briysh punctuated his displeasure with smashing a small wooden table.

"Stop destroying my room, Briysh," Kharshea scrubbed at his hair in frustration. "Wouldn't it be more effective for you to find a way to torment him invisibly, as opposed to me approaching him for all to see?"

Briysh didn't answer immediately. "I had planned to. I found him the day after his rude intrusion to my event. I had some ideas about handling the situation," Briysh smirked.

"Well?"

"Are you aware that he is well protected?"

"What difference does that make to you?"

Briysh swirled and flashed in the air, his agitation ramping up again.

He stopped abruptly. "Haven is well protected by brothers of *yours*..." Briysh hissed.

"*My* brothers...?"

"I am not invisible to them, nor can I overpower them." Briysh spun around, showing his father his back. He reached behind himself with both hands and grasped the edges of his back and pulled them apart, revealing a deep, squelching gouge from neck to tail bone. Kharshea could see the bright white of his vertebrae framed by torn muscle and sinew. "I know because I tried and got a taste of his sword down my spine." He released the flesh, both halves slapping back together again, and spun back to face his father.

Kharshea's mouth dropped open, speechless. This was the first he had heard of the arrival of what must be the holy Guardians on directive from Shalliyt.

Utter despair engulfed Kharshea. Shalliyt really was involved now. Whatever hope Kharshea may have held out that Dahka had been mistaken floated away. He needed to gather his brothers for a meeting, his fellow rebellious brothers, that is. They needed a better plan. Maybe they could plead with Shalliyt, if not for themselves, then for their sons.

"...Father? Are you listening to me?" Briysh's fists were clenched and he bared his teeth.

"Sorry, yes. I was unaware of the presence of my brothers in this, uh, capacity. It does present a challenge. I'll take care of it."

"See that you do." Briysh growled as he evaporated through the wall, leaving Kharshea in a pounding silence. He sank down wearily onto the edge of his bed.

42

Kharshea pushed himself forward off the tree he had been leaning against. He looked skyward, but any starlight was obliterated in the smog, a thick acrid blend of smoke and night dew that constantly hugged the valley. He raised one arm to get the attention of the men scattered around the clearing. About fifty Guardians gathered here in the woods, deep into the night. They began to amble toward Kharshea, their quiet talking dying down. He had summoned the group to search for solutions to their extremely serious problem. Several of their half-breed animal offspring wandered through the woods to make sure the Guardians weren't interrupted.

"So why are we here, Kharshea?" Torchlight glinted off the man's face, his features flattened in the low light. His tone didn't hold accusation, simply curiosity.

Kharshea folded his arms across his chest. "Brothers, we need to discuss the issues that are escalating around us." He cleared his throat, giving himself a moment to collect what he needed to get across. "We are cursed. Our sons are cursed—"

"That's just the Teller spouting his nonsense. What makes you think that's true?" one spoke out from the back.

"It's true. I spoke with Dahka regarding these things," Kharshea said.

"You returned to the mountains?"

"Briefly, to discover the whereabouts of my murdered son." He paused. "Men may think the Teller is of clouded mind, but that's not so. He is the mouth of Shalliyt. Our immortality is forfeit."

The Guardians grumbled, growing restless in the flickering light. A small degree of panic had set in, giving Kharshea hope that his brethren would finally listen. Then the conversation began shooting back and forth amongst them.

"Where is Aarkaos? Shouldn't he be the one to deal with this?"one shouted, referring to their leader who first set the plan of incursion into the valley in motion.

"He can fix this. It was his idea..."

"He never descended with us. He enjoys riding his new throne too much..."

Kharshea interrupted at this point. He no longer remains on that throne."He made eye contact with those around him. "Shalliyt has returned."

Dead silence followed that pronouncement.

"You have seen Shalliyt? Spoken with him? I thought he had abandoned us..."

"Kharshea is right. We have been dispossessed." All turned to the new speaker."I tried to return to the mountains, and I could not."

Kharshea spoke again."Dahka warned me that would be coming soon."He looked upward toward his old home."I have not seen or spoken to Shalliyt. I too have lost access above the mountain mists. But there is no question Shalliyt watches us. I suspect he always did, and Aarkaos...misled us on this."

"But how can you be sure?"

"I know what Dahka told me, what the Teller speaks regularly to the very few in the valley who still listen, and..."

All the Guardians were agitated now, as the reality of what Kharshea told them began to register.

"And?"

Kharshea clasped his hands behind his back as he delivered the last bit of his news, the bit that would be irrefutable in his argument."And...our brothers who chose not to rebel against our creator are here now."

"Here in the valley?"

"Yes. They remain untransformed. I believe they are protecting those loyal to Shalliyt."

"Protecting men from us? We have improved their lives. They should be grateful to have been raised from the base existence they had prior to our arrival."Kharshea couldn't see him in the shadows, but he knew that arrogance could only have come from Rhyima.

"I haven't spoken with them, but I suspect it isn't so much us they protect men from."Though we have murdered several of them in anger, he did not add, as it wasn't really the issue here.

"But probably from our sons who rage out of control, happily killing, plundering, and raping wherever they go."

The Guardians murmuring began to swell at this point. Kharshea knew the arguments happening—they weren't new. The Guardians who had not fathered sons yet were angry with the ones who had, accusing them of not keeping them under control, because their bad behavior was ruining everything. He gave them time to vent before he raised his arm again for silence.

"This brings me to the other problem we have. Our sons are spectacularly ill mannered, I suspect from the unnatural crossing we have done here. But they are our sons. They are our only future now, though even that will be cut short. They have begun to increasingly turn on one another. My own son was killed by another Offspring. Death is not their end, but it is infinitely worse than their life. They are exiled to the wilderness, tortured by pain and thirst and hunger." A few in the crowd nodded having experienced this with their own. "We need a plan to bring them to heel, before your sons meet the same fate as mine." Emotion clogged his throat, ending his plea.

A Guardian stepped forward from the shadow. "I don't think we can alter this. It is ordained."

"Explain what you mean," Kharshea said.

"According to the Teller, chaos, murder, and cannibalism is the natural path carved by Shalliyt for the Offspring to follow. They are doomed here and now, as well as eternally."

"You go and listen to the Teller?"

"No, not directly. I hear men talk about it."

Another stepped forward. "This all leads back to Shalliyt. We must approach him and ask him to change his mind. Remove the curses from both us and our offspring."

Another responded to this. "We rebelled against him, spoke of him as if he were dead. Why exactly do you think he would change our punishment?"

An angry outburst answered. "We rebelled? Really? Who created us with a lust for women and then offered us no outlet? Who put us in charge of guarding this race of men with beautiful daughters and then expected us to keep our hands off? His punishment is unfair. We never had a choice in the matter… we're driven by the nature with which he has endowed us. Only a tyrant would punish his own sons for doing what comes to them instinctively."

Kharshea winced at the blatant heresy voiced in that tantrum. But the discussion continued around him.

"He has relented in the past. When his mortal children asked forgiveness, he changed his planned retribution."

"He has never treated Guardians and men alike. I wouldn't assume he will now."

"Guardians do not repent. We are not weak like men."

Kharshea knew this was true. They were not designed the same as men. Forgiveness, given or received, was not intrinsic to their nature. "We must plead our case to Shalliyt. We have nothing to lose at this point." Kharshea's hands moved through the air while he spoke, explaining his plan. "We can use our superior abilities in logic and reasoning to remind our creator that we are his sons with inherent rights, even that we preceded men in the order of creation."

Some of the heads in the crowd bobbed in agreement. Guardians universally prided themselves on their ability to use logic, or to effectively twist it if need be.

Kharshea continued. "Our difficulty is that we have lost access to the throne room to present a petition of pardon."

The angry voice was back. "I will not beg before Shalliyt. We are not without our own resources, knowledge, wisdom. If we pull together and think this through, we can come up with a solution to avoid this curse, if it even exists."

He was quickly rebuked by another. "Brother, we have much power. But let's not repeat Aarkaos' mistake and style ourselves as gods. There are no rituals for achieving immortality, no cosmic manipulation for regaining our eternities if they have been taken from us. Shalliyt alone has the power of our creation…and our destruction."

Heavy silence momentarily doused the debate.

"The petition is our only option. We could approach our more *noble* brothers—they surely still have an audience before Shalliyt."

"We can try that." Kharshea said, "But I suspect they will not interact with us except in defense of their charges."

"They are still our brothers. They will not turn a deaf ear to our plight!"

Kharshea sighed. "We will find out, I suppose."

One Guardian who had remained quiet till now stepped forward. "The Teller can be our messenger. He clearly has the attention and favor of Shalliyt. We can ask him to deliver our petition."

And in the end, that is what they chose as their course of action.

43

Kharshea stood waiting at the Teller's door, his pride bruised by coming to this old man to ask a favor. A rather large favor. But there didn't seem to be an alternative.

He glanced around the interior of the vacant meeting cave, about the only dwelling in the entire valley with a sufficiently high ceiling. Or no ceiling at all possibly, as he looked up into the oppressive void that soared into darkened obscurity. He actually felt dwarfed by the space. It made him long for the open vault of the crystalline star-stippled sky.

"Yes?"

Kharshea startled, looking down from his cave ceiling rumination, to the old man whom he had not heard open the door, standing hunched on the platform before him. The contrast between the two men was vast—one was gnarled, wrinkled, bent over, with flowing gray hair and milky blue eyes staring out at nothing; the other tall, powerful, dark haired and black eyed. This was truly humiliating. However, he would be courteous.

"Teller, I would like to speak with you."

The Teller didn't ask who he was. Kharshea figured he already knew. Probably knew Kharshea was coming over before he had even arrived. The elderly man stepped back and motioned for him to come into his room.

Kharshea eyed the door that was about half his height.

"If it suits you, maybe we could sit out here." Kharshea waved slightly toward the benches in the meeting room. Not only the door height presented an issue, but the light from the open doorway to the cave somewhat illuminated the meeting room. The Teller's chamber looked black.

The Teller nodded and clopped stiffly across the platform with his staff and down to the first bench in the row. He slowly lowered himself to the cold stone of the seat. Kharshea sat several feet away from him. The steady dripping of the cave walls unnerved him. Green moss, that looked more like pond dross, oozed down the slick surface. Kharshea felt like it was slithering directly onto him, though the wall came nowhere near him. He shifted slightly to remove the irrational feeling that had unsettled him, when his mind suddenly processed and comprehended the nearly tactile response.

His brothers were here. Kharshea couldn't see them, but he could sense them. How stupid of him not to anticipate that the Teller, of all people, would have Guardian protection sent by Shalliyt.

"They aren't concerned about you, Kharshea. It is your son and his kind that attempt to harm me, interrupt my message. Kindly, state your business."

Kharshea nodded. "The Guardians have lost access to our creator because of some poor decisions made on our part."

The Teller said nothing but arched a single, grey-furred brow.

"Aarkaos misled us, and yes, we followed."

"If Aarkaos is the responsible one, why is he not here pleading the case of the fallen ones?"

"I suspect you know the answer to that better than I. He never descended with us." Kharshea shook his head. "I don't know why. For some reason he has chosen to locate himself in the wilderness with my son and those like him."

"He never intended to descend…to the valley or the wilderness." The Teller paused and looked blindly off, as if his mind traveled somewhere in thought. "Unlike you, his 'lust' is not for the daughters of men. His plan is much greater and unfathomably more evil."

Kharshea looked at the Teller, perplexed. This was not what he expected.

"Through his veins burns a hatred so bright and searing that it consumes his mind. All his brilliance, his wisdom, his ambition are twisted toward the destruction of those Shalliyt loves: the men of the valley."

"His fall from grace eons ago. The fall that shut men from the mountains." Kharshea murmured, starting to put the pieces together. "But there was no consequence to him, only to man and his part in it, so why the hatred from Aarkaos now"

"Oh, there was a consequence. The prophecy states that he will be punished by one born of man yet to come."

"A man?"

"His time is short and he knows it."The Teller tapped his staff on the hard floor. "He believes if he can destroy Shalliyt's creation, then none can be born to carry out the curse on him. Additionally, he thinks if he succeeds then he will be greater than his own creator."

Kharshea stared at the Teller in horror. "And he used us in hopes to accomplish this for him?"

"Yes. You were willing enough."

"But we are not here to destroy man. We want to live among them. We better their existence in exchange for allowing us into their homes and families."

"But you are destroying them."The Teller pinned him with his vacant stare. "You gave them wisdom from the mountains."

"That is not evil. It is simply information to improve their lives."

"You are correct. The wisdom is not inherently evil. But it was expressly given to your race, for your habitation. A boundary exists between man and Guardian, between the mountains and the valley. You have breached that boundary by introducing the wisdom of the mountains down here."

"Does Shalliyt not wish for man to prosper with this knowledge? Why does he want his children kept ignorant?"

"Shalliyt withheld this knowledge from man because he *knows* man will pervert it for evil. With knowledge comes responsibility. And this is a responsibility man will struggle with and mostly fail at. And…"

"What?"

"Look at what your unions have propagated—damaged, ruthless creatures that will ruin the valley and all that is in it. Your lust has done that. You have crossed another boundary that violates the basic structure of creation. This boundary was not one of location, but rather of your body.

"All things under the throne of Shalliyt reproduce after their own kind, from the lowly grass, to man in all his complexity. You and your brethren have mixed the kinds at the most basic level of reproduction and created abominations. Not only with man, but with the animals, too."

The Teller paused and looked down toward his gnarled hands. His voice hoarse from his long speech, he quietly stated,

"The Guardians have brought a curse on this valley. It will be destroyed because of you."

Kharshea shifted in his seat. He did see some truth in what the Teller said. But surely his assessment was overly dramatic. What Aarkaos had done was much worse than the Guardians pursuing their natural desires—with good motives to help out in the process. "Then Aarkaos should lose his immortality because of his attempt to overthrow Shalliyt. But we had no ill intent toward man. Our motives were pure."

"Your motive was lust."

Kharshea pressed on. "Our punishment is too much to bear."

The Teller shrugged.

"I…we…are asking you to present a petition to Shalliyt asking for a pardon, a rescindment of the curse placed upon us. A reprimand maybe…but he would cut us off altogether." Kharshea paused and looked away. The humiliation of saying this not only in front of the Teller, but his hidden brothers, who were without fault, nearly crippled him. He felt constriction in his chest at the thought of the enormity of what had been lost, what was at stake.

"And if not for us, at least our offspring. They had no part in our defection," he whispered. "I love my son." He looked back at the Teller. "I would ask mercy for my son, for all the sons." Kharshea felt the weight of the Teller's blank gaze on him. "They are all we have left if Shalliyt will not pardon us. Please appeal to him as a father. He is father of us all, we are his sons. All of us, both you and me…" His voice trailed off.

The Teller nodded. "I will present your petition." He rose on creaky joints and shuffled away while Kharshea sat in silence.

44

(One Week Later)

Kharshea strode swiftly along the path that followed the base of the mountain, his long legs pumping, moving him at great speed. Anger welled up within him, effectively crushing the despair that occasionally bled through. He was livid. He hadn't killed the Teller, but, oh, he had wanted to. Of course, the Teller was simply the conduit for the message. But he sat right there, in front of him, sanctimonious, pious, and calm. Kharshea could have stretched out his arm, wrapped his fingers around the old man's throat, and squeezed. The crusty elder probably wouldn't have even put up a fight.

Kharshea cracked his knuckles as he stalked, needing to dispel the energy from the fire building in his gut. He focused on the path he trod, his feet crushing curly-topped ferns that had overstepped their boundaries and flopped onto the cleared way. It would have been quicker to cut directly through the village to get to the eastern edge, but he knew he would encounter fewer people along this route. Fewer questioning glances. Fewer scenes of destruction and pathos that now littered the village. The words of the Teller had been impressed into his mind. No, seared fit better: painful and permanent.

"I presented your petition, and the answer appeared swiftly, that your petition will not be granted unto you throughout all the days of eternity, and that judgment has been passed upon the unholy Guardians. And you shall not ascend into the mountains unto all eternity, and in bonds of the earth the decree has gone forth to bind you for all the days of the world.

"Shalliyt presides in the great assembly; he has mounted the throne. He renders judgment among the Guardians

'I said, "You are the guardians; sons of the Most High.

"But you will die like mere mortals; you will fall like every other ruler."'"

217

The Teller showed no emotion as he delivered this message of ruination.

No quarter had been given. No grace extended. No hope.

Kharshea needed to get to Haven's quickly, needed to shut that boy down now. Kharshea tried to solve the Guardian and Offspring problem through honorable means. He had humbled himself. Humiliated himself for the sake of all the Guardians. That hadn't worked. It only confirmed what they already suspected and proved their creator had no mercy toward them. Now he would do whatever it took to get what help he could for his son. There was nothing left for him. His future, what may be left of it, was all he had to work with. But he would spend that time in service to Briysh and those like him.

The Teller had been no less harsh on his pronouncement for the Offspring.

"You have wrought great disaster upon the valley. And you shall have no peace nor forgiveness, and inasmuch as you delight yourself in your children, the murder of your beloved ones is all you shall see. Over the destruction of your children shall you lament and shall make supplication unto eternity, but mercy and peace shall you not attain. The destruction of your beloved sons shall torment you, and you shall have no pleasure in them, but they shall fall before you by violence.

"And to my holy Guardian that faithfully awaits me I said, 'Proceed against these children of fornication. Destroy the sons of fornication and of the Guardians from amongst the valley. Send the Offspring one against the other that they may destroy each other in violence, for length of days they shall not have. No request the fathers make shall be granted on their sons' behalf.'"

Not only would the sons continue to kill one another, but they would now be incited to higher peaks of frenzy and brutality by his own brothers, the Guardians who did not rebel. Those who remained the slavish minions to the creator would take part in the judgment of the Offspring. Kharshea growled, forcing air out between his lips in a feral expulsion.

As Kharshea neared Haven's cottage, he formulated a plan for how to deal with this presumptuous young man who dared to interfere with his own son's healing rituals. Knowing that Haven had Guardian protection meant he needed to go about this indirectly. He wouldn't be able to see his brothers unless he transformed out of his terrestrial body, but he should be able to sense them as he did in the Teller's cave.

Instead, he decided he would simply ignore them. Maybe they wouldn't realize what he was up to. No, he knew better than that. But if their only concern was Haven, then there were alternate, probably unprotected, routes.

Kharshea stood on Haven's stoop. He could see someone plowing with horses out in the field and assumed that was Haven. Some discreet checking around this morning taught him that Haven was the man of the family, his father dying from an illness when he was much younger.

Kharshea also learned, in a bizarre irony, that Haven had an interest in the daughter of the man whom he had commissioned to make the serpent statue. A man whom the fool Ashteala had killed recently in an act of unrestrained passion. Kharshea shook his head slightly—the murder was an unwise move. If it was discovered that a mountain dweller had committed this crime, they would all be in a difficult position. It was bad enough that their sons were acting so poorly amongst the men, but this would be even worse. Even if Shalliyt had completely rejected them, Kharshea still felt a desire to live in a semblance of peace with the men of the valley. It was irrevocably his home now, too.

Kharshea composed himself. He smoothed his shirt down and took some deep breaths. Removing all thoughts of the Teller, he focused on his mission of containing Haven's influence, and knocked firmly on the door. It opened, but the smile on the woman's face died as she looked from his chest all the way up to his face. He presumed this to be Haven's mother. Kharshea quickly smiled at her. "Ma'am?" He had no idea how much Haven had influenced her with the Teller's endless warnings, so this could be quite a challenge.

"Yes?" She blinked rapidly while her hands twisted in her apron.

"My name is Kharshea. I was a friend of your neighbor's, Jared." He allowed his smile to falter a bit at the sad reminder of her murdered neighbor.

"Oh. Okay." She paused, seemingly not having any idea how to handle the situation.

Kharshea smiled again, crinkling the corner of his eyes. "You are...?"

"Oh!" she huffed out a laugh. "My apologies. Where are my manners? I am Tirzah. I live...here."

Kharshea chuckled at how flustered this little woman was. "It's a great pleasure to meet you Tirzah. May I come in and speak with you and your husband?"

Tirzah stepped back allowing Kharshea to duck his head and step into the cottage. She motioned for him to sit on a chair that sat prominently in the sitting area. "My husband is deceased. But please have a seat. Can I get you some water or tea?"

"Please. Water is fine." And she scurried off. Kharshea glanced at the proffered chair that in no way would hold his large frame, and instead opted for a padded bench off to the side a bit that would work. He folded his legs and sat on it gingerly.

She returned and handed him a scratched and chipped glass filled with water. "Sir, how can I help you?" She settled herself at the other end of the bench, their knees almost touching. Kharshea didn't understand why she didn't take the chair, but this was much better.

"Actually, I'm here to see how I can be of service to you. Now that you have told me you are widowed, I am even more determined to help."

"Help?"

"Yes, with Jared gone, I know there will be much more work for you to do in the fields you share in common. I know he had no sons, and you with no husband..." He gently laid a hand on the edge of her knee. "I am in awe of you, Tirzah. How you have handled this all on our own. Your strength is inspiring." He kept direct eye contact with her.

Her pupils dilated and she rubbed her thumb absently back and forth across her lips. Kharshea buried the smirk he felt trying to twist at his lips. Clearly her son had no impact in warning his mother about strange tall men. "On my own? Oh, no, I'm not alone. My son, Haven, is a constant blessing to me and a very hard worker." She beamed at the obvious pride she had in him. She dropped her hand to her thigh where her fingers fidgeted near where Kharshea's hand rested on her knee. He wasn't sure if she was even aware of her own reaction to him.

"That's wonderful that you can depend upon your son." He squeezed her knee just a bit as he finished, "but still, it must be very lonely. A beautiful woman such as yourself, alone, to raise her child and run a farm." She blushed, but Kharshea thought it curious she had not reacted negatively at all to his rather inappropriate touching. Perhaps she was lonely for the attentions of a man after years of widowhood.

"I…I…"

"I would like to become involved, in honor of Jared, to help you with some of your work around here." Kharshea had no intention of working at all, but he could hire it out. Whatever it took to get in this old, lonely woman's good graces so that he could have access to influencing Haven. Even just keeping Haven busy by worrying about his mother and away from the other villagers would be helpful. But maybe he could talk some sense in to him, too.

Just then the front door opened, and a young woman stepped through, shaking barn dust and cobwebs from her hair. Kharshea yanked his hand back, completely surprised, thinking they were alone.

"Oh, Rachel. I'm glad you're here." Tirzah stood and walked to the girl.

Rachel nodded but couldn't tear her eyes away from the huge man in front of her. "Who is this?" she whispered.

"This is Kharshea. He was a friend of your father's." Turning to Kharshea, she finished with, "This is Jared's daughter, Rachel."

Kharshea could see the fear clouding Rachel's eyes. Kharshea stood and reached out to Rachel, thinking to quell her apprehension.

"No. Don't touch me. You need to leave." Rachel spun toward Tirzah. "He needs to leave, Tirzah. He will harm us."

"Rachel, you're being rude."

"It's okay," Kharshea interrupted. "How about if I just wait outside." He gave a sad smile and turned, leaving the room. He knew Tirzah would follow.

As Kharshea stepped off the stoop, he could clearly hear the women through an open window as they moved to another room.

"You need to calm down, my sweet girl. I'll be back in a few moments." Tirzah's lilting voice contrasted with the strained pleas of the younger woman.

"Do not go to him. Don't do it." Rachel's words came in gulps. "He'll hurt you."

"You are grief stricken because of your father, and I'm afraid my son's nonsense has gotten to you. He is a guest, Rachel, and deserves better than this, hmm?"

Kharshea stared off into the field where Haven, wholly unaware of the turmoil in his home, urged on his horses. The girl had been turned successfully by Haven, or simply by the death of her father, and now also needed to be dealt with. Had she witnessed the gruesome murder? Kharshea had sensed no protection on her from his still-allegiant brothers. He would have Briysh handle Rachel in a more...stealthy manner since she remained vulnerable. He grinned a little. Briysh's methods sometimes made the recipient question their own senses, or their sanity. Perfect.

Tirzah appeared next to him, looking nervous. "I'm sorry about Rachel's behavior—"

"No need to apologize at all. I understand the violence that has been done to her family. It is only natural for the girl to be afraid of new people."

"Well that's very gracious of you." She tucked a strand of hair behind her ear. "But, I'm afraid that my son has something to do with it." She looked off in the distance where Kharshea still looked at Haven going back and forth with the team of horses.

"Haven, right?"

"Yes, Haven. He has this...idea...about the newcomers in the valley. The tall men, like yourself." Her eyes flicked around a bit.

Kharshea reached down to grasp her hand in his. "It's alright, Tirzah. You can talk to me." His thumb stroked back and forth over the top of her hand as he hoped to ground her.

She visibly relaxed. "It's really very silly." She squeezed his hand a little and Kharshea offered her an encouraging smile to continue. "Oh, it's nothing. The old Teller just fills his head with ideas, and I think since Haven doesn't have a father, that he puts the Teller in that place. Maybe giving him more credence than should be given to an elderly man having visions of unknown source." Tirzah forced a light laugh. "And Haven scares Rachel with his talk. That's all."

"So maybe Haven could also benefit from a *responsible* paternal influence in his life?" Kharshea raised a brow.

Tirzah turned fully toward Kharshea and looked straight up into his eyes. "Why...yes. You would be that for him?"

"Absolutely."

45

Fear looked down at the sleeping woman in front of him. Black curls spilled across her pillow, glinting in the moonlight.

Fear had learned the best way of relieving his unending torment was through bathing himself in the anxiety and dread as felt by humans. It would wash over him providing a relief and excitement that didn't exist in the wilderness. He didn't care if it was a man or woman. But it worked better when it was someone of weak faith, someone easily rattled. He penetrated their minds with his and controlled them, played with them. And let their fear reach back into his. This had to be accomplished in the early hours of morning when the people were in a light sleep and their minds were wide open and accessible. As soon as they fully awoke, the access shut off.

Lust had sent him on this particular mission. Somehow this incredibly vulnerable-looking woman was a threat to Lust. Fear couldn't figure it out, but he actually didn't care. The young woman before him was in a particularly susceptible state since her father had recently died. Well, more like had been brutally murdered. Fear smirked. She would be overflowing with despair that he greatly desired to share with her!

Rachel's eyes fluttered open. She stared at the plaster ceiling, its dips and swells mostly obscured in heavy shadow. Only a slip of moonlight slanted through the unshuttered window. She could smell the humid earthy scent of a recently plowed field wafting in on a soft breeze. New leaves from the oak by the window murmured on the breath of air.

She strained her ears. Nothing. She didn't know what had awakened her so abruptly in the deep of the night. The leaves' shadow flickered at the top of the wall where it joined the ceiling in her view. She stared at the dancing shapes.

Movement at her feet had her eyes swiveling down toward the end of the bed. Alarm shot through her body, pricking hairs on her arms and scalp. A scream formed deep in her soul, expanded, billowed, filled her mind, and then died in the back of her throat. Her pupils dilated in terror at the realization that she couldn't open her mouth. Blood pumped faster through her body flushing her cheeks. Grunting, screeching, sobbing all ended the same...silence. They were simply thoughts pounding at the edges of her mind. Her body lay limp, unresponsive, quiet. With the exception of her eyes, she could move nothing.

A broad grin spread across the face of the...thing... standing at the foot of her bed. Her eyes focused on that lipless smirk. This was not a joyful smile meant to ease her, but an expression of conquest by the victor. Waves of hatred emanated from her intruder, surging over her in a thick cloud she could feel brush against her skin. She stared hard through the dimness trying to see its eyes, her own eyes aching and watering with strain. Only black holes looked back at her, deep holes set in a smooth face, a face brilliant white like polished bone. Some sort of skin and flesh covered the forehead, cheeks, nose, and chin, but it was thin and stretched taut, melded with the bone beneath. So white, almost glowing in the flicker of moonshine. Its body flowed with a white robe or gown, also thin and gauzy like the skin.

Its smile faded and the black holes of eyes—somehow— intensified, searing deep into her. She had the odd thought that it could hear her screaming even though no sound escaped her numb body. She fought to move an arm, leg, anything.

Rachel began to rise up into the air. Slowly. Flat as a plank she hovered, her only view the ceiling a few inches in front of her face. Then her left hip dipped and she spun, suspended now with her back to the ceiling. Below her was the bed, the covering mussed up and lumpy...lumpy with someone lying in her bed under the covers. Confusion clouded her mind as she tried to process who slept in her bed below her, flat on her back, face up and eyes closed.

A wave of malignancy rushed through her. She couldn't see the intruder in this position, but she felt his presence acutely. Something in the fetid tendrils winding through her mind spoke to her. "My name is Fear" it said, and "I will have you."

Panic zipped down her spine and she was spun once again. Now facing the wall, she hovered, tension bolting through her. Suddenly, the plastered stone wall came rushing to her at high speed. In her mind she screamed, "Haven! Haven!" Her lips and voice were useless. Then just before impact, her plea changed to "Shalliyt!"

As the word "Shalliyt" flowed into Fear's mind, he was suddenly thrown back with a searing pain shooting behind his eyes, and his connection with the woman severed. He cursed his luck that she would turn to faith during his roamings in her mind, but it wasn't a total loss—he did feel some relief coursing through him. He grumbled to himself as he flew away. He would try again elsewhere.

Rachel sat up in bed, panting. What just happened didn't make any sense, but it wasn't a dream—she was sure of it. She felt like she had been attacked or violated. She thought about how she had looked down at herself in the bed. It had to have been a dream. But it was so realistic. Maybe it was just the heavy burden she carried from her father's death. She briefly considered going to wake Haven or his mother to tell them what had happened. She chided herself on being silly, and instead lay back down, pulling her covers tightly around herself. She stared at the dark wall till the rising sun allowed her to safely fall back to sleep.

46

Haven sat on a bale of hay, leaning back against the wall of the stable. Shiloh and Sheba noisily ate their morning feed.

The door to the stable opened, and Rachel's dark, curly head appeared around the edge of it. "There you are. I was looking for you." She walked over to Haven and sat down next to him. She picked at a piece of hay and twirled it between her fingers. She seemed weary again. She had been doing better since Jared's death, but something clearly occupied her thoughts.

"Are you alright, Rachel?"

She sighed, nodded, and immediately changed the subject. "Why were you so upset the other night when you got home?" She moved closer to him, and he put an arm around her shoulders. He knew she referred to the night he had gone to the derelict hut with the serpent and had been humiliatingly ignored by those in danger and thrown out by the man-voiced woman and her guard...things. He still couldn't wrap his mind around those beings, or the whole evening actually. He was never sure how much he should share with Rachel. He didn't want to frighten her unnecessarily, but he did not want her ignorant of the dangers, either. He leaned over toward her, putting his nose to her hair, and inhaled. She smelled fresh and clean, and innocent. He closed his eyes and took comfort from her nearness.

"Please talk to me, Haven." She stroked her thumb across his brow and he opened his eyes.

"You know I love you, Rachel." He didn't smile.

"I do know that. And I love you, too, and you're not answering my question." She placed her palm on his chest over his heart.

Then he did begin to smile, a little. "That's the first time you've said you loved me."

She rolled her eyes. "I've loved you since I was a child... and you know that, silly!"

Haven arched an eyebrow and stared at her.

Her cheeks pinkened. "And now," she whispered, "I have fallen in love with you."

A much larger smile spread across Haven's face.

Rachel closed her eyes and leaned into him, kissing him on his cheek.

He hugged her close with the one arm around her shoulder and nuzzled against her, down the side of her face, into the crook of her neck. His senses were overloaded with her scent and her softness. He lifted his head and gently kissed her on the mouth, then leaned back against the wall, attempting to put some distance between them.

"I saw your father's serpent that night." He stretched his long legs out in front of him.

"Where were you?"

"I went to the gathering for a healing in the western forest." Haven paused and dragged a hand through his hair. "They, the people who wanted to be healed, were worshiping it." Haven shook his head.

"Why would they do that?" Rachel laughed as she said it.

"Because they believe it heals them somehow. They also seemed to worship the priestess leading the ritual, and another man, who never came out of the hut. A man who's an offspring of a Guardian. I was escorted out before I saw very much of what happens."

Rachel, still stuck on the serpent, said, "Why would they think something my father carved out of wood could possibly heal them? That makes no sense."

Haven folded his hands together on his lap, tapping his index fingers together. "I don't know. They have been tricked somehow. It doesn't really matter. It's an abomination to Shalliyt. It will lead to their deaths."

"Did you tell them that?" Rachel was finally catching on to the gravity of the situation. Her hands were fisting in the material of her dress. She reached out to Haven and tugged on his shirt. "Haven, you have to warn them. You can't let them do this. If they've been tricked, they are innocent."

Haven removed her hand from his shirt and held it in his. "I did tell them. Over and over. That's why I was forced to leave." He furrowed his brow and looked down to the ground. "And not a single one left with me when I pleaded with them."

He sighed. "The Guardians and their offspring have this ability to sway people, to blind them."

Rachel didn't speak. She seemed intently focused on something on the other side of the stable.

"What is it?" Haven reached over and turned her chin his way.

"It's nothing."

"It's something. Tell me."

"I can't. Not yet. I made a promise."

Haven didn't like those kind of promises. Secrecy never led to anything good. But he wouldn't push her on it now—she had been through so much.

They sat in silence for awhile, lost in their own thoughts, still holding hands. The horses shifted around in their stalls, anxious to get out to pasture.

Haven let go of Rachel and stood up to take out the horses. "I need to go talk to the Teller. Tell him what I saw at the ritual. Can you get the door?"

Rachel slid open the larger door for the horses, and Haven led them out, reaching high to grasp them each by their mane, and guided them to the pasture. Rachel opened the gate for him there, and they both leaned against the fence and watched the horses trot off with steam huffing from their nostrils in the early morning air. The smell of smoke was thick in the mistiness. It had a tinge of another stench. Rotting and decay. Or, Haven mused, all that burdened his mind was impacting his sense of smell now.

"So the Teller…" Rachel began, but then paused.

"Yes. Although he probably already knows everything that I just learned. But I feel the need to go talk to him."

"Can I go with you?"

Haven glanced down at her. "Why?"

"I, um, feel the need, too." She looked away and back to where the horses had stopped and begun grazing.

Haven kept staring at her, then slowly nodded. "Okay. We'll go later today."

Haven sat cross-legged on the stone floor of the Teller's cave room. Rachel perched on the edge of the chair by the pile of scrolls on the desk, and the Teller sat on the edge of his bed.

Haven had just finished recounting the entire scene at the healing. During the description, which was more in-depth than Haven had given her at the stable, Rachel appeared at times shocked and then quiet. Very quiet. All three sat silently while the only candle illuminating the room flickered, unaffected by the story.

Haven looked away from the mesmerizing candle to the Teller. "Sir, can you tell me why the prostitute spoke with the voice of the man? I've heard her speak before, and that was not her voice."

"No, it wasn't." The Teller stroked his long beard. "The voice belonged to the Guardian offspring Briysh whom you met in the street."

"So it was a trick? They made it seem like his voice came from her mouth?" Haven asked.

The Teller shook his head. "Briysh is dead. Was killed awhile back by another Offspring." He paused.

Rachel and Haven looked at each other in confusion.

The Teller continued. "Leah was possessed by him. The Guardians have taught some the knowledge of allowing the Afflicted access to human minds and bodies to use them as one would use an empty vessel. The people have been fooled into thinking they are their gods."

"The Afflicted?" Rachel asked softly.

"The Afflicted are the spirits of the Offspring once they leave their terrestrial bodies. Briysh died—his body died—but his soul is still active. His soul is the essence of who he is: personality, emotion, mind, and spirit. He craves a body to feel any peace, and he will do whatever is required to feel whole again. His soul can take over Leah's body and he speaks and acts through her. Not just him, but others are doing this as well. They go after those whose faith in Shalliyt is weak or altogether missing."

Slowly dripping water pinged somewhere outside of the candle's small glowing circle. Almost like it counted time.

"Rachel, you have also encountered one of the Afflicted?"

Haven's head swung around and up to look at her.

"I…I have?" Rachel seemed confused, as she looked back and forth between Haven with his raised eyebrows and the Teller's perfectly placid face.

The Teller spoke softly. "His name was Fear. Do you remember?"

Rachel gasped. "I…It was just a dream?" she whispered. She looked away from Haven. "But, no, it wasn't…"

Haven knew she was probably feeling embarrassed or badly about whatever happened to her in connection with the Teller saying it happened to those of weak faith. He felt so much compassion well up inside him for her. He longed to reach for her. "Rachel, what happened?"

But the Teller interrupted, "She can share it with you later. And Rachel, you should tell Haven these things."

Rachel looked down, nodding.

He continued his explanation of the Afflicted. "When we die, the souls of those who are chosen will wait patiently for the resurrection of our bodies. There is no resurrection for the Afflicted. As part Guardian, part human, they are doomed from conception. They were not created by the will of Shalliyt, but rather through the disobedience of his sons and daughters. The Guardians who have perpetrated this abomination will be eternally punished. The humans who allowed themselves to be part of it will also face judgment. The Afflicted will experience neither. They will simply cease to exist when Shalliyt brings order back to the valley one day."

"So he will be bringing back peace to us the way it used to be?" Rachel swiped at her tears.

"Yes. It will be even better than it ever was in ways we cannot imagine. But, Rachel, the valley will be completely destroyed first. All abomination will be eradicated completely, all iniquity removed. Those who have transgressed Shalliyt's law will be destroyed with no hope of resurrection. This time of distress will be an exceedingly painful process."

At this proclamation Rachel paled, her expression stricken. Haven laid a hand on her foot, the only part of her he could reach, and gently squeezed.

Even blind, the Teller seemed to sense the change in Rachel's demeanor. "What is it my dear? What do you fear?"

Silent tears began to flow down Rachel's pale cheeks. "I am one of them," she whispered. "I have transgressed. I doubted Haven, I doubted you, and I doubted Shalliyt. Is there no hope for me?"

Haven crawled over to her and pulled her from the chair. He wrapped her in an embrace on his lap on the floor.

"You confess your wrongdoing?" The Teller said.

"Yes," she gasped.

"Will you place your trust in the words of Shalliyt and follow them no matter the consequences?"

"Yes!" She sobbed out, all misery consuming her. Haven held her tight against his chest and stroked her hair, trying to comfort her.

The Teller kept on. "Then you will be delivered through the coming crucible. Haven will be your husband and protect your life for now, and Shalliyt will be your God and protect your soul for eternity."

Haven kept hold of Rachel as she sobbed, relief coursing through him that she would be saved, and joy sparking in his brain at the thought of her as his wife to cherish and protect for the rest of his life.

"Haven, you, and now Rachel also, have Guardian protection. But there is one in your household at risk."

Haven's head jerked back. This could not be true. "I'm supposed to accept help and protection from a Guardian?"

"Most of the Guardians are still faithful to Shalliyt. It is they who protect you, have been protecting you for awhile now. There is nothing for you to 'accept.' It is Shalliyt's will. You won't be able to see them—unlike the fallen ones, the holy ones retain their spiritual state."

"So if we can see them, then they are not holy ones?"

Haven thought that was an odd question coming from Rachel. Surely, she could not have any possible question about Ashteala's intentions.

The Teller responded, "At this time, that is correct. Would you like to share your concern with Haven?"

Haven looked at Rachel. He didn't think he could handle any more revelations.

"I promised not to say anything, yet," she whispered.

"Rachel, what? Who?"

Haven turned to the Teller. "Wait, you said one in my household is at risk."

He looked down at Rachel and pushed her back to his arm's length. "My mother. Is she in danger?"

"Yesterday when I came in from chores, she was speaking with a man in the sitting room." She paused and took a deep breath. "A very tall man. As tall as Ashteala."

Haven's mouth dropped open.

"I'm sure he was a Guardian. And your mother was very defensive of him when I tried to warn her."

"Has she not heard *anything* I've said to her?"

"She was going to tell you and what it was he wanted. I don't know what that was, she didn't say. But she asked me not to tell you yet. I'm sorry."

"Please Rachel, no more secrets between us. It's too dangerous."

She nodded and he held her tight to his chest.

The Teller spoke, addressing his comments to Haven. "I don't know when the end of the valley will come, but it will be soon. When you feel the earth tremble, and the mountains look to topple, come to me immediately. I will show you how to pass through safely."

"Into the wilderness?"

"Yes. It won't be easy, but Shalliyt will be with you. He will speak directly to you in the days after. He shall give you the strength and courage to rebuild a life with Rachel."

"But you will be with us, too. You are Shalliyt's faithful prophet!"

"I will do the will of Shalliyt."

"And others? Will there be others to come with us?"

"As many as repent may come with you, and I will guide you all to safety. But Haven," He paused, pursing his lips, "there won't be many. The faith of man is failing quickly."

Haven had never felt such a mix of emotions before. Rachel was his! But his mother. Oh, his heart ached for his mother. Fear and unease threatened to overwhelm him. If he were to have strength and courage as the Teller said, it could only come from Shalliyt, because it seemed none was to be found within him now.

47

Haven stepped carefully over small piles of rubble that littered the cobbled street. The air reeked of a noxious combination of burnt wood and decomposition. Animal or human, he wasn't sure, and at this point he didn't want to find out. He needed to find Jon.

They had separated unspeaking after the incident with the animal/boy creature in the cart. Haven shook his head at the memory. He loved Jon and needed to impress upon him the seriousness of what was happening in the valley. Why wouldn't anyone listen to him? All they had to do was look around to see everything falling apart. But more importantly, he had to make sure Jon was safe. Something very bad had occurred in this part of the village.

After his last visit with the Teller a few days earlier, Haven understood better what was happening, and what was yet to come. He hadn't been able to speak to his mother yet. He'd been busy with the fields—although he wasn't sure what the point was any more. But he had a desperate need for some normalcy in his life with everything feeling like it was crashing down around him. His long hours out in the field and caring for the animals calmed him a bit, allowed him to talk himself out of what his mother could possibly be doing entertaining a Guardian. It was probably just a one-time thing. There was no way she would have ignored everything he had warned her about. When he would return to the house, exhausted, she would already be in bed for the night. He would talk to her, he had to, but first he needed to take care of Jon.

Haven turned a corner on the deserted street and almost tripped over several dogs. They snarled and snapped at a lump on the ground that had their full attention. Against his earlier resolve, he stopped and looked hard at the object of the canines' interest. The smell of rot was powerful, squeezing his stomach. Flies buzzed all around, landing on the flesh, yes flesh, the moment the dogs paused to glance at Haven. They turned from him and enthusiastically dove back into their meal, sending the flies back up into a buzzing haze above them. Haven stumbled, bending over and vomiting off to the side. He wiped at his mouth and took off, leaping over more mounds of debris. He was almost to Jon's place.

Jon was an apprentice at a sign-maker's shop in the village and lived in the apartment over top of it with another worker. But this part of the village lay in ruins around him. Was the shop even still here? And where were all the people who live here?

Haven took the next turn more carefully, wary of more surprises. He stopped and looked down the abandoned street. No one. A roof of one building still smoked a bit; the other roofs were mostly missing except for exposed charred crossbeams. He saw the sign-makers sign off to the right several buildings up. It swung gently by only one side, twisting in the foul-smelling heat of the afternoon. *Oh, Jon,* Haven thought. *Please be alright.*

Blood splashed into Shet-Tsebeh's eyes and on his forehead, making him cackle with glee. This was the most merriment he had had in…forever! He wrapped the six fingers of his right hand tighter around the forged iron chain he wielded. He locked his thumb in place and swung it in a circle over his head before bringing it down once again against the backs of the three men lined up in front of him. They wailed at the same time. At least the ones that still lived. He glanced over at Semqat to see if he also received joy with his display of strength and dominance.

Semqat drooled with anticipation as he rubbed his hands up and down on his thighs. "Come on, finish it."

"Patience. You need to enjoy the process as much as the reward." Shet-Tsebeh strutted back and forth as a smile stretched across his face. And enjoy it he had. He twirled the iron chain on the floor by his feet.

Vacant shops, and even some homes and inns, were now scattered throughout the village. Some had burned, some vandalized beyond habitability, some abandoned for no apparent reason. These two Offspring had located a still-standing shop in the center of a large area of burnt-out buildings. This shop had no roof, and the second floor had partially collapsed in, but the timbers were still plenty strong to tie weak men to. Townspeople avoided the whole section in general now, making it an ideal location for their illicit activities. For their sport.

"Let me have a turn with the chain." Semqat bounced from foot to foot.

"P-P-Please st-stop." One of the restrained, kneeling figures begged quietly. His head hung down with his face pulpy and torn from where the end of the chain had snatched at it.

The Offspring both sniggered. "Okay, Semqat. It's your turn." Shet-Tsebeh laughed and tossed the chain to him.

Semqat caught and coiled the chain around his hand and arm as he sauntered over to the broken young man bleeding all over the stone floor.

"What's your name, huh?" Semqat squatted down next to him.

The much smaller man shook violently but didn't answer.

"Come, play along. What's your name?" Semqat poked at the man's shoulder repeatedly. "Tell me," he whined.

Silence.

"You aren't going to let him get away with that, are you?" Shet-Tsebeh folded his arms across his chest and lifted an eyebrow.

Semqat looked uncertain for a moment. Then he raised his chain encased fist and brought it down on the back of the man's leg. The bone snapped audibly.

"JON!" the young man screamed. "It's Jon…" and his voice trailed off into wracking sobs.

"JON. It's Jon…"

No, No, NO. Haven had been watching through a broken window from outside on the street for only a few moments. He had immediately seen the dark-skinned man, who looked quite a bit like his friend. But with the damage to his body and his awkward bent over position, it had been impossible to be sure. But the voice…there was no doubting that. And the name.

Haven was beyond thinking reasonably. He took the few quick steps to the doorway that held no door and ran into the room hollering as loud as he could. Both young giants spun around in surprise at this intrusion. Haven ran straight for Jon, but Shet-Tsebeh stood between them.

237

The Offspring started to smile, reaching to scoop up the interloper.

Haven ran into him and shoved. Shet-Tsebeh laughed, but was knocked slightly off balance by the screaming lunatic half his weight. He took a recovery step backward and stumbled over a canted floorboard. The smile disappeared from his face as his arms began to flail. In what felt like a suspended moment, Shet-Tsebeh hung off-balance in the air. He came crashing down on his back, his head connecting powerfully with a large rock that protruded from the wall.

Haven, Semqat still on his knees, and Jon twisting his body to follow the action, all watched as Shet-Tsebeh's head cleaved in two and its mucilaginous contents slithered onto the shop floor.

Semqat glanced up at Haven.

Taking a deep breath, Haven got moving again and skirted Semqat to get to Jon.

"No you don't." Semqat rolled from his knees up to his full height. "You can't hurt him and get away with it. Join your friend and we will all play with my chain some more."

Haven swallowed the bile crawling up his throat and, ignoring the serious threat uncoiling the heavy chain from his arm, knelt by Jon. He gently laid his hands on Jon's torn cheeks and turned his face toward him. Jon's eyes were swollen to narrow slits. He must have been badly beaten before being restrained.

"Hold on, Jon. I'm going to get you out of here."

"Haven." Tears leaked from Jon's eyes. "Please." His voice was hoarse.

Jon suddenly looked up behind Haven. Haven turned and saw Semqat raising the uncoiled chain. Keeping his eye on Semqat, he hugged Jon to his body to protect him from further blows. Jon shuddered in Haven's embrace.

Semqat reached back with his chain, his eyes blazing at Haven. He brought his arm forward. Haven squeezed his eyes shut. And…nothing happened. Haven opened his eyes to see Semqat staring at the broken ceiling above him where his chain had somehow snagged around a beam.

Semqat growled and yanked on the stuck chain. It didn't budge. He yanked harder, throwing all his weight into it.

The ceiling creaked, then groaned. After a few beats of silence, a huge ripping vibration pulsed through the shop as the beam suddenly broke free, swung down, and struck Semqat directly in the center of his face. He dropped to the floor, instantly dead. The building quieted.

Haven and Jon looked at each other. Haven shrugged. He began to unbind Jon's arms.

"Shalliyt is very good to you," Jon whispered.

"Yes, he is. Let me check on the others." Haven stood and checked the other two men, but they were both dead now. "Come on. I need to get you out of here."

Haven started to gather Jon up in his arms.

"No, Haven, don't."

He set him back down gently and looked at his friend questioningly.

"I'm not going to make it." Jon lifted the front of his torn shirt and showed Haven the lethal damage that had been done to his abdomen. "Just sit and talk with me," he whispered.

Haven inhaled on a sob, but swallowed it. He removed his shirt and balled it up. He carefully maneuvered Jon down onto his side and slid the shirt under his head for a pillow. Then he stretched alongside Jon.

"Jon—"

"Wait, Haven. Let me talk while I still can." Jon's voice was a rasp, barely there. "I was wrong. Wrong about everything." He coughed, speckles of blood coating his lips. "I should have listened to you. I turned my back on you, on the wisdom from the Teller, on Shalliyt. Now it's too late."

Haven could barely hear him, his voice was so soft. He hugged Jon to him, chest to chest. "It is NOT too late. Shalliyt knows your heart. He sees your repentance and he forgives." He spoke directly into his ear.

A wet sigh bubbled from between Jon's lips, and he nodded slightly. "And you?"

Haven pulled back and looked into Jon's nearly swelled shut eyes. "You are my best friend, Jon. I have loved you since we were kids and you were a terrible brat back then."

Jon smiled a little at that.

"And I will always love you." Haven hugged him close and heard him exhale.

He was gone.

48

Haven rounded the bend of the footpath and his home came into view. He saw Rachel standing outside the cottage, looking his way and twisting the material of her skirt in both hands. He knew something must be wrong. He quickly swiped his sleeve across his face to remove the wetness from the tears that had been steadily streaming down his cheeks the whole way back after holding Jon while he died.

Haven felt horrible for leaving Jon back there, but he didn't know what else to do. With his muscles straining nearly to the breaking point, he had slowly dragged the bodies of the Offspring out of the ruined building and left them exposed on the walk way. Then he unchained the other two men who had been tortured to death and laid them next to John, carefully covering them with a ragged blanket he'd found. And finally, he put up a barricade over the open doorway to prevent the dogs from coming in and getting at his friend's body. It wasn't even close to enough. But the urgency to get home and talk to his mother, to protect her from the unfathomable evil, had begun building in his gut.

He hurried up to Rachel. "What's wrong? Is it my mother?"

Rachel paused in the twisting of her skirt and looked directly at Haven. "What happened? You've been crying," she spoke softly, searching his eyes.

"Those monsters." He quickly swiped across his face again. "They killed Jon. There was nothing I could do…"

"Oh, Haven." She threw her arms around him and buried her face in his neck. "I'm so sorry."

Haven gently pulled her away from him. "What's going on here? You looked upset."

"He's here," she whispered. "The man I told you about. His name is Kharshea, and your mother is feeding him dinner right now."

"No," Haven growled and stepped around Rachel. With long strides he approached the stoop, hopped up, and banged through the front door.

"Mother!"

Tirzah appeared around the corner from the kitchen. "Haven," she smiled. "There you are. I was just about—"

"Where is he?" He pushed past his mother and stalked into the kitchen.

Haven came to an abrupt halt. Before him was a huge man sitting at *his* kitchen table, eating *his* food, off *his* plate, which *his* mother had prepared. And this evil giant smirked at him.

Haven's hands fisted at his sides. "Get out." His voice was remarkably restrained.

"Haven? What are you doing?" His mother came through the doorway behind him.

"Be quiet, mother." Haven's stare never left the man. "Get out of my home, now." He took a step forward.

"Haven, stop it. You're being rude." His mother's hand laid on his arm imploringly.

Haven spun around to face her. "And you are behaving like a fool," he hissed.

"Haven, that's enough." Kharshea rose to his feet, his head nearly brushing the ceiling. "You shall not speak to your mother that way." His voice was calm, concerned. "Tirzah, why don't you wait in the sitting room and let Haven and me have some time to get acquainted." He smiled.

Haven's blood boiled through his veins.

Tirzah nodded and gave Haven's arm a small squeeze. "Behave yourself, Son," she whispered. She left the room.

Haven was torn between his astonishment at his mother's naivete and his fury at this Guardian who just *reprimanded* him.

Haven had to crane his neck up now to look into Kharshea's eyes. Black, flat, eyes. He kept his voice low. "You will get out of my house, and you will stay away from my mother." He knew this man, no, not a man, could kill him with one strike if he so wished. But righteous indignation flooded his senses and his heart pounded in his chest.

Kharshea reached around Haven, pulled out a chair from the table, and gently shoved Haven back into it. "Sit there and conduct yourself civilly. We *will* talk."

242

Haven's breath panted in and out. He gripped the chair arms till his fingers turned white. "What do you want?" he ground out between his clenched jaws.

"I'm here to help, Haven. Both you and your mother." Kharshea raised a hand to silence Haven when it was clear he was going to interrupt. "Clearly, you have a predetermined notion that I mean you harm. You could not be further from the truth—I am no threat to either of you. I am simply a friend in the time of your need." Kharshea leaned back in his chair with a placating smile on his face. As if Haven were a child.

"You are no friend. Your offspring murdered my friend this day." Haven turned and spit on the floor. "One of your kind killed the father of the woman I love—"

"I'm sorry about your friend, Haven." Kharshea crossed his arms over his chest. "But that was not my offspring. I had only one son and he, too, was killed."

Haven watched in disbelief as Kharshea's eyes appeared to well up a bit. Did Guardians actually feel loss? Was this just some act? Haven was horrified to realize he felt a wisp of sympathy toward Kharshea's loss of a son. "Your son was killed? Why?" Suspicion laced his voice.

Kharshea exhaled. "I don't know for sure." He tugged at his ear before continuing. "He was being bullied by some local boys who were jealous of his superior size and strength. I think they ganged up on him. Crushed his skull."

Haven deflated. What could he say to that? He had never counted on these creatures having human-like *emotions*.

Kharshea continued on, seemingly lost in his own thoughts now. "Briysh is my boy. I love him…"

Haven blinked once, then again. Briysh?

Briysh, the ruffian who burned Eli and his home and fields? Briysh? The man who attacked him and the prostitute in the alley by Jared's shop. Briysh?? The dead being who was taking possession of people and demanding worship in the clearing in the forest. That Briysh? How many Briysh's could there be? Only one with that odd of a name. Haven leapt from his seat.

"…he wasn't perfect, but he was my son. I will do—"

Haven was on Kharshea in a second. He completely surprised the bigger man, knocking him over in his chair. Haven went down with him, on top of him. "Your son is an abomination," he hissed into Kharshea's startled face. "*You* are an abomination." Haven wondered through his haze of anger why Kharshea wasn't reacting. "You are a fallen Guardian disgraced and rejected by his creator. Your final end is coming. Judgment before the throne of Shalliyt and an eternity of separation await you." Spit was flying from Haven's mouth. He pummeled the larger man's chest while he straddled him there on the floor. Kharshea had begun grunting a bit, but still made no move to defend himself. The hatred blooming in the larger man's eyes, though, was unmistakable. "And you will NOT be taking my mother down with you."

Suddenly, Rachel and Tirzah were on Haven, grabbing his arms and pulling him off Kharshea. The women pushed Haven back toward a wall, and Haven fought desperately to get a hold of his wildly swinging emotions. He glanced at Rachel and saw tears pouring from her eyes. It sobered him up immediately. Haven leaned back against the wall and bent over to rest his hands on his knees while he caught his breath. He could hear Tirzah talking to Kharshea, helping him up.

Kharshea seemed sluggish and speechless at first. Then he suddenly roused himself, pushed away from Tirzah, and fled the kitchen. Haven heard the front door slam and then a primal roar ripped through the outside air. Haven, Tirzah, and Rachel all stopped what they were doing and looked at each other. It sounded like a wild animal being tortured, and the hair at the back of Haven's neck stood on end.

Haven never saw the smack coming. His mother hit him across the face with the flat of her hand, hard.

"You went too far," she rasped out. Then Tirzah turned and ran out of the kitchen. The front door slammed again.

Haven absently rubbed at this stinging spot on his cheek. "No," he whispered brokenly.

He tried to go after her, but Rachel enfolded him in her arms. "Let her calm down, then we will go get her." She rubbed her hand against Haven's chest. "You will only push her farther away if you follow her now."

Haven slumped into the chair by the table. He felt utterly defeated.

Kharshea ran through the forest, leaping over fallen logs, heedless of the branches whipping at his face. His fury coursed through him like molten lava. He may have still been bellowing. He wasn't even sure.

Then he stopped abruptly. He leaned against the trunk of a tree and slid down till he was sitting at the base of it, his breath sawing in and out of his lungs. He had been made a fool of. Following so close on the heels of the condemnation from the Teller, this degradation dug deeper.

He had been forced to sit there and listen to that ungrateful whelp rail against him and against his beloved son. Haven had laid hands on him, shoved him, punched him! He would have smashed the slug's face in, but he had been unfairly restrained. Restrained and muted. The minute Haven leapt onto him—apparently that had been a mistake mentioning Briysh's name—Kharshea felt his brothers bind his arms tightly and shut his mouth. He couldn't see them, but there was no mistaking their presence and their strength. They held him immobile and defenseless against Haven's attack. Then, to add to that insult, after they released him, Kharshea felt the hot prick of the sword as they had herded him out the door like a squealing pig.

His fists still clenched in impotent rage. His teeth grated in his mouth. He would get that boy somehow. Not just for the offense against Briysh and the ritual, but for him now, too. Obviously direct interaction wouldn't work. But there would be a way, an opening. And he would take it.

Kharshea cracked his knuckles in an attempt to release some of the tension that cramped them.

That's when he heard it.

Someone calling his name.

Tirzah.

Tirzah was most likely following the wide swath he'd left through the trees in his flight.

Tirzah was coming after him. Kharshea laughed darkly.

What a stupid woman. And what a brilliant solution.

"Tirzah! I'm over here," Kharshea called out.

The sun had begun to set, leaving a creeping darkness under the trees' canopy. Dappled light filtered through in a few spots yet. Kharshea heaved his body up and began to walk toward Tirzah before the senseless cow could get herself lost

245

in the gathering dusk. He heard her footsteps crackling over broken branches. "Follow the sound of my voice, sweet woman."

Within a few minutes, she was close. Kharshea stopped and waited for her to approach. She came into view but didn't see him yet as her eyes kept track of her feet overstepping obstacles.

"Tirzah," he spoke on a breath. "My lovely, Tirzah."

She startled at how close he was, but then immediately reached out a hand to him.

He grasped it and brought it to his lips. "Tirzah, I am so sorry for what happened," he murmured over her hand. "Can you forgive me?" He was thankful for the dark, since he wasn't sure he was masking his anger well enough yet.

She began shaking her head. "No Kharshea. This is my son's fault, not yours." She gripped his hand tightly. Her hand trembled, as did her voice. "I can't believe the horrible things he said about you and your beloved son whom you lost so violently."

"Let me walk you home. The darkness is upon us." He turned her easily and still holding her hand, he put his other arm around her shoulders.

She continued speaking as she snuggled up against him. "It's that Teller. I told you he'd been a bad influence on Haven."

"You did." He rubbed her arm as the temperature began to cool. "The Teller has made him angry, unreasonable." They walked lost in their own thoughts for a few moments. It became clear that she could not see at all where she was going now, so Kharshea gently led her along the path. "So do you believe the Teller speaks for Shalliyt?"

"No, not at all." She spoke with vehemence. "My god would not be the source of such anger…and violence. I cannot believe how Haven attacked you!"

"Hmmm. That's a valid point." Kharshea could see a lantern off in the distance. He needed to wrap this up. "Let me ask you Tirzah, if you discovered that your god was a god of violence. A god of condemnation. Of judgment. What would you do?"

He could feel her shake her head. "I would only follow a god of love."

"Excellent," he whispered. "I see a lantern up ahead. I suspect it is Haven looking for you. Why don't you call to him so he aims for us properly, then I will hand you over safely."

"Thank you, Kharshea." Tirzah looked up toward Kharshea's face. He heard longing in her voice. "You have been such a gentleman," she whispered.

He leaned over and gently kissed her on the mouth. "Call your boy."

She turned away from Kharshea toward the spot of yellow light. "Haven! I'm over here."

"I'm coming, Mother. Please don't move." Haven began crashing through the underbrush more quickly.

Kharshea moved behind Tirzah. He placed a hand on her shoulder, squeezing gently. He reached his other hand around her front and cupped her chin. He rubbed his thumb along the smooth skin there. Then he tightened his grip and jerked her head, snapping her neck. He gently lowered her into the leaf mold below.

In a way he wanted to stay and see Haven's reaction. But he also remembered the sting of his brothers' sword that accompanied Haven, so self-preservation had him moving quickly along.

He was quite a distance away when he finally heard the piercing cry as the sniveling boy must have discovered his dead mother. God of love indeed.

Kharshea melted into the night.

49

Briysh raised his fists as the pulse of triumph throbbed through his body. It was the prostitute Leah's body, but it was all his now. She had finally tipped her mind over the edge with the mushrooms and botanicals that he prescribed for her, and now her essence cowered deeply in the recesses of her soul, unaware of her surroundings and with no control over her actions. Briysh would no longer need to vacate the body or borrow it temporarily; it was his. Power and pleasure surged through him, alleviating all remnants of his painful existence.

He had spoken with his father earlier and learned that the voice of dissent, Haven, had been quenched and his mother killed. Kharshea seemed out of sorts to Briysh, but he didn't really care—he had taken care of his problem. It almost felt like his father hovered at the edge of madness with an uncharacteristic darting of the eyes and excess movements as he paced while relaying the story to his son. Kharshea normally possessed a placid countenance and a potent strength of character and purpose. But now something below the surface of his father's expression crumbled, his force of personality, disintegrating. Oh the irony if his father were to descend into lunacy while Briysh took on his new mantle of power. Briysh ascends to godhood as his father, a true son of god, becomes a fool. Delicious.

Briysh lifted his head to gaze between his upraised fists at the full-bellied white moon suspended overhead. Fortuitous circumstances had aligned a full moon, a newly trembling earth, and Briysh's escalation of form and power. The masses flocked to his clearing in the woods. They were terrified.

Behind him, in the hut, Briysh could sense the frenetic movement of the serpent. It now held a multitude of the Afflicted who were being fed a surfeit supply of human blood and fear. The faithful were slicing their forearms in frenzy, letting the blood run freely down the wooden scales that glistened wetly in a sliver of moonlight. The blood ran down the coils and dripped, uselessly, onto the corpses of babies stacked below. Some of the faithful, mostly women, spewed a constant gibberish from their mouths as they allowed the Afflicted to express their glee through them. Other's howled, in pain or pleasure it was hard to know. One woman kneeled silently, unmoving, blood running down her arms, tears down her face, as she kept one outstretched hand on the rotting body of her newborn and one on the serpent. Briysh knew the woman because she had been here for several days. Unlike the other babies under the serpent, this one had not been sacrificed, but died of natural causes. Its mother begged for it to be brought to life. Briysh admonished her for weak faith and sent her to the altar to remedy that.

Briysh roared and brought his fists back down, swiveling his eyes to the throng assembled before him. As one, they fell to the ground on their faces. Hundreds had found their way to the meadow tonight. Recently, the half-beast progeny had enlarged the clearing by ripping down surrounding trees. Yet, it was at capacity again.

As if on cue, the earth shivered after Briysh's roar died down. "Do you feel that?" He spoke softly, immediately causing all present to hone in on him. There was some soft crying, muffled by the grass. Women in ritual ecstasy could be heard murmuring in the background. "The world is coming apart at the seams." The meadow floor cooperated by rippling again. "This Valley of Shalliyt is shaking apart. Where is the Lord of the valley?" Briysh paused.

He allowed a smile to crawl across his face. "I think perhaps our god has journeyed away. Or mayhap he is sleeping?"

The people remained face down, shaking in their fear. The quaking earth was new, and only added to the rest of the turmoil building in the village and their neighborhoods. It added to the darkened skies and smoky air. Violence, upheaval, and now instability below their feet. Their foundation unstable beneath them.

Someone near the front of the crowd crawled toward Briysh, head hung low. He reached a hand out and laid it on Briysh's foot. "You can save us." His voice croaked.

Briysh jerked his foot back, but then launched into the opening given him by the desperate man. "I CAN save you." Briysh began to methodically pace back and forth while he spoke. "And ONLY I can save you. If you are faithful to me. If you…worship me." The people began to moan and sway. "I will be your god!"

Throughout the rest of the evening and night, Briysh spoke to his followers walking back and forth under the cold moon. A breeze had come earlier in the day and blown away the persistent smoky haze, revealing the brightness of the moon and stars. It all lent power to Briysh's argument. And the people believed with all their heart. At times they responded with moaning and weeping, at times with joy and hope. But they were now his. All his. Heart and soul. Briysh wallowed in pleasure and ecstasy. The other Afflicted in attendance also benefited from the human adoration, empowering them to perform multiple feats of strength and what appeared as miracles to the people.

The people would never turn away from the new gods. Gods they had never known. Tonight they fully embraced them. They would bleed for them. They would kill for them.

The earthquakes began the night of Tirzah's murder. They weren't ravaging, pounding, or shattering, to mirror the upheaval felt through Haven's household. They rumbled quietly, barely there. At first, just a stuttering vibration quivered across the valley. Some of the people didn't notice. Most were either preoccupied by the escalating violence in the village or the bizarre behavior of the animals in the countryside, who seemed to have no problem feeling the tremors.

Rachel reached out and placed her hand against the wall as she glanced over at the flickering candle on the windowsill. There definitely was a long, low quivering coming from the earth. She pulled her hand back and turned her attention to Haven.

She had no idea what to do. He sat very still on his chair. He stared right through her, like she wasn't there. It was almost better before as he had clutched his mother's broken body to his chest and carried her home, howling and sobbing like a wounded animal.

Haven had carefully laid her in her bed, pulled up the quilt, and straightened her hair, tucking the stray hairs behind her ears. With trembling fingers he attempted to drag her eyelids down to cover the glassy stare. That didn't work, so he bent over and kissed above her eyelids. Then Haven simply stopped. The tears stopped. The desperate pleas for his mother to respond stopped. He sat back in a chair near the bed, a dazed expression across his face.

Rachel kneeled in front of him and placed her hands on his thighs. "Haven. Haven!" She gently jostled his legs.

His eyes drifted toward her face but didn't seem very focused.

"The earth is trembling, just as the Teller said it would." She lowered her voice to a whisper. "It is beginning. The end is coming." She squeezed his legs a bit. "Please come back to me."

He showed no reaction at all to her words. Rachel feared he was adrift in his mind, unable to swallow the horror of the death of his mother. Having recently lost her father, she understood. But she needed Haven with her now. With her in both mind and body.

As the days passed, Haven moved through the motions of living. But he never spoke. Never really acknowledged Rachel. He dug a grave for his mother. He ate what Rachel put in front of him. He laid in bed at night, but Rachel couldn't tell if he actually slept. He didn't seem to notice the increasing frequency and strength of the shifting earth.

He took care of the horses until the third day when they were taken. Their stable had been knocked down, more like ripped to shreds. Boards were torn in half. Blood coated some of the wood and splashed across bales of hay that remained stacked on one side.

Rachel found Haven tugging at his hair as he stared at the destruction. She glanced at all the blood as she grabbed at Haven's elbow to lead him back inside. Where were the horses? It was obvious at least one of them had been killed, maybe both—there was so much blood—but where were the bodies? Why would someone take dead horses with them? "I can't believe we didn't hear anything," she murmured.

As they began to climb the stoop into the cottage, an explosion burst forth in the distance. They both turned toward it. In the north, the top of a section of mountain had gone missing. Fire shot from the rocky stump and a thick flaming liquid cascaded down the sides. Black smoke rose from the base of the mountain. "The forest must be catching fire beneath," Haven whispered.

Rachel looked at Haven. Her emotions tumbled within her. Haven finally spoke! But their world was exploding before their eyes.

Haven reached out and touched Rachel's jaw, his thumb rubbing over it. His eyes were focused and intense. "It is time, little one."

Rachel just nodded. She turned to run inside the cottage. She needed to pack and get ready for their journey. She needed to prepare food and supplies for the uncertain future. She needed to make haste—but Haven grabbed her arm and yanked her back before she got through the door. "We don't have much time, Haven. I need to be quick."

"No, we have no time. We go now."

"But how will we manage? What will we eat?" Rachel sputtered as Haven began dragging her to the path that would lead along the mountain base and toward the Teller's cave.

Haven came to an abrupt stop and grasped both of Rachel's arms. Then…he smiled. "Shalliyt." He leaned forward and kissed her. "Now we watch how he cares for us. We need to trust him, Rachel. He has promised us."

They both stared at each other. Rachel, so thrilled that Haven was fully back to her, worked to comprehend what he was saying. Could she trust to that degree? Trust Shalliyt with her very life? Another explosion rocked the valley. It was farther away but when the two turned they could see more fire shooting into the sky. Haven looked back at Rachel and arched his eyebrow in a silent question. Rachel took a deep breath and nodded. Hand in hand they ran.

50

The way to the Teller's cave from Haven's cottage usually took a twenty-minute walk. Quicker at a run. But there was nothing usual about this trek. Fairly soon on the path, Haven noticed wide bloody streaks in the dirt. His first thought was his horses. He slowed down to a walk and cocked his ear to listen for any signs of people around. It was difficult to hear over the distant roar of the blazing mountain and the now constant shaking of the valley floor below them. Rachel heard something first.

She pointed off to the side of the path where it turned into a heavily wooded area. It was also the direction the bloody drag marks went.

"Stay here," Haven whispered, then turned and crouch walked into the woods.

Rachel had no intention of being left alone, so she placed a hand on Haven's back and followed him on silent feet.

It was fewer than twenty steps till they got a view into a small opening in the copse. Haven and Rachel both stood and stared in horror at what laid before them. Two half-beast creatures with furred haunches and hooves for feet tugged a huge chunk of white-hided bloodied meat back and forth between them with gory hands. A third man, a tall, young man sat apart from them sniggering as he chomped on a heart. A raw heart the size of a man's head. The size of a horse's heart.

Rachel pulled away from Haven, fell to her knees, and began retching. All three of the creatures heard and turned toward the pair. Haven grabbed Rachel's arm and began to run, dragging her back to the path. The sound of heavy bodies crashing through trees sounded behind them, but once Rachel and Haven hit the path they had the advantage over the engorged monsters stumbling behind them.

The ground shifted underneath their feet as Haven and Rachel sprinted along the path. Pebbles cascaded down the side of the mountain, bouncing and skittering along the slippery sides. Huge fissures webbed out above their heads through the solid stone. Haven could hear louder cracking booming through the valley and imagined larger pieces of rock would soon begin to fall.

Rachel started coughing as the smoke thickened in the air, and her steps began to falter and slow.

Haven slowed down and grabbed her hand. "Rachel, keep running. It's all coming down! We have to get to the Teller's cave." Rachel clutched at his hand with both of hers and began to pull backward. Haven saw her dilated eyes, her breath wheezing in and out. She was panicking. He stepped forward, scooped her up, and tossed her over his shoulder.

A sheep-sized rock crashed in front of Haven, sending out a spray of small chips. He dodged around it and ran as fast as he could, Rachel's nails digging into his back as she clung to him. His shins burned where several shards had embedded themselves. It was just as well Rachel had her face buried in his back, Haven thought, as he leapt over two bloodied bodies grotesquely splayed on the path. An explosion ripped through the air, just as Haven reached the entrance to the Teller's cave. The concussion from the blast shoved Haven through the door where he landed on his knees, nearly crushing Rachel beneath him. The stone doorway behind him collapsed, sealing them inside the mountain. In the dark.

"Rachel, are you alright?" Haven groped along her arms and her torso, up to her face, to assure himself that he hadn't hurt her in the fall.

Her breathing sounded heavy and loud in the black hollow space. "I...I'm fine." She took a deep breath. "I think the air is better in here." Normally dank and moldy smelling, the air was at least free of smoke, and the dampness might soothe some of the irritation in her throat.

Haven shifted off his bruised knees onto his seat and pulled Rachel to him, embracing her as her wheezing subsided some. Overhead it sounded like the whole mountain was coming down on top of them. The ground vibrated more forcefully underneath them.

"We're going to die," Rachel whispered, burying her face into Haven's neck.

Haven gripped her chin and lifted it up. "Where is your faith, little one?" With his other hand he stroked through her curls, gently pulling out leaves and twigs that had lodged there.

"We are trapped in a cave, alone, in the dark, with the mountain about to come down on us." She shivered violently. "The sun has been blotted out for days, and the moon has run away! The valley is on fire. The people are slaughtered." She sobbed inconsolably. "Where is our hope?"

Haven smoothed his thumb along first one cheek, then the other, wiping away the tears as they fell. "The question should be 'who is our hope'? Hmm?"

Rachel settled, hiccupping. She whispered, "Shalliyt?" Haven didn't speak. "Shalliyt," she said with more conviction.

"Yes." He leaned forward and lightly kissed her on the mouth. "He doesn't break his promises. He just doesn't always carry through on them the way we expect." Haven could feel Rachel nodding slightly, as she began to relax into him.

"Haven. Rachel. Come over here." The two of them startled at the Teller's voice. It didn't sound as powerful as it normally did.

"Sir, we're here." Haven pulled himself to his feet, dragging Rachel up with him. "Keep talking. It's dark in here."

The earth shook violently, then, knocking them both back to the floor.

"Follow my voice. I'll light a candle…" His voice faded as he must have gone back into his chamber.

It was enough for Haven to get his bearings, as he maneuvered himself and Rachel around the meeting benches and toward the Teller's door at a half crouch to keep his balance on the heaving floor. Then a small light bloomed brightly in the blackness. Rachel picked up speed then, heading toward it.

The Teller stood at the entrance to his room, the light from the candle in his hand dancing across his long beard and white robe.

Haven could see the wrinkles dragging down across his face in heavy folds, his deep-set eyes hid in shadows. Haven laid his hand on the Teller's arm when he and Rachel reached him

The older man turned and walked into his chamber. "Follow me."

A mighty boom rumbled through the mountain around them. Rachel shrieked but then clamped her mouth shut on any

257

words. Haven wrapped his arm around her shoulder, accepting the candle the Teller handed him. They could hear rock plunging down from the high ceiling of the meeting room. The floor heaved again, and the Teller stumbled toward his bed and collapsed onto it.

"Sir, what do we do now?" Haven tried to keep his voice sounding confident, though tendrils of fear were coursing through his veins now. He just needed to keep focused. Hear what the plan was. Move forward.

The Teller righted himself, sitting on the edge of the bed. "Come here, both of you. It is time for you to be wed."

Haven looked over at Rachel and reached his hand out for her. She took his hand, but clearly had a look on her face that she thought this to be less than the appropriate timing. Haven smiled at that. Usually he was the practical one, but for the first time in days, he felt himself release his fears. He pulled her close so they could help prop each other up on the rolling floor. He reached over and set the candle on the desk.

"Yes, sir. We're ready." Haven spoke loud enough to be heard.

The Teller looked at Rachel and waited. She looked up at Haven, took a deep breath, and smiled. She nodded her head.

In that uncanny way of his, the Teller knew without his sight that she agreed, and he began to speak.

"Your right hands." The Teller said.

They let go of holding hands, and each put out their right hand. The Teller reached into a pocket in his robe and withdrew a long, narrow, sharpened rock. With his other hand he grasped Haven's outstretched hand, and with no warning, sliced Haven's hand from the base of the small finger, diagonal across his calloused palm to the base of the thumb. The Teller quickly grabbed Rachel's hand before she could yank it back, and sliced her in the same fashion. The cuts were shallow, but a dark red stripe of blood welled up along the wounds. He pressed their palms together and quickly wrapped a rag around them, knotting it. Then he leaned forward and placed his hands on both their heads.

"You are now one blood, one flesh, consecrated to one another, holy and wed in the eyes of Shalliyt. Be faithful to one another unto death."

Haven realized this very nontraditional ceremony was over and he looked down at Rachel. She looked a little like she needed to vomit. He gently squeezed her palm that was wrapped with his. She looked up at him, tears in the corner of her eyes, then gave him a big, though a bit shaky, grin. He leaned forward and placed a quick kiss on her still smiling lips. He tucked a loose strand of hair behind her ear with his left hand and stroked her cheek with his thumb. "I love you, Rachel."

Rachel turned her face into his open palm and kissed him there, her eyes fluttering shut in a way that made Haven's blood feel warmer in his veins. "I love you, Haven." She murmured.

"We are short on time." The Teller pulled them from any romantic feelings that may have been building. "Give me your hands again." He untied the rag, folded it, and wiped the smears of blood from their palms. "It is done."

The Teller laid back and pulled a blanket over his body. "Shalliyt will lead you from here, as he has led you all along. The two of you be ready to act on his lead."

"That's it? That's the plan?" Rachel's voice came out in a squeak.

"Wait." Haven interrupted. He sat on the bed next to the Teller's prone body. He gripped the man's hand in his. "You need to come with us!"

The Teller sighed. "My duties are done here, son. I am very tired. I expect Shalliyt to call me home soon." His voice grew noticeably weaker and harder to hear over the cacophony coming from the cave behind them and the mountain around them. "Go through the blanket there and…" He motioned to the blanket acting as a door separating his bedroom from whatever lay beyond. "Come here, Rachel." He motioned for her and waited for her to sit alongside Haven. Then he took her hand, and as he held them both he blessed them in a raspy voice. "Trust. Trust in Shalliyt; be strong and let your heart take courage; he is your help and your shield. He will keep you, and you shall inherit the land." He released their hands, his head falling back again onto the bed, eyes closed. "Now go." And he slipped into unconsciousness.

Haven sat there stunned, tears filling his eyes. In a momentary calm of the collapsing mountain, he could hear Rachel beginning to cry softly. He pulled her to him and held her tightly. He had no words.

The stillness abruptly ended with a thunderous crack echoing through the chamber, and a massive jagged cleft opened in the wall beside them. It was over. The mountain was coming down on them.

"Rachel now! Run now!" Haven hollered over the deafening noise. He pulled her behind him and headed to the hanging blanket the Teller had indicated. He grabbed the candle from the desk, the flame threatening to gutter out altogether in the billows of rock dust raining down on them. They pushed aside the blanket and found themselves dashing through a long hallway of sorts, hewn into the solid stone. The heaving ground pitched them up against the sides as they ran, nearly blind, through the unknown tunnel. They could hear the rock piling up behind them—there was no going back. Forward, and fast, was the only option. So they lurched and ran in the near darkness.

After several tense minutes, and many more cuts and bruises from banging into the unforgiving, but crumbling walls, Haven and Rachel reached the end. The end of the passageway. A stone wall prevented any further progress.

"No…No!" Rachel wailed as her fists pounded against the wall.

Haven dropped the candle, plunging them into heavy blackness. He grabbed her fists and yanked her into his embrace. An unnatural calm came over him. He could hear the tunnel collapsing behind them and Rachel sobbing into his chest. "Shhh…" he whispered into her ear. "Shh…" Then not much louder and barely audible over the din, he said simply, "Shalliyt. Save us."

A thunderous explosion made him squeeze his eyes shut and lean over to protect Rachel's body with his the best he could, waiting for the impact.

Then silence.

Haven opened his eyes to a blinding light coming through a large crack in the wall before them. It was wide enough for them to fit through. "Rachel. Rachel! Look!"

She lifted her head from his chest and turned toward the brilliant light shining through. Her hand flew up to protect her eyes. She laughed and looked back at Haven's dirt-smeared face, his own smile beaming broadly.

The mountain boomed and rocked around them, immediately shaking them from their surprise.

"Run!" Haven shoved at Rachel.

She turned sideways and shimmied through the opening, Haven right behind her. They leapt out onto the sandy wasteland of the wilderness. Holding hands, fingers entwined, they ran.

EPILOGUE

Lust squatted on a boulder, slowly dragging his long yellowed fingernails of one hand up the opposite arm, leaving bloody pus-filled furrows in its wake. It didn't help the unending itchiness that plagued him, but that didn't stop him from trying. He looked back at the young girl splashing at the water's edge about twenty yards away from him. She paused in her play to reach up and swat aside a dark black curl hanging low on her forehead. She was a beauty, just like her mother. At just four summers old, it was clear what she would grow into as a woman, and Lust could imagine it well. He licked his chapped lips in anticipation.

Behind the girl stood a tall, robed Guardian. The girl couldn't see him, but Lust could. Lust glanced up at the Guardian's face to see the armed soldier glaring at him. A sword hung at his side, with his hand never far from the hilt. Lust had felt the tip of that sword across his back several times when he had ventured too close to the girl, and it stung fiercely. Lust spit toward the Guardian. The glob pathetically landed just in front of Lust's feet. The Guardian ignored him.

The little girl squealed in glee as she slapped her hands against the cool water. She frolicked along a small pond formed from a fresh stream that burbled up from the ground among an outcropping of rocks. Small green plants surrounded the edge. Rachel knelt a short distance away, scraping a sheepskin to prepare it for drying. She looked over at her daughter fondly and went back to her task. To the other side of her, her two boys, her first and second born, were both bent over on hands and knees moving very slowly…stalking a lizard presumably. Haven was off in the distance, breaking ground for a new garden.

Lust hated looking at this family, all day, every day. But what else was there to do? Once the valley had been leveled, buried in layers and layers of rock, Lust had lost access to Leah.

Lost access to his relief, to his pleasure, to his power. Everyone had died, except Haven and Rachel.

Lust picked at his nose, caked and grimy with the desert debris. His life was nothing but misery. Shalliyt showered blessings on Haven and Rachel: provided them a small oasis in the wilderness to live in, brought them some wandering animals to sustain themselves, gave Rachel an exceedingly fruitful womb. He also gave them a cadre of protectors—the Guardians-- that made Lust's life wretched and the solution, access to the people, impossible. These weren't helpful Guardians like his father. These were the faithful minions of Shalliyt. It was the first time in centuries that these lackeys had been given a task involving humans.

Lust thought about his father. He didn't miss him, but he did miss what his father could do for him—get access to his own relief. The day the valley collapsed, all of the Guardians living in it simply vanished. Lust had no idea where they went. The people all lay dead, crushed under the rocks; the Guardians vanished; and the Offspring that still lived as humans were also killed and then reappeared disembodied in the wilderness alongside of him.

Except Aarkaos. He had survived and still wandered the wilderness. But he wouldn't come anywhere near the Guardians protecting the family. He was still bossy as ever.

Lust had been told by his father that he would not have immortality, but apparently for Lust and those like him, time wasn't up yet. Which brought him back to considering his intense need for easing his own situation—the hunger that continuously burned through his body, the thirst, the cravings.

And that brought him back to the pretty little girl splashing away nearby. He grinned. She and her family may be protected right now. But one day the Guardians would move on to a different assignment, or get sloppy and leave an opening, and then he and his horde would go in and take over. Take over their minds. Take over their bodies. Steal their chance at immortality. Lust knew it wouldn't be Haven and Rachel. They were too dedicated to that accursed divinity that supported them. But the children…the children wouldn't remember the valley and what happened there, both before and during the catastrophe. They would forget Shalliyt's faithfulness to their parents, forget his warnings, forget him. Lust believed they could be easily convinced to seek out wealth and power and pleasure at any expense. And Lust would be ready for them.

ACKNOWLEDGEMENTS

I would like to thank my husband, David, who has spent many hours with me through the years hashing over the biblical concepts covered in this story. I also appreciate his patience and support as I would disappear for hours, or even days, to go write with my writing groups!

Many thanks to the ladies in my two writing groups: Sara, Tracey, and Mandy for slogging through one chapter at a time over two years offering invaluable advice. Then for reading it through yet once again for their final thoughts. And Kelly and Susan for being my test audience on that final read-through. I'd also like to thank Kelly for her editing expertise.

Thanks to the professionals in the business, author Mike Dellosso and Christian fiction reviewer Peter Younghusband, who offered me support and encouragement just when I needed it. Their assistance to new authors is a real blessing.

I would like to recognize Dr. Michael S. Heiser who got the ball rolling in my mind many years ago. I've benefited from his scholarly analysis on these topics through his online classes, books, and podcasts. I especially recommend his non-fiction book *The Unseen Realm* to anyone interested in a greater understanding of the supernatural passages in the Bible.

And finally, I thank my Lord Jesus Christ who gifts us with calling, creativity, and curiosity. Without these, there would be no book.

ABOUT THE AUTHOR

J.S. Helms is a married mother of two grown daughters. She owns a curriculum store serving home educators and is also a free-lance editor and writer. She resides in South Central Pennsylvania on a small farm with her husband, cat, dog, chickens, sheep, and goats. This is her first novel.

Visit her website at GodsTheyHadNeverKnown.com or email with any comments to PACEbooks@live.com